THE MURDEROUS VIILLAIN ROSCO PITT

Ross McDermott

Copyright © 2024 Ross McDermott

All rights reserved

The characters and events portrayed in this book are fictitious. Any similarity to real persons, living or dead, is coincidental and not intended by the author.

No part of this book may be reproduced, or stored in a retrieval system, or transmitted in any form or by any means, electronic, mechanical, photocopying, recording, or otherwise, without express written permission of the publisher.

Cover design by: Emma McDermott
ISBN: 9798333846419
Printed in the United States of America

For the friends of my youth, cowboys each and everyone of us, for those brief moments in time. Yeeha!

PROLOGUE

Rare it is to find the words of a man such as this. A man who turned his back on the world and found solace in the empty whisper of granite and stone beneath the unrelenting wind that is life.

The words you are about to read are the words of the man himself. A man who crossed the land when laws were for the weak and borders knew no bounds. His sirens were the coyote, the wolf and the buzzard; his cohorts were the ghosts of his past, who beckon in dreams and torture his soul. He was one of thousands, lost and forever wandering, destined to be faceless and nameless, unknown. Then he came down that mountain, and became a legend.

This is his story...

CHAPTER 1

Best get back down

It is cold in the shadow of the mountain. The clearing stretches out before our eyes in the fading light of the day. Already the sun has dipped below the lofty peak that looms to our backs high, draped in icy mist at the apex of its tip. The mountain seems to bid me adieu, but I don't turn from the flame that crackles low but warm at the edge of the trees.

MissT. That's the name I've given that crag of pointed rock that filled my view for much of the many years I've spent exploring the folds of her skirt. Even now, while I'm turned away from her never-changing countenance, I can feel her chilling breath raise the hairs on the back of my neck. Being both enemy and foe, the mountain and I had formed the closest of bonds that I could ever attest to having. Granted, I've never joined the ranks of those who lose their minds in the high country, so I knows that bond is not a thing we can touch, it has nothing for me to point to and say, 'there it is,' and MissT feels nothing but cold stone cracking and sweeping winds. Her ways are arbitrary, which though appear fickle at times, bends not for my needs, or wants. This I know. But, in the past just recently done, I've found myself speaking to MissT, starting to expel the breath required to make sound as I address her – aloud. Even Mr. Andrews' ears seem to prickle with uncertainty when I speak to the mountain.

Mr. Andrews is my horse, and a fine one at that. That was the name on the saddle when I found him and that's the name I've called him ever since. He's a good cavalry horse and next to MissT, pretty much my best friend. His footing was steady and sure, as we picked our way down the mountain, and my trust in that Appaloosa was just as firm, that much I can say. But how's I come across him is a story for another time, another telling, if the opportunity ever presents itself.

Back to addressing MissT. Now, this aint like the lengthy conversations I've had with Mr. Andrews, no sir. My words are short when the mountain listens and I hear her tell me I best get back down. It's not right, MissT seemed to whisper, when a man starts to think she's anything more than the jagged rocks that scrape the sky. "Best get down Rosco." I'm sure that carried on the wind. Which is another darn good reason to best get back down.

So, I'm telling this gently to McTavish. Lachey, we call him. Laughlin McTavish. He's a man I met a few years back, riding the north ridge of the mountain's wide waist, hunting the goats that cling like acrobats to the razor thin ledges that mark the sheer rock face. He is and was then, a wiry Scotsman, short but stout with ruddy cheeks and twinkling blue eyes. Beneath his often-worn cap of racoon, which McTavish only removes while sleeping, was a thick, curly mess as red as any flame, a scalp he'd done well to keep as its rusty curls would honour the post of any brave's lodge. His beard, a common growth worn for warmth and shared by many of us who dwell up high, was like the wire of a heavy brush as red as the hair of his head, and it framed a smile of an infectious nature when he spoke with his thick Scottish drawl.

Our paths had crossed on occasion as we wandered the trails, both forged and existing, through the thick, tall pines and hidden valleys of the mountain. And though we join up for barely a season all told, we'd learnt enough of each as men to see an ally in each other's eyes and hear a tone of trust ring clear in our words. And now, again our paths had crossed at the base of MissT's rise, and for one last time we shared a fire, and sat silent, gazing across the snow-patched clearing to the opposing line of trees who's tops still glowed yellow in the hidden but setting sun. I spoke short, to the point. The news of my departure had fallen on Lachey's ears and was what brought on the silence of the moment.

"We all come to the time, Pitt," Lachey replied after some reflection. "When the mountain beckons us no more and the world below, if a man can recall, casts its net on the weary mind."

"You ever thought of going back down, Lachey? I mean more permanent like?" I asked.

"Not on your life," the burly Scotsman replied, without any hesitation. Lachey stared at the flame, as was always the way of the man. His coon hat covered the head of fire and his Sharps rifle sat close to hand.

"Aye. I'll tell you something laddie. I will not deny there's been a few moments when the wind tells me things. Maybe my time among the Blackfoot has made me dismiss any misgivings. I listen. When the wind talks, it's no a sign of madness boy, no up here where men are few and far between and to hear your own tongue spoken back can bring a man to tears. Listen to it, Pitt. Some say it's the voice of God, I suppose, but again to the Blackfoot, it is the voice of the mountain, and either one is the best council a man can have."

Lachey shifted his position, stretching out his legs and leaning back on a single elbow. I watch him reach in his jacket and begin preparing his pipe. The man had brought the rabbit, which now turned on the spit over our small, warm fire. He gave it a quick inspection, and satisfied with its roasting progress, turned his blue eyes my way again.

"You've never told me Pitt, and no response is required the noo if you so choose to keep it to yourself. My own reason is not one I will share so do not ask, but what brought you west? What brought you so high, Pitt? Though still green when I met you, you were no a man easily filled with wonder, even back when we first sought the goats, you were young, aye, but even then, raw with something."

I chuckle a bit, not at anything particularly humorous, but simply at the remembering, so suddenly, of something buried so deep. The rabbit spat its juice, crackling the fire and the moment of quiet. I notice the darkness has grown colder and the patches of snow in the field abroad turned a tinge of blue in the fading light. Saying nothing, I get up and add wood to the flame. With the ensuing dark the cold will descend and though another winter approaches there is still warmth in the light of day while the night grips a man tight with its chill. I sit back down and watch the flames grow and feel the warmth radiate. I reach and move the roasting rabbit from the directness of the flame, finally meeting Lachey's eye.

"The war," I tell him. "It was the war when I thinks on it now. Sure, there was much more I experienced between then and now. I'd been a stable hand, a mule skinner, a bar fly and a thief; a rustler, a scout, and I even delivered the mail for a spell, and I've seen the cruelty of this world taking many forms. Men speak of justice, kindness, truth. To be clear, I'd seen far too little of any of that in my days down below, in my days after the war."

I pause for a moment, reflecting further, and Lachey watches as if knowing my mind. Being not one to speak of oneself in any detail, I did not proceed to do so now, but I had done much more than my oral resume had stated, things not fit to remember, things best left unsaid. My Scottish friend knew this, just as he refused to speak of his life, before the question had even been asked. But that's the way it was, the way it had always been between us.

Behind us the thick stand of bristling cedars looms dark and our small fire casts our twisted shadows across the trunks. Before us, the clearing is lit by an open sky and the full, unblemished moon that shimmers, providing a clear view if anything should choose to move across the land in the night. Night comes quickly on the mountain.

"But now that you ask," I continue my response. "I know what it was, what pushed me so far west and so high, as you say. It was that day on the beach. That one hellish day on the sands of Carolina."

I pause again. The memories burst the banks of the river in my mind. I feel my eyes dart quickly between Lachey and the flames of the fire. The Scotsman is patient, and I'm grateful, as I'd never spoken these words until now. And as I speak them, it becomes real again and I force myself back to face the horror:

"I'm scared," I told him, as if he and I were there together, back in that war. "Not the foolish fear of a boy in the night; not startled by the glimpse of a jacket hung on a chair in the dark; not the hair-raising alarm of 'what is that?' Nope. For the first time in my life, I know what fear is in its most primitive sense."

Lachey sits up – a captivated audience for my tale.

"My bowels loosen as I bury my head in the sand. The blasts are horrendous and relentless, screaming through the air to burst with an earth-shaking rumble spraying beach into the morning sky. I can hear the screams of the men, so many screams and so many men; the screams of the horses; the smell of blood and powder is thick, even with my face pressed tight against the earth."

I pause for a moment. My eyes fall on Lachey as I try to measure the depth of his reckoning. I see his eyes narrow, and he nods. Then I'm back on the beach.

"A near-miss. The concussion sends my world buzzing with blindness. I feel my bowels release, my crotch grows warm and wet. The smells of the battle are joined by another stink, hideous but somehow complimentary to my situation. I don't care."

I tell him how the onslaught continued, how the men caught in the open had no choice but to dig where they fell and pray face down in the dirt, and how the morning is filled with the sounds of fury, agony, and death. Gradually the cannons subside and just the sporadic cracks of rifle fire lend their voices to the mortal choir of moans and cries.

"I raise my head to look up and down the line, now broken and littered with crooked limbs and bloodied torsos." I pause again, my throat grows tight with the memory.

"Their guns had found the distance and rained hell down on us. Smoke shrouds the beach that stretches from the dunes to my rear all the way to the distant walls of the rebel fort that stands as a sentinel on this coast of the Carolina's. The ocean breeze makes short work of the smoke, that drifts and clears the eyes so again I see the walls of the Confederate stronghold. Its a structure of stone and mud, wood, and bags of sand dot the ramparts and encase the gun placements."

In detail I describe a simple thing, "the thin hairs of smoke from the cannon still drift thread-like from these portals of fiery reckoning." Lachey nods solemnly as I relate how those cannons, in minutes, had left a mark on our numbers, "but the word was we numbered a thousand at least, and even that would be an estimate of the lowest proportion," I said.

"The bugle beckoned our retreat. I watch those who could moan and crawl, others more foolish than brave, stood and ran back to the cover of the dunes. I stay on my belly and make myself small, sliding like a snake through the sand, which suddenly puffs into little clouds beside me followed by the rifle's report behind me. Well, that gets me up and running with the rest.

"I don't talk, as you know, Lachey. I join the ranks in silence as I've generally done since signing up. I learned quickly that my southern mannerisms were an oddity and a threat to my northern friends. I may speak one word here or there, most times in a quick response to a command, and in cases of camaraderie I found a smile, a nod, or a shrug to be usually sufficient.

"I move among the men sitting on the sand, crouching with an overt caution despite the cover of the dunes that now surrounds us. I sit close to the Colonel. I don't rightly know his name. I'm sure it had been spoken but I paid no mind, we just call him Colonel, but I'd heard the first lieutenant call him Raymond on occasion. But then, as I imagine now-a-days, a man's name is mainly only needed for the mark above his grave, so I don't bother much about such small matters. He's a young man, this Colonel, only about a season older than myself so I wonder how, in such youth, a man could be fit to hold in his hands the lives of so many?"

Lachey is patient with my digression, which I push aside and take us back to the beach. "The air screams again: once then twice – but the explosions roar far short of our cover and reverberate outside of our protective dunes. The occasional rifle crack sounds off and occasionally brings a distant response but other than that the sea of union blue sits quietly on the sand.

"I'm close enough to command to pick up their words. I see a man address the Colonel. 'The gap is wide. The sand is loose. Their heavy guns will tear us apart before we crossed even a third of the ground. Another charge would be suicide Colonel.' I hear the man say it, and I'm apt to agree. He has captain's bars on his shoulders. A thin trickle of blood tracks down from beneath his hairline, tinging orange the blonde hairs of his scraggly bangs, but his cold blue eyes are clear and firm as he addresses his commanding officer, again, who I can only see from behind.

"'Send the coloured,' said the Colonel. 'We're in this fight for them. Even Lincoln, I believe, would say now is a time good as any for these darkies to demonstrate some gratitude. Don't you think?'"

I shake my head at the recollection. Even now, so many years gone, those words of that Colonel sadden me. Lachey's jaw clenches firm. "Only a fool weighs the worth of a man by the glance of an eye and the word of another," he nodded, as did I.

I told Lachey how the Colonel's voice sounded matter of fact, like a chat in a barber's chair while getting a shave, and how my younger self was saddened by his shortcomings in his compassion for his coloured soldiers, who fought and bled side by side over every inch of ground the troops had wandered. "I spat out the rotten taste of betrayal. It landed red, blood on the sand."

Lachey shook his head for a moment. He recalled, and he spoke it now plainly, I'd spoken once of being from the south, "how is it you found yourself fighting for the Union?"

"Well, that would be a story to tell at another telling," I told him, but I did my best to provide a quick summation:

"Being a southerner, I knew too well the plight of the negro, ever since we started plucking them from their Africa, and chaining them as slaves to toil on our land. I was raised on a small farm. Just me, my Ma and Pa. Pa had built three cottages on the land and had purchased three coloured families to occupy them. He'd traded a plow, two mules, and a one fifth share of our next season's crop to Mr. Jacobs on the next farm down the road. It was a good trade for Mr. Jacobs, my Pa had said, and a good trade for us, using the word 'equitable,' which to this day I still like the ring of – 'equitable.'

"The families all had the last name, Jacobs, as was common for the slave to take the surname of the master, and each family brought a child or two into our midst. They helped us work the land, not as slaves but as partners, and shared equally in the fruits of our labour – equitable. Of course, my Pa was careful to treat them as property when they'd go to town, but back on the farm it was the sharing of hard work and genuine kinship."

I felt my face smile, and Lachey's grin grew broad as well, as I recalled making fast friends with the children of those families, the ones old enough to hoot and holler and rough house around the farm.

"I spent many hours of my childhood playing with Nickle and Fanny and Allbright. Never had I ever any reason to reckon that they were any less or different than me, other than the colour of their skin, which I fancied and found reminiscent of chocolate, I told them laughingly, and they neither felt slighted nor found ill will in my teasing humour."

"Chocolate!" Lachey exclaimed. "Ah, it's been many a moment since my mouth's had the pleasure of such a morsel. Shut your trap Pitt, or I'll be coming doon with ya."

Like I'd said, the man was infectious, and my laughter joined his to sweep across the clearing and bounce around the forest to our backs. After a few moments, we settled back down, and I continued my response.

Ma, who had been a schoolteacher, decided to set up a classroom and me and Nickle and Fanny and Allbright attended half day every day, and learned our arithmetics, readings and writings and such."

It had been through this mechanism, I explained, that I formed my opinion much like my father's, that the coloureds were no different than we white folk, and in fact were equal or better at many things in this world.

"So, when Lincoln signed his proclamation and this hellish war broke out, it didn't sit right in my mind and heart and I did not agree with the moods of my southern brothers in respect to the negros, so, with the encouragement of my father I rode north to the state of New York and signed my commission to serve the Union Army. That's how I found myself on that beach surrounded by bluebellies and hearing the command express a mindset similar to the Confederacy he's fighting. Again, it doesn't sit right in my heart and mind, and I know I don't belong here with the Union any more than I belonged with the Confederates.

"I watch the coloureds rise and take formation – their lines are straight and their motions strictly regimental as their sergeant bellows his commands. I don't look at their eyes. I can't. But I can hear the taunts of the soldiers still sitting in the sands – mocked encouragement and slights against their very humanity. I'm ashamed of myself, of my people, but still, I can't bring myself to raise my head and look them in the eyes as they march by. But inside, I knew those that could were lesser in moral standing before the eyes of God.

"Still not looking them in their eyes, I stand up and move to the column of men and slinging my rifle over my shoulder, I join the ranks of the coloured brigade. I saw the blue eyes, the brown eyes, the hazel eyes – the white eyes – of men look away when they spotted me marching among the negros."

"You were a fool for your morals, man," Lachey stared in disbelief. "But its no a bad thing, I suppose," he continued. "Can't say I would have done the same."

I described to him the column of men moving out, each man marching in-step with the man ahead and the man behind. The ripple of the drums and the sweet song of the flute provide the rhythm for the march. My eyes settle on the back of the man in front of me. The dunes move past slowly, the sand a loose surface for a soldier's march.

"And as I lift my head to look forward, I see the point of the column passing by the final rise of the sand – into the open, into the grinder we march.

"I can hear them still. The cannons sounded and the screams announced the approach of the shots. The first one struck, and men flew scattered through the air, tumbling and twisting then lost in the dust.

"'Chaaaarge!!! Double time, double time!' The cry wrang out. We broke ranks and the sound of feet pounding the sand to my right and left filled my ears. Men before me stumbled and fell over the bodies that had fallen before them. Rifle fire rung out from the walls of the fort and the cannons continued their relentless volleys, raining balls of iron and deadly cannisters upon us."

I paused then, the brim of my worn-out Union hat, though frayed and tattered, darkening my eyes before the flames, eyes which I now raised to look at my companion with solemn recall.

"The coloureds didn't scream, I noticed. They died and suffered silently, not that their sounds would have been heard amidst the cacophony of battle. In moments, the beach had become an abattoir. The carnage was fresh and seemed to be moving, writhing beneath the continuous concussions of the Confederate's barrage."

My words landed heavy. I could see it in the shine that now glistened from Lachey's blue eyes. I continued, recounting my dash across the sand, how I saw the walls of the fort drawing nearer. I had yet to fire a shot and continued to run towards the enemy that fired too many. When I reached the point where I had to angle my neck to look up to the top of the battlements, like many men around me, bloodied and glistening with sweat, the ground fell away from beneath my feet, and I felt myself tumbling down a sandy slope then bumping to a stop at the level bottom.

"Around me the men were scrambling." I see it plainly as I remember, my hands forming claws that scrape at the air. Lachey watches, mesmerized.

"I stood up to see a deep trench had been my downfall and many had suffered a similar fate. I joined the men scrambling up the forward bank of this treacherous trap. The sand was loose and slipped beneath my feet. The slope of the bank was steep and the number of men attempting the climb only lent to the impediment of progress for any one individual. The bottom of the trench had found the water and quickly became thick mud. The harder I tried to climb the bank the more sand I displaced. Contrary to my best efforts, I was gaining no ground. The matter grew worse as the men that neared the top discovered a near vertical rise at the pinnacle of the embankment and tumbled back down to the place where they started. And all the while, more men tumbled into the trap and the trench began to fill and we were crowded and pressed close together.

"Unbeknownst to us men at the bottom of the trench, the fort of the Confederacy above on the beach had opened its gates and released the outpouring of blood-thirsty grey-coats. Though I couldn't see them, yet. I could hear their high-pitched rebel yells approaching the top of the trench. I knew what was about to happen but there was nothing to be done. We were worse than fish in a barrel for those rebel guns and they soon appeared in a celebratory line across the top of the trench, hootin' and grinnin' – firing at will and again, as quick as they could reload."

There were no words, as was evident by the slack-jawed stare that Lachey tossed my way. In the end I was wounded, buried alive and lost to the light of day.

"I hear the gunshots, over and over, bullets seeking and finding the flesh of the trapped men. I hear a few shots of return fire, but they are silenced quickly on the heels of a rebel yell and a sudden volley from above. The cannons are still sounding, finding its fodder across the beach where the rest of the Union force has begun its charge. I can hear the trampling of the feet approaching and the promised shouts of retribution. Then I hear nothing. The light is gone. For me, at least, this battle is over."

I had heard later, after being freed from the sand and the piling of bodies, by men I did not recognize, men of an entirely different regiment, that the charge upon which we had been so recklessly ordered was one that could have, that should have waited. The Colonel had decided to mount the charge seeking glory on the field of battle, some had said. The man had known the navy was to arrive offshore by mid-morning, but he'd ordered the charge anyway. About an hour after the smoke had cleared and the slaughter had subsided, the Union Navy drifted close to the shore and hammered the fort with a rain of fire, silencing the Confederate guns that had proven so lethal.

"That was the day," I concluded.

I could never view men in the same light again, "the savagery of this garden, once referred to as Eden in those cherished scriptures, was a deep gash to my soul."

Lachey understood and expressed himself as such. Those down below think the men who fled to the high country were rejected by the world, he said, but in truth, as any man in the high country will tell you, "It is we who reject that world below, and turn our backs on that savage garden of which you so eloquently speak."

Lachey reached and grabbed the spit, steam rising as he tore away a strip of rabbit and tossed the roast to my eager hands. Somewhere, high above our backs, the rock of MissT rises high into the night, but down here where the foothills become the downward slope to the Valley of Many Rivers, the evenings hold a man with cold, damp arms.

We eat quietly, my mind re-playing the charge of the fort and the trap of the sand that day on that Carolina beach. It would replay now, over and over, keeping me restless through much of the night. I know my eyes closed and felt heavy at times, but I could not testify truthfully to having found any real rest in my tossing slumber.

Despite my doubts sleep must have found me, for I awake in the morning and I find myself alone, the fire but dying embers and no sign of my old friend Lauchlin McTavish. I see his tracks moving off. My eyes follow his trail for a moment – back into the trees, up to the high country. MissT's never-changing countenance stares stone-cold back down upon me. She bids me adieu, and this time, I nod and return the gesture.

CHAPTER 2

12-Shot Trevor and Terrible Ted

Personally, I'd never heard a spit about the Trowley brothers, and as events would soon dictate, I strongly wish I never had. Despite their lack of notoriety in my mind, they sure seemed quite full of themselves when they bolted their mounts from behind a thorny thicket and blocked the trail that Mr. Andrews and I had spent such a pleasant morning following, up until then.

MissT had sunken out of sight, the deeper the trees drew us in and the further down we moved on the trail. To be honest, I was not surprised by their sudden appearance. Mr. Andrews and I had caught their scent at least an hour back on the trail and knew just seconds before the underbrush started crashing that we were drawing closer to the point where we were sure to meet. And we did.

Maybe I'd been up high too long but I had to give my head a shake when the boys barged roughly onto the trail. The smaller of the two, acting bigger than his britches, drew his mount close to the shoulder of Mr. Andrews, which made him uncomfortable, and that made me uncomfortable. The trail was narrow, but the aggressive little fellow urged his horse forward and barged his way by, taking up position to my rear. That was,

I would soon learn, 12-Shot Trevor, on account of the twin six-shooters that swung from his hips. The other, the bigger fella, owned the moniker of Terrible Ted, more of a reflection of his quick-to-anger attitude than his lack of daily cleansing, though the latter was quite evident given my proximity downwind.

They dressed like those Pinkertons, as I recall: tight, formal pinstriped jackets and funny, round hats with barely a brim to speak of. They each sported identical mustaches, and while Ted sat squarely and firmly in the saddle, I could hear little Trevor shifting agitated behind me. The soft and familiar sound of metal slipping from leather whispered in my ear. I knew Trevor had drawn on me and now pointed one of them Colts at my back.

"You best be polishing that pistol," I said, not turning to look back at Trevor but keeping my gaze firmly on his bigger brother. I moved my hand slowly up to rest on the grip of my dependable, Colt six-shot, Army Issue 1860, which protrudes clean from just beneath the hem of my deer-skinned waist coat. I cock it quiet and slow. I see Ted's eyes fall on my hand, on my holstered weapon. I see his Adam's Apple bulge, which will happen to a man when he realizes he's bitten off more than he can chew. Ted keeps his hands away from everything. His eyes dart over my shoulder at his brother, Trevor, behind me.

"Put your gun away now, Trev," Ted says, slow and careful. "This fella aint gonna be no trouble. Are you mister?"

I take a breath and lean back in the saddle. I hear the leather again as Trevor holsters his pistol behind me. I level my gaze at Ted and nod. "I don't deal in trouble mister. Me and Mr. Andrews here, well we've been riding all morning without a hitch or hint of trouble. Can honestly say it's not on our list of things to find."

Ted eyes my mount – like something he would covet. "Well. Mr. Andrews is a mighty fine-looking horse. We're the Trowley brothers. The Terrible Trowley brothers. That fella behind is my brother Trevor, 12-Shot Trevor, and I'm Ted. That's right, Terrible Ted Trowley. Expect you might have heard of us." Ted seemed to sit taller in the saddle with the ending of his statement. From behind, Trevor steered his horse back around, again bumping the shoulder of Mr. Andrews, which again made Mr. Andrews uncomfortable and, as I've said, made me uncomfortable.

He sides up beside his brother and the resemblance is uncanny. I laugh, shake my head, and tell them as much, then break the news, with a level of somberness, that the Trowley name leaves no mark on my mind, and I am unfamiliar with their perceived fame. "What's there to know?" I ask, explaining my recent descent from the high country and my prolonged absence from the world below.

"Why hell, mister," Trevor pushed the bowl of a hat back on his head and scratched. "Our exploits are told by John Maximilian! We're legendary and immortalized in the pages of the dime-store novels he writes and sells in all the big towns back east. We's famous." Trevor grins broad and nods at his brother, as he speaks the last two words.

I didn't rightly know what he meant. The word, 'famous,' is as foreign to my ears as the jumbled words of the Blackfoot, which I never bothered to take the time to learn, seeing no need given my solitary ways. But being familiar as are most, with the boastful ways of men, I feigned my sudden recognition and mockingly nodded.

"John Maximilian, you say! Dime-store novels, well get on and get out! Why didn't you say so?" I smiled at the boys, and they both smiled back, seeming pleased that I had accepted their celebratory status. Then, as I'm sometimes prone to do, I pull out my proverbial pin and pop their proverbial balloon. The smile left my face and like there was butter in my holster I draw down on them boys with my pistol and shoot little Trevor in the knee cap.

"Never heard of him," I said. Turning my aim on Ted while watching Trevor fall from the saddle to squirm painfully around on the ground.

"Trevor!" Ted shouts, his hand moves for his holster, but I click my tongue nice and loud, a sound that was fond to the ears of Mr. Andrews, who wasted not a moment and bolted up the path, knocking both Trevor's and Ted's horses out of the way.

Mr. Andrews kept up his furious pace, racing and winding down the trail and through the trees. A rise on the land to my left catches my eye and I steer Mr. Andrews towards it, slowing his pace as we leave the trail and quickly pick our way through the undergrowth. We mount the rise and grabbing my rifle from its scabbard, I dismount on the run and send Mr. Andrews down the other side where he can find cover.

I fall flat to the ground and look down the sights of my Winchester, back to the trail to spy the brothers' pursuit – there was none. At least one of them was still back where I'd left them, but both, no doubt, were left stunned by my sudden assault and just as sudden escape. I could hear the soft moans of Trevor drifting through the trees and imagined him rolling on the ground grasping his knee. I'm sure I shattered the cap with that shot and there's no denying 12-Shot Trevor would spend the remainder of his life walking with an ever-present limp, at best.

Ted, it seems, has a bigger brain than I'd a given him credit for. I hears him bush-whacking his way through the trees as opposed to charging up the trail like an easy target. He's moving slowly, loudly, but coming straight my way like he knows I'd be sitting here waiting.

I look down the hill and I see Mr. Andrews, quietly and calmly munching on some shrubs. My Sharps rifle is in my bed roll, but I wished I'd grabbed it, seeing now that my foes are providing me with the time to aim. None-the-less, I turn my sights to the noise in the forest and in just a few seconds I catch a glimpse of old Ted's pinstriped suit and funny, round hat, sitting in the saddle and swaying as he picks his way through the trees.

I really had no want to kill these fellas. I'd just as soon get on my horse and ride, leaving their missteps behind and letting bygones be bygones, so the saying goes. I hadn't come down the mountain looking for trouble and I'd only been below for a few meagre hours and already I had half the mind to go back and return to the majesty of MissT. But my other half of mind, well, it was peering through the crude sights of my Winchester repeater and sure enough, had found the form of Terrible Ted. Once, twice, three times that funny hat bounced up into the sight and a squeeze of the trigger could have ended it all, but I'd never been a malicious man, and the proof of that was clearly demonstrated by Trevor's wounded knee.

I fired off one shot. It ricocheted off the trunk of a tree, close to that funny hat on Ted's head – close enough to startle his horse and force the man to fall and land heavily on the ground. I hear him scampering through the underbrush. The man was sobbing, it sounded like. Fear has a way of reaching in and stroking our gentler side and I assumed that was Teddy's plight right now. I could see him, but he couldn't see me. I knew it. He knew it. And he knew that I knew it. I quickly assessed, given my skillful marksmanship, that Ted's fear was completely justified.

"Ted. I could have killed you and your brother." My voice sounded loud in the quiet of the forest. Even the birds had ceased their songs to listen. "I told you all, trouble was not on my list of things to find, but you-all just had to make it so."

I could see his head bobbing back among the trees. He was trying to follow my voice and get a bead on my position. I fired another shot to puff up the ground just a hair from the man's left ankle.

"Could a killed you again Ted. Let's not be stupid and see this to what appears to be the inevitable end. My next bullet will be in your brain, I swear. Or, and I know you're a smart man Ted, at least when measured beside that fool of a brother you got, you can relieve yourself of all your weapons and walk out to the trail with your hands in the air. I won't shoot you. I promise. In fact, you do as I ask, I will return with you to your brother and help him with that nasty scrape on his knee. I've got a kit in my saddle that'll fix him up good. Least until you get him to some doctoring. What'd ya say Ted, fair enough?"

It was less than a moment when Ted's voice came drifting back. "Okay," he said. "I'm coming out. I'm doing like you asked. Don't shoot."

I stayed belly down and watched him move to the trail

through the sights of my rifle. When he was almost there, I moved down the hill and whistled. Mr. Andrews rounded the small hill behind which he had enjoyed his shrubs and joined me on the path with Terrible Ted.

He had done as was asked. He stood with his hands up and was unarmed. Ted leads the way back to his brother, I follow with my pistol levelled to his back, and without a word we walk back to see how little Trevor is fairing. At first glance, judging by the blood that stained the ground and the permanent grimace on Trevor's face, not too well was my immediate summation.

I look at Ted hard. His eyes fall level with mine for a moment then drop to the ground, unable to hold my gaze. I look down at his brother. Trevor lay still with his eyes closed, only the frantic rise and fall of his chest and the stifled sobs of pain give any sign of awareness. His knee, unfortunately, was pretty much gone, and I realized his proximity to my pistol had been the ultimate downfall to that much treasured part of human anatomy.

"Afraid I have to break my promise Ted," I said quite sincere, pulling my eyes from his brother to look Ted plainly in the face. "There's nothing in my saddle to fix that mangled mess. I'm awfully sorry Ted. I really am. I misjudged my proximity and did much more damage than I intended."

Ted looked at his brother, then raised his eyes to mine. Seemed the "terrible" part had abandoned him for a moment as his hard, dark eyes seemed to soften. He tilted his head, and I smirked a little, despite the circumstances. For a moment Ted fondly reminded me of Mr. Andrews when I said something too fast, and the darned horse couldn't comprehend.

"You're a strange man," he said. "I believe and accept your apology mister… what's your name? Or would you prefer I call you Mr. Sincerity, as you've made me so inclined?"

Ted smiled. I laughed. Trevor trembled and moaned.

"Pitt," I said, raising my chin, showing my eyes clear, not caring to remove my cap at this juncture. "Rosco Pitt. Expect you-all to have heard of me," I replied with a grin, which produced a wider smile across Ted's face.

After a moment's discussion, and a shake of the hands, a pledge as strong as any other, I busied myself applying a quick tourniquet to the moaning Trevor then threw together a ramshackle stretcher upon which to pull Ted's wounded kin. The branches and bows were a flimsy bed, and the bounce of the trail was sure to repel a comfortable ride, but Ted would see his brother home to his mother where the man would lose what he'd have to lose, or have the rest turn green and fester. It was a fair ride east, Ted had said, assuring me I would be welcomed while apologizing in advance for the assault his mother was sure to rain down upon me, once told it was Rosco Pitt, the man on that very horse, who had shot her youngest son so viciously.

I side-eyed him and looked with shame down at the form of his suffering brother whose head bounced and bobbed with every trot of the horse. Despite my life in the wilds of the mountains, and my escapades on its very slopes, and despite the bloody struggles I've seen and made no effort to avoid, I never took pleasure in the death of any man, though my hatred at the moment of some souls' passings was quick to vanish once their hearts ceased to beat. I discovered quite quickly, after joining the Union, that despite my passive raising and my tendency to give the benefit of doubt to my fellow man, I was proficient at killing, be it gun, blade or bare of hand, and though I excel at many things, killing was the one thing I could do best. Though I'd waged no war with the peoples of the mountain, I'd had my share of scrapes with both Crow and Blackfoot, and others of such earthly tribes I could not guess to name, but they were the struggles of men, the hunter and the hunted, the challenger and the challenged, often sought out and often arbitrary, but always resolved beneath the never-changing countenance of MissT.

We rode for a while in silence. Mr. Andrews coughed now and then, reminding me he was still right there between my legs, and was not pleased with my lack of addressing him with my queries as is common on a day's ride. But I stayed quiet, as seemed respectful, given Ted's furtive glances back at his brother and the film of sweat that now glistened on the young man's skin. The tourniquet would slow the bleeding, but it was no use against the putrid infection that now ran through the boy's body like a raging blaze on a grassy plain. It was still a quarter of an hour till we got to the boy's home, and even then, I thought with concern, the saw best be sharp, and the leg taken quick.

I was growing keenly aware of Ted's rising emotions. I watched his turns increase in frequency and his constant frown form deep furrows cross his brow. Thinking I'd ease his mind for a spell, I drew my own mind from my own wicked ways and pondered to the man in hopes of distraction.

"Say," I said to Ted, who glances over his shoulder to acknowledge my address. "You and your brother, you don't seem all that bad of a sort. What's with the names? Terrible Ted and 12-Shot Trevor? From what I can tell you two couldn't rob a blind man of his cane without his deaf friend hearing you coming."

"I'm of no mind to tell you my tale, least not at this time, Mr. Pitt, Rosco if I may," Ted replied without turning around. "Now in the case of 12-Shot there," he threw his head in a backward direction, drawing my eyes once again to his tortured brother, "well there's debate among many on how he came to claim that moniker. There are those who say, quite accurately I might add, it's on account of the twin six shooters he carries on his hips."

Ted pauses for a moment, whether for theatrics or because he is truly distracted by the buzzard that circles high above I cannot say for certain, but it has the desired effect on my anticipation of what is the alternative to the 12-shot explanation. Finally, after what seems to my mind an eternity, he finishes his thought and ends my mental torture.

"While there are others who say he's earned the name of 12-Shot, because generally, in the calmest of moments, it takes him all twelve shots to finally, if he even does, hit the object at which he is aiming. Now I'm not taking one side or the other Rosco, and I would never be one to speak lowly of my brother, but based on your experience with the man who now moans from a bullet you blasted through his now shattered knee, why do you think my esteemed next of kin would deserve the moniker 12-Shot Trevor?"

He pulled up on his reigns and brought his horse to a stop, eyeing me as I moved up level. His smile was genuine, and he knew my uncertainty to the question he'd countered with loomed large in my mind. Ted smiled so broadly. He had revealed my gullible nature, a product that I now realized was a direct result of more than five years in the high country and a failure to have remained familiar with the linguistic joust that is, in educated circles, I'm certain I've read, referred to as sarcasm.

Ted pulled his horse close and reached out to pat his hand on my shoulder. His sudden display of camaraderie set my mind back. I was once again half a mind to turn tail and run back to MissT, but his face was flush with genuine amusement, and I felt a kinship forming with Terrible Ted. If things went well, maybe, I thought with some hope, maybe I could convince the man to take a bath.

"Just up over this next rise," Ted said, interrupting my daydreaming, nodding his chin ahead. "At the top, the trees grown thin down to the meadow and Plitter-Plop Crick, where my Ma's shack sits before the drooping branches of the Widow's Wailing Willow. Ma says it's a haunted tree, but don't pay her no mind. Just you know she will be ornery, but don't worry, I got you covered Rosco."

We reached the top of the next rise and sure enough Ted was true to his word. The trees grew thin the land opened wide and greeted the eyes with the sweetest meadow I'd seen in years. The grass sloped green and plush, down to the banks of the winding creek that wound its way like a bending ribbon, from one stand of trees to the next. It curled around the crooked, one-story shack that sat on a patch of worn dirt from decades of foot falls. Dots darted at the front of the structure, ducks or chickens or fowl of some sort, and my eyes caught the corner of a crooked fence, extending off the side and disappearing behind the box of sticks these boys called home. Behind it stood a similarly crooked barn, and the shack had a porch, so I rested easier knowing Mr. Andrews would or could have a roof over his head this night, if Ma sees fit.

We nudged our horses, both Ted and me at the same time, and down the hill we rode at a measured pace, mindful of Trevor bouncing on the stretcher. As we drew closer the front door opened and a woman stepped out. Ma, I presume, waited to greet us. Once again I had half a mind to turn tail and run, preferring the wrath of MissT to the ominous threat that now stood in-waiting on the twisted porch of the crooked shack in the valley of Plitter-Plop Crick.

CHAPTER 3

Cupid's wings

I've never been one to romanticize, but I gotta say as we trotted down the gradual incline to cross the dirt-packed yard at the front of the shack, the woman, who I assumed to be Ma, struck quite the figure standing ready on the porch, cradling 12-gauges of reckoning and setting her jaw as square and firm as any man would, defending what's his.

I noticed the closer we got her countenance shifted, but her defensive stance remained poised, and though dressed as a man hard at his day-to-days, the womanliness of her form was not lost on my scrutiny of the scene. The sun at my back enhanced the sight and I could not pull my eyes away. Her face was smooth and flushed by the effort of some recent exertions. Her eyes were as chestnuts, large and round, and the locks thick and sandy, cascaded round her head, frosted white at the tips; a testament not to her age, but somehow her wisdom. Her eyes fell on me offering no warmth as should be expected given the stranger that I was, and the state of her youngest being slung cross the ground in some serious measure of despair.

"Theodore?" She spoke the name as a question, those dark eyes flashing up to her oldest boy who now was climbing off the saddle. The sound of her voice dripped in my ears, sweet as a batch of fresh-rendered honey. It had been years since I'd heard the English spoken with such soft tones, like a song, with a subtle scratch to the vocalizations weighted heavy with emotions. She was a woman who would wear her heart on her sleeve, I thought, and would make no qualms when it came to expressing herself, regardless of her cause or need. And I'm sure her actions would come with equal lack of consideration, as I noted her finger still stroking that shotgun's trigger and the barrel still pointed my way, though her eyes now followed Ted's dismount.

I begin to dismount myself when I feels her eyes dart back my way and hear the hammer of that 12-gauge cock. I freezes, my eyes shooting up to meet hers, my foot, once lowering, now hovering just inches from the ground. With one foot still in the stirrup and one hand on the saddle horn, I dangle on the side of Mr. Andrews, who brays his displeasure at the sudden unequitable distribution of my considerable weight.

"It's okay Ma."

The sound of Ted's voice carries some relief for me, for a moment, but that thought is fleeting. I'm still clinging to the saddle horn and Ma's eyes have not wavered, nor has the finger, such a tiny, delicate appendage, stopped stroking that trigger.

"What happed to Trevor?" Her voice was even and tempered, but her eyes threatened with the dark clouds of an approaching storm. I begins to have my doubts about Ted's previous re-assurances, and though an early-evening breeze cools the air, I can feel the beads of nervous sweat forming beneath my worn-out army cap.

"He got shot Ma." Ted moved closer, slowly, with his hands in the air. A might strange, I thought, not the way a boy would normally approach his mother. I pondered on the chance that Ma might shoot old Ted and began to feel my bent knee protest and my hand losing its grip on the horn of the saddle. The fact that Mr. Andrews seemed not to care that my very life was dependent on his immediate cooperation, dancing in place and throwing his head back with a muffled whiny, only made my cap grow damper across the brow. I saw her eyes glance at Ted for a moment, and took the opportunity to complete my dismount, finally freed from my statuesque pose. I square my shoulders and look up at the woman on the porch, who once again stares hard my way, and her eyes don't leave me, still staring over Ted's shoulder as he finds her in a warm embrace and coaxes her to lower the gun.

I nodded at those chestnut eyes, and my heart, I swear, skipped a beat or two. I felt my mind slipping deep into those warm, brown pools of promise – no longer hard but now wet and soft with a mother's pain.

Ted moved back and stood beside his mother. He nodded his head down my way and placed a gentle son's arm around her shoulder. Ma seemed to have wilted slightly, and now stood less threatening with the gun dangling, forgotten at her side.

"This here is Rosco Pitt, Ma. He put that tourni-cat round Trevor's leg. Probably saved him, stopped him from bleeding out. But Trev's got some fection, Ma. Something hot and nasty in his blood."

I was grateful to Ted. He failed to mention that I was the one who shot her son, at least for now, and in doing so the woman, who now hurried to Trevor's side, was unaware the boy would be in no need of that tourniquet I applied, had I not first applied my pistol to his knee cap.

She didn't turn to look but just belted out instructions. After a quick inspection of the boy's non-existent knee, and a hurried press of her hand to his forehead, she told us concisely to gently carry Trevor to the barn out back, clear off the work bench and lay him to rest. With that said, she got up and disappeared into the shack.

Ted and I unhitched the stretcher from the back of his horse and commenced dragging Trevor back to the barn. We laid him on the straw-strewn floor for just a moment, while Ted lit a lamp hanging on the wall and I wiped off the work bench that looked in the dark like a madman's table of torture. But it looked fine in the light, after I cleared it of debris, and I whistled sharply.

Mr. Andrews came bounding round the side of the shack and stopped to stand still at the door of the barn. I unpacked my duster and grabbed my Winchester from its scabbard, as was my habit. I whispered to Mr. Andrews, thanking him for his quick response, stroking his muscled neck and promising to rid him of that saddle shortly. Leaning my rifle against a knotted post, I draped my duster over the work bench and bent my back to help Ted lift poor Trevor to the flatness of the tabletop.

As soon as we'd finished that task Ma came rushing into the barn. Torch light or sun light, it mattered not, my breath was truly taken by the woman's earthly beauty. She had changed her manly, white shirt for a womanly, printed frock, sleeveless and rather small for her adequate curves, I assume it was better suited to the messy task at hand. Her trousers was the grey of a southern soldier, faded by years, but a rebel's pants just the same. My eyes did not lie, and the memory of Johnny Reb's legs at the top of the trench was etched in my mind for a time immeasurable.

She paid no mind to Ted or me. I nodded at the man, who nodded back then moved close to watch his mother work. She placed a black bag of leather on the table and began removing rolls of cloth, small, shiny blades, and a jar of what looked a moldy mucus, to my ignorant eye, but was obviously a poultice of sorts. Upon opening its stench carried quickly across the small space of the barn and penetrated my nostrils as the remnants of unwashed feet.

With my hosts being otherwise occupied and the light fading quickly from the cloud-scattered sky, I took the opportunity to fulfil my promise to Mr. Andrews and freed him from the burden of the saddle. He brayed and sputtered his thick, horse lips with appreciation, then galloped off to explore the creek and the meadow, with the last of the light of day.

I pondered the day, and all that had unfolded, and with saddle in arms, I moved towards the Widow's Wailing Willow and the gentle bend of Plitter-Plop Crick. My glances repeatedly drift to the glow of light from the barn. I readied my camp by the haunted tree and the lapping sounds of the creek that plittered-n-plopped on the rocks as it wound its way.

My mind keeps turning as I build my fire. I spent much of the day, reflecting, thinking and looking back up to MissT, and now my night was filled with the thoughts of another lady, one to whom I have yet to be formally introduced, and yet, has already, it seems, made an indelible mark on my villainous heart.

Like I said, I've never been one to romanticize, but I have had one other occasion when such a thing has stolen my mind and took hostage my heart. But that was so long ago I'd almost forgotten those simple days when Steph had bumbled into my life and edged her womanly ways into my every waking thought. It was another time, not long after the war, wanted as both a deserter and traitor, and wandering lost, I found some solace in barely-the-town of Worsley, and earned a meagre pay under the name of James Carmicheal. There was some contentment in those days, as I recall. The job of stable hand paid little, but I didn't need nor want for much, having only the meagre life of a soldier to draw from.

A harvest dance, and she looked so pretty. I remembered her dark ringlets of hair smelled of lilacs as we danced, and her pouting mouth spread in a smile that made the ground drop from beneath my feet every time she graced me with such expression.

From that night on we stole our moments, and each one was as, or more precious than the moments before. We were young and full of fancy future, we thought, but her daddy had a different view, and after weeks of heart-felt bliss and gentle joinings, his possessive rage got the better of the man.

One night, as I finished up my day-to-days, be damned if the fool didn't barge into the stable and thinking not for a second of the consequences, pulled out the biggest knife I'd seen till that very moment. Well, I was still a sprite in my judgements and Steph's Pa, well he was a beast of a man and considerably larger than my malnourished youth, and I don't deny the shimmer of that blade in the dim light of the stable made me shiver.

I didn't fool with the man. My pistol rested firmly on my hip and with the hand of a war-hardened, seasoned killer, I pulled it fast and dropped him quicker, leaving a clean, round hole in the centre of his head. And so ended my whirl-wind romance and my days of content in barely-the-town of Worsley.

I sees her like it was yesterday: Steph in her flowered dress twirling and twirling on a sunny afternoon; Steph, smiling wide like she did, and laughing at my southern drawl and 'peculiar' manners in expressing myself. I had told her I loved her, and she laughed, her eyes looking up at me in earnest, she said she felt the same.

My memories of the moment spring fresh, and despite my age and weathered mind, I tear just a little – "damn smoke," I mumble, blaming the flame for the loss that suddenly welled up to pool in my eyes. I never said goodbye to the girl. Before her Pa's blood had a chance to dry, I was quick to the saddle and fast out of town, not once looking back with my physical eyes, but drifting to her once again, and often, in my mind.

I hear voices and it disrupts my deep thoughts. In the light from the door of the barn I see two figures gesturing with their hands, and hurried words, though garbled by distance, find my ears. The two figures part and one approaches. The other, who by the height of his form and length of his gate proves to be Ted, I see moseying back up to the shack and disappearing inside. Ma walks steadily to my fire, without a word the woman sits cross legged across from me and stares at my blinking eyes.

"You shot my boy," she said plainly. "Explain your actions. Theodore told me but he's as dense as a bear-path's thicket. I want to hear it from you, Mr. Pitt, and then my judgement will follow, as is my prerogative being the boy's mother. Why did you shoot my boy?"

Dripping honey. Again, I must shake my head. I try to respond but my tongue feels twisted and tied in a thousand knots. I find it harder to look at her, the longer my silence lingers. Finally, I find my words, and could only hope this woman was as sweet as her voice and as fair as the flawless face that glowed by the flames of my fire.

"I sincerely apologize for the infliction I've imposed on your son, Ma'am. As I'm sure Ted has told you, I've been years in the high country and my angst when it comes to confrontations has grown frayed, tattered, and quick to break."

She watched me as I spoke, and while I was fully engaged with the eloquence of my recitation, a boy inside me squirmed with sheepish pleasure, feeling the warmth of her scrutinizing gaze. Her eyes moved over my face, following every line and crease that etched their paths across my forehead, at the corners of my mouth, and that crinkled when I grinned, at the corners of my eyes. Her gaze moved up to my cap, and down to my trousers, then lingered with a sense of admiration at my buckskinned waist coat, that I had fashioned and stitched with the ligaments of the very same animal.

"To be frank Miss... I'm sorry, I would like to address you with the respect you deserve, Ma'am. I could assume you carry the name Trowley, as do your boys, but my daddy taught me never to assume when meeting a new friend, ask and learn and cherish the building of the bond. What is your proper name, Ma'am?"

"I'm Mrs. Trowley to most round these parts. You can call me that, or Ma'am is just fine. My given name is Marjorie, but I'm not too fond of that sound so I'd be pleased if you'd keep it from your lips, Mr. Pitt."

She could talk all night and I'd be just fine with that. "Thank you, Mrs. Trowley," I said. "You can call me Rosco if you're so inclined. I've always been fond of its sound and to hear your honey voice say it would sure enough make my night a blissful one."

I saw her shift slightly at my words, and though I couldn't be certain by just the light of the fire, I swear she smiled just a little, as I remarked on the charms of her soothing tones.

"As to your boys," I continued, having re-found some of my natural confidence, "they was trying to rob me, and though I don't fault them for that, as I know men are mostly driven to do such dastardly acts in difficult times, but Trevor's knee came about after the boy passed me by from an eye to eye encounter, to settle in behind and aim at least one of those twin Colts he sports at my back. Now, not sure where you-all come from, but back in Missouri, where I spawned to this world, back shooters are dealt with harshly, and Trevor should count himself lucky it was me who took offense to his low-down ploy, and not some other back-country vermin who wouldn't think twice about busting a skull as opposed to the cap of a knee."

"So, I should be grateful, you saying? Huh. Guess I never thought on it that way, Mr. Pitt. Gee, maybe tomorrow you can shoot Theodore in the stomach and then tell me to be thankful he's only gut shot as opposed to spitting up blood from a bleeding heart."

I could sense her anger rising, and like the waters of a river after a heavy rain, there was no stopping it.

"You spent too much time up high, Mr. Pitt, if that's your opinion on morality. Where I come from, Mr. Pitt, any assault on my kin is an assault on me, and maybe you haven't noticed quite yet, but I'm not one to take too kindly to any affront on my well-being. Anybody hurts my boys and I hurt them. God knows if their pappy was still alive, he'd have you skinned and quartered and hanging in the barn by now."

Her eyes again lingered on my Union garb. "Missouri?" she continued. "Thems Union colours you're wearing?"

I chuckle and nod. "Yep. Yes, they are," I respond. "Didn't quite see eye to eye with my southern compadres. We's all gots to pick a side Ma'am."

"My Thomas died in that war," she said quietly. "He picked his side, but I understand what you mean Mr. Pitt. He picked his side, though he had no stake in the matter. He followed his friends and his brother. He didn't even know what a slave was or even cared about the politics of the north or the south. We were simple, Mr. Pitt, happy people until the war brought its blood and death to our door. There was no side in that war, until, like my man Thomas, once the fighting became more than the odd skirmish in the hills or on the road, we followed our kin and picked our side."

She leaned forward closer to the fire, emphasizing her words without changing their tones. "I supported my man Mr. Pitt, and every man that served the Confederacy, but us folks around here had no thought of the particulars. We never bothered to ask the reason why. We are drawn to what is familiar, Mr. Pitt, and fearful of what is not. That's what my pappy used to say was healthy living."

Our eyes locked. I sat forward trying to relay that her words were important, and made more sense, other than my own, than any words anyone had uttered since I turned my back on the low-lands and headed high to walk on the bending spine of the earth. I told her how she'd spoken true, and how sorry I was for the loss of her Thomas. Again, I apologized for shooting Trevor, and I gave her my word, "to harm as such was not my intent."

"The boy's an idiot!" Mrs. Trowley blurted the words then laughed like the soft sound of a bell ringing to my ears, a small, tinkling, tiny bell, changing the mood of what had become a tense conversation. She pressed her face to her hands and made a frustrated, sobbing sound. "But I'm glad you didn't kill him," she added, raising her face once again to grace me with the expression of a contrite yet dark and furious angel. "Them boys are too much their father and I've always known they have bad intentions for the world in general. Trevor don't think, that's his problem. From the sounds of it, and just like Theodore said, seems he had it coming."

She sighed, and glanced around the darkness of the meadow, which had fallen thick and unnoticed as we had conversed. A silence fell then, but it was well-suited and not one of discomfort. In the light of the fire, I assessed her again, and was not swayed from my initial inclination towards Mrs. Trowley. In fact, I warmed to the woman even more, having gained a sense of her person and her heart. Both measured well in my assessment.

Without a word she stood, and looked down at me quietly, for a moment. She glanced back at the shack, then turned back to smile at my eyes. Apologetically, she explained the size of the shack would not permit my lodging inside, but she offered the barn as suitable shelter and a fine breakfast at the table in the morning.

"Well thank you Mrs. Trowley. I am in your debt. I'm apt to pass on the barn. The skies and the stars are a shelter I cherish, so I'll just bed down here by this willow if that's alright. Mr. Andrews, on the other hand, prefers a roof overhead when he beds down for the night – be it the bows of a tree or an overhanging ridgeline. Don't ask me why, I don't rightly know, but that horse of mine will not sleep a wink, or allow me to either, if he don't have a roof over his head. He's been that way ever since I got him, and that is another story whose telling is best left for another time."

"Well, hopefully you stay long enough to maybe share that tale with me sometime. I sense you're a good man, and I'd be lying if I said I wouldn't welcome your company, Rosco."

She said it. She said it and I heard it and just as I imagined, the sound of my name on her lips moved more than just my bursting heart. She spun and walked away but without turning around she called back over her shoulder. "Marjorie. You can call me Marjorie, Rosco, until I tells ya you can't."

I watched her shadow move up to the shack and dissolve in the shadow of its lopsided frame. I prepared my bed and whistled for Mr. Andrews, but I should've known he was already inside the barn, bedded down in a dark corner, secure and safe with a roof over his head. I nestled into my bed beneath the Widow's Wailing Willow and listened to the plitter-plop of the creek bubbling over the rocks. In my mind I saw her – Marjorie, Mrs. Trowley – and she wore a flowered dress and spun around and around on a warm, sunny day. I closed my eyes, and I just knew, for the first time in a long time, I might sleep without waking.

CHAPTER 4

A bone to pick

A gentle rumble, closer and louder, then fading again. I hear the bubbling of the creek and feel, as happens sometimes when one first wakes on a frosty morning, the urgent need to relieve my bladder, but my eyelids flutter in earnest protest refusing to open and welcome the day.

I hear it again, that gentle rumble, moving closer and getting louder as before, but suddenly stopping and kicking up dirt, specks of which rain down of my face. I feel, and I hear Mr. Andrews, one snort soft and subdued, bidding me to rise and start the day, and suddenly I recall my bladder was telling me the same.

I scampered from the warmth of my bedding, and B-lined for the Widow's Wailing Willow, moving behind putting the large old weeper between me and the distant windows of the shack. Behind me, the creek gurgles low on the rocks and the song of a morning lark enhances both flows of water that now reach my ears.

My plan was to go to town today, maybe move on my wandering way. I believe I suffered what's called "infatuation," on this evening just past, in regard to my feelings for Marjorie. A good night's sleep had put my mind right, and I reasoned, as

I leaned on the Widow's Wailing Willow relieving myself, that perhaps this sudden "infatuation" was the effects of missing the mountain, the never-changing countenance of MissT. And besides, Mr. Andrews was in need of some proper stabling, and I was itching for a bath and, seeing how I planned to be moving amongst the living, I thought a shave would be in order. I was a might bit curious myself, to see my many faces without the fur that guarded against the cold, harsh breath of MissT over the seasons gone by.

I'd busied myself in the preparations for my departure. My focus was such I'd lost track of the time. When I heard her voice drifting across the meadow, the morning was half gone, and I saw her in the window of the shack, that faced back towards the creek, waving an arm.

"Hey! I see you mister," her shout drifted through the air, complimenting the quiet solace of the mid-morning meadow. I placed my pistol down on the swath of leather I'd spread on the ground for cleaning the gun, the brush and the wire fell from my lap as I pushed my way up. Then I moved a few feet away from the shadow of the willow and waved back at the woman once I was clearly in view.

"Good morning, Mrs. Trowley," I hollered back. "And a fine one it is, now that I've heard your song on the wind."

I could tell from her motions in the window that she laughed softly, bringing her hand to her mouth to cover her smile. I'd cleaned up as best I could so I approached the woman in the window, who I must confess, by simple manifestation gave a strong argument for a man to linger, even when his heart pulls toward the wander of the world. Her hair fell and cascaded down upon her shoulders. I saw that pouty grin as I drew close, and those chestnut eyes flashed at my heart like a beacon in a blizzard offering shelter.

"Well, you-all coming in for breakfast, Rosco?" She was wearing a dress, I noticed. She stood in the window like a picture in a frame, the shack's interior behind her was a dark, swirly backdrop that framed her perfectly in the light of the morning.

Again, she smiled, and seemed embarrassed by her display, lowering her head slightly but keeping her gaze level with my own.

"Breakfast sounds very nice, ma'am," I replied, maintaining a respectful distance, as I believe a gentleman should, and removing my cap for reasons much the same. "I'll be right in."

Inside the shack the dimness was at once suffocating. I could see Marjorie plainly, seeming breathless in the kitchen, twirling in her flower-print dress, suddenly unsure of a safe place to rest her eyes in the known crannies of her own home.

"Oh my, I do apologize Rosco. I'm… we're not accustomed to entertaining in our home and…well, never mind. Please," she moved suddenly but still gracefully and pulled back a chair before a finely set place at the table. "Have a seat Rosco. I've got the ham warming on the stove, and I'll fry up the eggs as needed when we's ready to eat."

I felt her hand come to rest on my shoulder as she ended her words, standing behind the chair in which I now sat. It was then that I noticed good old Ted, sitting in the darkened corner in a worn-out lounger that had seen the rain more than a few times, I assessed.

"Well, good morning young fella?" My greeting was short but cordial. I sensed a change in Ted's disposition. I assumed the night had not been kind to his brother, and Ted, in the most certain of terms, informed me of just such in short order. His greeting in return was not cordial.

"I'll give you the fact the sun is up, so yes, it is a morning indeed. I hope you had a pleasant night's rest down by the haunted tree, Rosco." Ted raised his hands to his ears and made spidery gestures with his fingers. "Glad to see no ghosties came a-wailing to get ya."

Well, there it is. It seems Ted was going back to the sarcasm and being the considerate fellow that I am, I listened to his grievance out of respect for his brother's situation – but even without a limb, my sympathies in that matter were wearing thin. He told me Trevor moaned all night and mumbled at things only he could see. He told me his brother was no longer tormented by the pain of his wound, now that the leg was gone, but the fever would not break, and the poultice applied was spent and devoid of any healing properties.

"So, I hope you slept well Rosco. I can forgive you for shooting him in the knee, but if he dies, I can't forgive that," Ted spoke with finality, leaning forward in his chair and bringing his face into the light.

"You hush now Theodore," Marjorie spoke to my defence and moved from her place at my back to stand before her son. "I told you to fetch me more," she wagged her finger in admonishment. "I need the willow bark and I can make more. You're as lazy as a mule Theodore."

"There's a willow right down there by the creek, Ma. Why you yelling at me to fetch it?"

To be clear, I had heard no voices raised, so whatever Ted was referring to remains lost on me, but I sensed the volume would soon increase, as Marjorie, her voice no longer sweet as fresh-rendered honey, took in a deep breath before her response.

"I told you Theodore, we cannot touch the Widow's Wailing Willow. Don't you even think about scratching the bark of that tree. There's lots of willows dotting the banks of this creek, or to the river in the valley just yonder. Get off your lazy ass and go gather. I need five lengthy, or wide, strips of bark and I can make medicine. We will rid that boy of that fever, Theodore, just get me the fixin's to do it."

Ted rose from his chair to tower and glare at me over his mother. She moved forward and had wrapped her arms around his waist. "Just go get the bark," she breathed. "Ok?"

She pulled back from her son, who still glared at my spot at the table. "Alright, Ma," Ted said, turning and walking out the door. Marjorie remained facing the door until she heard Ted mount his horse and gallop off to the east with pace. Only then did she turn, and with a wavering smile, moved to join me sitting at the table.

The coffee poured thick, black, and steaming from the iron

pot she tilted, filling both my cup and hers with a generous helping of the fragrant brew. She offered me sugar, which I politely declined.

"Don't pay no mind to him, Rosco," she said, after we'd each had a taste of the coffee. "I swear the neither of them has ever grow'd up to behave the way a man should. He's thirty-years old, Rosco, yet here he is still living with his mother in this tiny, run-down shack..."

I raise my hand to offer my objections, mild as they may be, to the conditions of her living quarters, but Marjorie would have none of that and shut me up with a look and carried on with her verbal tirade. She knew where she lived and the way people judged, but it was her home, as it had been her Thomas's home. She was comfortable in this "box of sticks" and could give a spit about the judging eyes of others.

As she complained, once again, about the inadequacies of her offspring, her voice, once so sweet, became a scornful buzz rising and falling in crescendo, unintelligible, and droning in my ears. Seeking solace, my mind turned to MissT. She never uttered a word, out loud, harsh, or otherwise, and while the voices that whisper in our minds can be straining, I now recall the sounds of a woman scorned can be grating on the very sanity that even the strongest of man can possess.

When she was all said and done and out of breath, flushed from her oral exertions, she looked at me with soft, brown eyes, and damned if her voice didn't suddenly and again glisten with honey as her smile reappeared and she whispered: "Sorry, Rosco."

I was quick to forgive. It came easy. She reached her hand out and grasped mine and forgiveness was a done deal. "No apologies needed," I said simply, watching her stand up from the table.

"How many eggs you want, Rosco?"

I held up three fingers then watched the woman work. She moved around the kitchen, and she knew I was watching. Her face betrayed her enjoyment, and while some might say she liked to cook, I'd beg to differ in the reasons behind those stolen glances, sheepish grins, and the brush of the light fabric of her dress against the imagined softness of her skin, as she subtly twirled on the balls of her bared feet.

Maybe I'd stick around for a spell after all.

The breakfast was consumed, at least on my part, with a vigor reflective of my lack of a meal indoors, home cooked and served on an actual table, as opposed to the lap of my crossed legs and the bare bit of ground I could find close by.

We talked small pleasantries, commented on the fairness of the morning and the day ahead. I thanked her profusely for her hospitality, of which I was sincerely grateful. I told her the breakfast was delicious and her company just as pleasant, especially to a man badly in need of both. I told her how pretty she looked in her flowered dress, recalling briefly on the only other woman from my past, who once wore a dress similar and stole my heart with her loving countenance and tender ways.

"You scared I'll steal your heart, Rosco?" Marjorie posed the question playfully, but I heard behind the words an anticipation more urgent then required for a flirty remark, as she waited for my response.

"I'm scared you already have, Marjorie." I said it before I realized I was saying it, but too late, there it was, cards on the table as were my eyes, unable to face her on the heels of such confession.

When I finally stirred up the courage to look, I saw her, face flushed, mouth open, which she quickly covered with the delicate fingers I've come to notice she possessed. Her eyes, as quickening to my heart as they'd ever been, opened wide and glistened with appreciation for my compliment.

She spun on her chair and faced me, placing both hands on the table. Slowly she rose from her chair and rounded the table to stand above me. I looked up at her smiling and I watched her bend down, her arms slowly creeping to snake their way around the back of my neck, and she pressed her lips to mine. They moved like worms beneath my lips, and contrary to my abysmal attempt at description, it was not a feeling that was unpleasant. I felt something in my mouth, flick between my teeth and tongue, and realized, somewhat surprised, but again, not unpleasantly, that it was her probing tongue.

I felt her body lower, daring not to open my eyes, and she nestled herself in my lap and pulled herself close, so close I could feel the slightest curves of her body beneath that flowered dress and the press of her bosom sent my mind reeling.

My hands found that tangle of blonde locks and my fingers explored her golden tresses. I sent my own tongue darting into her moist mouth. She gasped and seemed to spasm for a moment.

I heard them before she did, but I let her carry on for a second or two. Then the horses announced their arrival with the pounding of their hooves, and she sprang from my lap and commenced to fixing her hair and her dress, quite frazzled, which was a departure from her usual contained composure.

She darted to the window and peered through the moth-eaten curtains. "Shit!" she said beneath her breath, not pleased with whomever had just ridden up to the front of the shack.

"It's Theordore and his loathsome Uncle Casper," she turned to look at me, still sitting at my spot at the table, Union cap perched beside me, and I'm sure a confused look on my face as to what the fuss might be all about. Marjorie eyed my Union cap.

"You gotta make that scarce, Rosco. Casper is a southern man," she explained, darting behind a curtain at the far end of the room.

"He thinks the war's still worth fighting and if he catches wind of your Union affiliations, well, I just don't even want think what would happen."

After a moment of unseen rustling, she burst back through the curtain, no longer donning the pretty, flowered dress, but strapped down in tan-hide pants and a crisp, blue shirt that squeezed tight against her chest, but otherwise hung on her as such a thing would, being meant for a man.

She wore a tanned, wide-brimmed hat and on her hips

hanging visible was the friendly end of a pistol, the dangerous part still hidden inside the black, leather holster.

"Know this," she said, spinning to face me as the footfalls of the men outside mounted the porch and approached the door. "I do not like this man. He's Tom's brother not mine, and ever since Thomas passed, that man has been sniffing on me like a hungry hound on the trail of a fat, briar-patch rabbit. He's an angry man, and always had a bone to pick, Rosco, and like I said, an undying Son of the Confederacy. He's a dangerous man, Rosco. Just stay quiet, will you please?" She looked at me with pleading eyes. "Please."

I nodded and turned and went and sat back down at the table, poured myself another cup of coffee, and watched as Theordore moved through the now open door, graced me with a shit-eating grin, then stepped aside to fill my face with the form of Casper, the not-so friendly uncle.

He was a tall drink of dirty water, this Casper. Black hat, black coat, black tie, white shirt, black vest. His pants were, you guessed it, black, and his high-polished boots that needed some trail dust to make them right, in my assessment, were also Casper's predominant colour of the day: black. He had no hair, that I could tell of, or maybe just some wisps of grey drifting here and there from beneath his hat, but his eyes were a cold aqua-blue, bluer than any sky that ever stretched over the land and colder than the stiffest gust to plague the tallest of summits.

The man glanced at me briefly, then his eyes fell on Marjorie, and they twinkled with a light that made me uneasy. He gazed down at the wife of his now dead brother and extended his arms to embrace.

"C'mon now Marjorie. How's about a hug for your Uncle Casper." His smile was two thin lips stretched over teeth badly stained by the smoke of a pipe. I leaned back and drank my coffee and assessed the man fully, and after some brief consideration I came to the conclusion his value to this world was very little. I'm sure he was quick to anger, and perhaps just as quick with the six-shooter that hung low on his hip, hanging half out of the holster, ready to pull.

I knew a gunfighter when I saw one and I was pretty much sure I was looking at one now. Though, given my assessment I honestly believe that a showdown between me and him would prove to be less of a fight and more of a mercy killing. That is what I'd be granting him if I ended his miserable life quickly with a chunk of hot lead from my Colt. That was my assessment.

"You're not my uncle, Casper, and stop with your bullshit. What do you want? Wait, strike that. I know what you want, and I've made it quite clear. So, why else are you here?"

Marjorie wasted no time getting right to her point, and I grinned openly at her boldness. I'm sure I was the only one to notice, but as she spoke, her hand slowly, imperceptibly, edged its way up to the holster to rest lightly on the grip of her gun.

"I brought him here, Ma. On account of this here bluebelly, and my little brother dying out in the barn. You are too busy playing house with this high-country hick, to take care of your own, so I went and found kin to help. That's him, Casper. That's the bluebelly that shot Trevor and is trying to weasel in on our land."

Well now. After Ted's little speech, which burned my ears badly, so full of personal slights and insults to my honour it was, I leaned back in my chair and commenced rolling some tobacco. The man in black, Casper, moved further into the light, closer to what was swiftly becoming my designated spot at the table. His face was stone. Dead eyes didn't waver from mine, and he moved by inches and with steady purpose. With purpose of my own – I knows this game well – I pull my eyes from the man and focus on my smoke.

"Don't you cause no trouble in my home Casper!" Marjorie's plea carries a threat, but at least this time, Casper, it seems, will not be deterred.

"Shut your mouth, woman." He growled low, not taking his eyes of my place, where I focus, head down, on striking the match. With the flare of the flame at the end of the match I raise my hand to my smoke and my eyes follow upwards, the brownness of them catching the flame's reflection and gleaming accordingly as they fall flatly on the face of Casper – I know this game well. I puff out a cloud of thick, blue smoke and, leaning back slowly, I take another deep, long haul and extend my hand, offering the man a chair.

Not moving an inch, Casper declined my offer with a shake of his head. A smile played on his lips. He beckoned me to stand, without a word, just a rising motion of his hand. His stance broadened as did his smile. He watched me rise slowly out of what had become my favourite chair.

In the dimness of the shack, I heard a flurry of activity, but neither me nor Casper were distracted by the sounds of Ted and Marjorie dropping low to the floor and ducking behind furniture.

"I don't want to kill you in front of your kin, mister," I said, with not a hint of emotion. "Maybe we do this someplace else? Someplace where our ghosts won't linger to bother the living?"

"I don't believe in ghosts. And if my kin don't want to watch, they can leave. You count or I count, either way, at the count of three, I'm going to kill you." he replied.

Now, if there had been a clock on the wall, the ticking would have been quite effective, but there wasn't, so, and this is something I've always found peculiar, like gunfighters seemed prone to do, we just stood there staring at each other for a long time. I watched the beads of sweat form on the man's forehead and start to drip into his cold, blue eyes. Well, I gotta say, I'm getting tired of waiting, and he did mention at the count of three so I starts counting in my head and I know he can't hear but I'm just so tired of waiting for him to make a move that my mind says three and my hand, like it was on the wrist of a younger man, flashed my Colt too quick to see, and while the shot was still ringing I watched Casper fall in a heap to the floor.

I stood staring for a minute. Stunned, as I always was right after taking a man's life and remained as such while Marjorie paced back and forth in a panic, and Ted remained cowering behind the lounger, peaking out to see if I was still holding my pistol.

"Oh. Oh no, Rosco," Marjorie was growing in her agitation. She pointed at Casper, dead on the floor, the tidiest of holes round and red in the middle of his forehead. His face was frozen with that thin-lipped smile and cold, staring aqua-blue eyes. "That's just more trouble for you, Rosco," she shook her head, close to tears. "Bad trouble." With that she ran to me, and as natural as breathing, my arms open wide to embrace her.

"You've got to go, Rosco. There's no staying now. You've got to go." Her sobs dampened my chest with the tears and while she told me to go, I felt her embrace grow tighter.

"Damn right you gots to go," Ted finally spoke up, though he still cowered behind the chair. "The Sons of the Confederacy hear tell of this, every man in the county will be after your hide. The Sons is strong in these parts. Yes sir. You gots to go, Rosco!"

I look over at him and he ducks behind the chair. In my arms the boy's mother is sobbing, and all I can think about is how much I'd like to shoot that boy and shut him up for good. But I don't.

Gently I ease Marjorie's head from my shoulder. I gave her shoulders a shake and when I catch her eye, I nod firm. I move quickly to the door, outside and whistle for Mr. Andrews, who trots from a stand of trees to join me as I make my way down to the Widow's Wailing Willow and my gear. I saddle him up quickly, pack up my things, then move to the barn to retrieve my duster, which I'm sure is now covered in blood and the sweat of Trevor's fever. I cross the barn to the table and see the boy's motionless body. It's pale as the moon, and though I expect to feel the heat of fever rising, the boy lies cold and stiff. His eyes, which stare open, are the eyes of the dead. My mind twists at the sight. I have no time to ponder the loss and pull hard on my duster, freeing it from beneath the now-cold body. In doing so, dead Trevor rolled off the work bench and dropped heavily to the straw-strewn floor with a thud, as dead bodies commonly do when dropped from even a short distance.

I climbed into the saddle, and Mr. Andrews, having endured

the absence of my weight, vigorously nodded his head, happy to feel my familiar form once more upon his back. I urge him on, and we ride, but before we could even get beyond the yard of the shack, I pull him up to a stop as I see Marjorie, mounted on the dark stallion that had been Casper's, looking like a rough-rider ready for the trail.

"I'm coming with you," she said. She stared at me and shook her head. "Uh uh, I'm not asking," she said, ignoring the complaints of Ted who stood dumbfounded and helpless.

"What about Trevor, Ma? What about me? What you doing Ma?"

I glanced at him for a moment, "Trevor's dead," I said flatly, not knowing how to say it quickly any other way.

I see Marjorie cringe, but she holds on to herself and nods at my concern. I look back to Ted and bid him adieu with a touch on the brim of my hat, a wide-brimmed Stetson to replace my Union cap, as I thought would be advisable. That hat, that just seemed to nestle on my sandy, shaggy head, happened to be black, and once sat on the head of the recently departed and forever notorious Casper Trowley. I had considered the boots, but he had feet that were wide and long, and I'd be apt to break an ankle, or worse, trying to fill that man's shoes.

I turned back to Marjorie who had trotted up beside me. She sat tall in the saddle, a higher mount than the one afforded by Mr. Andrews, who I now soothed with strokes and soft words, in an attempt to ease his envious agitation.

"Alright then, pretty lady. Get on there...hiya!"

We rode away from the box of sticks in the meadow, and the Widow's Wailing Willow, and the charming sounds of Plitter-Plop Crick. And though she'd spent the better part of her life there, from what I could tell, Marjorie did not look back

"Don't worry, Rosco," she shouted over the pounding of the horses' hooves.

Despite the loss of a son and whatever Casper had been, I guess she looked genuinely at ease riding fine in the saddle. I sensed Marjorie may have had her first real taste of freedom. I lingered for a moment on the thought and after seconds of brief consideration I realize, I can't imagine life without it.

CHAPTER 5

Sons of the Confederacy

It was, perhaps, not a good choice but I thought it best to find a low spot amongst the denseness of the forest where we could burn a decent fire without fear of eyes finding the flame in the night. Marjorie had proven resourceful when we'd finally ended our hell-bent ride southwest away from Plitter-Plop Crick. I was unfamiliar with a helping hand and found the task of setting camp less burdensome and completed with a velocity that I truly believe only a woman could accomplish. Unfortunately, the frigid damp of the forest crept low in the night, as I knew it had a tendency to do, and its fingers found our bedding in the low-lying hollow, and we awoke with a shiver, embracing each other more for warmth than affection, though there had been plenty of the latter, I'm pleased to convey, when we'd finally lay together in the flicker of flames.

When the chill of morning and the fading embers finally drove us from the contentment of each other's arms, she rose first and commenced to brewing a pot of black death, so I calls it, as the coffee I carry is weak and more of dirt than grinds.

Mr. Andrews seemed rather disappointed that he had missed an opportunity to kick dirt in my face but amused himself with the taunting of the large, black stallion now stood hitched to a tree, disgruntled at the sight of that Appaloosa running wild through the forest. I feel for that stallion, and as I watch Marjorie move to the fire, re-stoked and blazing, and sit across to sip her brew, I ask the first question that comes to mind.

"Does that horse have a name?"

Marjorie turns to look over her shoulder at the large beast. It is a beautiful animal, shimmering black as night, and I'm moved by his regal posture, standing tall and alert, the steam from his snorted breath streaming from the flared nostrils, while behind him in the distance I see Mr. Andrews frolicking like the fool, barebacked and spirited. Undignified in the best of ways, a child in his later years, that horse never fails to make me crack a grin.

"I believe Casper called him 'Jax' on account he won him in a poker game with three Jacks and two other matches. He called it a 'full house,' as I recall, but I don't know much about such things. Why Mr. Andrews?" Marjorie asked at the end of her reply. And I told her, like I've said before, "That's a tale for telling another time. The telling itself would take most of the day, and something tells me we're going to have other business to attend to for a spell."

Marjorie nodded, eyes staring at the flame. "I still can't believe you shot him," she said, glancing her eyes more direct-like. "You don't really know what you've done, do you?"

I looked at her, puzzled. She was there. I didn't understand how she still couldn't believe I had shot the man. It had been a simple thing and had happened before her eyes. Then, shaking my head of its early morning fog, I understood her meaning clearer. She was expressing her disbelief that I actually had it in me to shoot a man dead as quick as I did. The word 'gall' came to mind, and I must confess, I've never been scarce when it comes to audacity.

"He's…or he was, Casper Trowley, Rosco. You aint never heard of him on your travels?"

"What's with you Trowleys? Y'all thinks you're famous." I sipped my coffee and gave her a wink, assuming she too had known of the exploits of the Terrible Trowleys, as told in the dime-store novels of John Maximillian. Her questioning look made me realize she did not, but as opposed to speaking words that would only lead down a long and arduous path, I rephrased my verbalisms.

"Apologies Miss Marjorie. I make jest at a time that perhaps I should not. I do not, have not, and did not know of this man named Casper Trowley, any more than I was familiar with the name of his fine horse, up until you told me just now. Please miss, do proceed to thrill me with the exploits of this man as I'm afraid Mr. Maximillian may have been remiss in his inclusion of this historied figure in the chronicles he composes for the masses."

Myself, I was quite proud at my most recent stab at sarcasm, but I could see by the countenance of Marjorie's tear-drop face, that my attempt had left her even more puzzled than she'd been before. Her eyes, as deep as they may be, stared at me all cold and serious-like.

"Casper is not a man to make light of, alive or dead. He come up in all those rough towns, in and around Texas, right after the Mexican wars, Rosco." Marjorie leaned in closer, getting set to tell the tale. I leaned back and crossed my ankles, commenced to rolling a cigarette, which I thought would be a warranted compliment to my weak cup of coffee and the fine story this woman was, I was certain, about to tell.

"He made his name with the likes of Burly Bill Campbell and Ronnie Favor, down around Santa Fe, and when the thrill of the feud ran dry in those parts, he found his gun and his predatory nature well suited to the pinstripes of the Pinkertons, and set his sights on 'hunting down vermin,' Thomas used to say, 'the lowest of the low and the scummiest of the scum.'

"During the war between the north and the south, he remained a Pinkerton and, back in Georgia where's we originally resided, he joined a company of 'regulators' and brought to justice the scared and confused boys who deserted the Confederacy, not wanting or willing to fight in a feud which they, for the most part, had no stake, other than the vitriol that was more than enough to call harder men to arms.

"After the war," Marjorie continued, sipping her coffee, and reaching across to request a draw from my smoke, a request I obliged in silence, not wanting to break her trail of recall, "when Tommy got back, just a shell of a man he once was…" Her voice trailed off then, and I could see her eyes moving as she looked up to my left at apparently nothing, like she was seeing a memory come to life, in her mind.

"When he got back from the war it wasn't long before the Northern victory began to spoil badly in the mouths of the men who still cherished the grey, and still donned the uniform with pride. After a short year of post-war anguish, a large group of those like-minded people formed a party of sorts and set off for greener pastures, away from the scornful gazes that now befell us.

'Disgraced sons of a beaten Confederacy,' someone cat-called us, as our wagon train moved out on that warm, summer morning. And I think, if I'm not mistaken, that's when the Sons of the Confederacy was born, in Casper's always-plotting mind. Though he hadn't fought in the war, he somehow saw fit to lead us, and I will confess we may not have made it without the mettle of that man.

"The trail had been hard, Rosco," she said, pausing to gaze at me with fearful wonder. "A few had died on that trail of lost redemption, some from sheer madness and some from the fever, and others just lost all hope with the hunger that plagued them and the wolves that howled so boldly in the night. Some, like them, just wandered away never to be seen again.

"The trail seemed unending, and we scuffled often among ourselves along the way." Marjorie paused here and smiled, purposeful and mischievous.

"I've seen your eyes, mister. I've seen them move over my form. It's not an unfamiliar thing, as I've seen it in the eyes of many men, but let me tell you something, Rosco, you think I can twirl a skirt now, you should-a seen me in my youthful days. I was a flower forever in bloom if I do say so myself."

I did not doubt her claim, not for one second, and I told her as much with deep seriousness and commitment to my words.

"Well, as such, being the womanly woman that I was and am, many of those scuffles was the result of unwanted advances from some of the lonely fellas who joined the party. Now, my Thomas, as I've said, did not come back the man he was, not just seeming to lose a piece of his mind in that godforsaken war, but also minus and arm and a leg. So, needless to say, there was little he could do but rage, when it came to warding off the less-than honourable men. It was his brother, Casper, who defended me from such ravenous eyes and each time it came to gun play, Casper was the fastest I'd ever seen pulling his pistol from his holster."

"Not anymore I reckon," I interjected, not raising my eyes to gauge her reaction. She ignored my observation and carried on with the story.

"After what seemed an eternity, we came to find the Valley of Many Rivers, and more specifically, this winding creek and rolling, grassy meadow which I myself gave the name of Plitter-Plop Crick.

Casper declared it the promised land, and it was one of the few times that I found myself in agreement with the man. We settled in quickly, and finally found peace in the solitude provided us by our long journey so far north and so far west. We learned how far north quickly, when that first winter came reckoning. But by then we had established a loosely scattered community, and under the direction of the man you killed yesterday, even managed to build up a town of sorts, and governed ourselves under the guise of Casper's brainchild, Sons of the Confederacy. He was our leader, Rosco. And to this very day the people of these parts owe him a depth of gratitude for leading us to this promise land. He was still their leader up until yesterday, and Ted was right when he pointed out that every man in the county will now be after your hide."

"Hmm," I said, contemplating the ramifications of my justified and defensive actions in the dim interior of that box of sticks. To be clear, I did not regret, for even an instant, punching that man's skull with the hot lead of my pistol, but I was heightened in my alertness by her words.

"The Sons is strong and many," Marjorie continued. "Right abouts now I would imagine their gathering at my shack, listening to Theodore spin wicked lies about how you shot Casper in cold blood and kidnapped me for your pleasure. He'll be telling them of your bluebelly tendencies, and if that aint enough, which it is, he'll tell them how you ravaged me brutally, ambushed him and Trevor on the trail, and shot his little brother through the cap of his knee which resulted in the young man's untimely death. He'll paint Casper the fallen hero, and you the dastardly villain, and them boys will come riding hard looking with ferocity to run you down."

"Hmm," again I contemplate. My instincts would be to ride on back to that shack and end what needs not to be a long serenade; end their lives quick, and as many as I can, then ride for the hills with a certainty that those I left alive would be sufficiently deterred from further pursuit. But, having listened to Marjorie's wise council, I sees the reasoning behind her advisements.

"You saying we should maybe become scarce to the eyes, and the nose. Well, you're as wise as beautiful darling, and I'm all in for that. We could travel north from here, head back up to the high-country. That's as scarce as a man can get, I reckon. Unless you got something better floating in that mind of yours, Marjorie." My cheeks stretch as I look at her, my eyes never grow tired of what my heart believes to be God's greatest creation. And I have every confidence in this woman, who I've known for less than a day, yet would follow her to the devil's doorstep, if she bid me to so oblige.

"I know a place, Rosco. But it's dangerously close to town. We'd have to stay real low for a few days at least, let the blood of the south simmer down, and the freshness of our tracks to fade." She stood up, suddenly, like it had been decided, and as she started to saddle the regal Jax, my next question seemed to give her pause.

"What place is this, Marjorie? I kind of likes the idea of keeping low right under their noses. It appeals to my senses, which often rise in the face of risky adventures. But I'm not one to rush in blindly, well, on consideration I am, but I ride alone no more, and I've got this pretty little Georgia peach to consider, and it would break my heart if my haste were to lead to even the splitting of a single hair on her head."

She took three strides and fell into my arms. "I do love you, Rosco Pitt. I don't know how or why, and I don't care, cause I do." She pulled her head back and told me what I'd asked.

"It's a small boarding house, just at the edge of Randy River. I know the woman who runs the house, Millie, Millie Bonner, her and her brother, and she's always been kind and considerate to my widow's plight. She's got a cellar, she showed me once, and has provided sanctuary before, I know, to the few wandering souls who travel this far north and this far west, all them harbouring secrets and running from something. I trust her, Rosco. She's never had a kind word for the Sons of the Confederacy and will not betray us to such scoundrels."

"Might there be a bath and a shave at this place of hospitality, waiting for a man in need?" I asked.

"There might," she responded, playfully raising her eyebrows, and crinkling her nose at some perceived stink.

I laughed and pulled her close again, kissed her hard on the mouth then whistled for Mr. Andrews. In short order we was back on the trail, skirting wide around the meadow where the Sons of the Confederacy may be massing, and picked our way carefully down the gentle inclines, and rolling path that led to the settlement of Randy River, and The Bonner House, for tired eyes and weary souls.

CHAPTER 6

The indelible stain

I toy with my Sharps rifle. It had been a while since I held it in my hands, and it felt good. I set my eye through the sights and get a clearer view of the man I spied from the edge of the trees that ended at the settlement of Randy River. This time of year, the sun sets, and the shadows grow long early, and with the late-day sun at my back, the man stands out bolder than a blooming boil on a sow's backside, despite his effort at concealment.

Beneath me is Mr. Andrews, quiet and calm, accustomed to my stealthy ways. Beside me is Marjorie, though just learning my ways of moving unseen, also maintains a quiet composure, while the horse beneath her, the magnificent steed that is Jax, scuffed at the ground and huffed out heavy winds, agitated at being forced to stand so still in the shadows, not comprehending the urgency for silence in our present situation.

The man was mounted and tucked beneath the drooping branches and creepy shadows of another weeping willow. This valley seemed to have a penchant for these types of trees, and while my eyes had taken note of such timber in the past, having been in proximity of two in as many days has left me unmoved by their ominous presence on the land, where as before, I had found their drooping countenance to be quite poetic, in a metaphoric sense.

This man, who much to my dismay wore the full uniform of a Confederate soldier, sentineled a short distance beyond The Bonner House – For Tired Eyes 'N Weary Souls, the sign said. Fortunately, the boarding house stood before the bulk of town-proper took shape, and we would not have to ride by so many eyes to reach our destination. But the eyes of that man would spot us quick, if we attempted to slip from these trees across the open path to the porch of said boarding house.

He had been an officer, when the Confederacy was an engine of war, and not some lost cause clung to desperately by a people unwilling to embrace any change, not seeming to care for the overall well-being of the collective Americas. I could see this by the fancy embroidery that garnished the sleeve of his long, grey cloak, and by the style of hat he wore on his head. A colonel, I reckon, as my eyes find his sabre hanging down his side, the decorative hilt dangles with tassels, yellow and bright in the setting sun, and I'd be willing to bet its blade had seen more butter than it ever did blood.

"We wait," I said quietly, dismounting and nodding to Marjorie to follow. We move back, deeper into the trees, tie off both horses, to which Mr. Andrews does not protest, as like I, he knows this game well.

Together, Marjorie and I crouch low and creep back to the edge of the trees. Together, Marjorie and I crawl belly-down, and again I sight on the grey coat. The ember glows at the end of his smoke, and my mouth waters for one of the same. I pass the Sharps to Marjorie, "Just look, don't shoot," I says, then commence to making a smoke of my own. Course, when I'm done, I realize I can't light the cursed thing and toss it aside in frustration.

"That's Calvin," Marjorie says, her big, brown eye peering through the sight. I'd ranged it already, and thought with some alarm, he'd be in her crosshairs and if she just pulls the trigger he'd hit the ground before he knew he was dead. Fortunately, she did not, both for her and for the distant figure of the mounted soldier, as while she may have hit the target, the distance between the butt of the Sharps and her delicate shoulder would have resulted in a painful dislocation of that joint, and undoubtedly, painful cries from the woman who was the object of my affections. She passed the rifle back my way.

"He, Calvin, was Casper's right-hand man," Marjorie told me. "I imagine, with Casper gone, Calvin could be the new, self-proclaimed leader of the Sons of the Confederacy. He's a rough type too, Rosco. I hear tells he was there at Gettysburg and was one of the few to survive, from the Confederate side at least, the Battle of Little Round Hill. Sure dressed fancy," she added. "He must have borrowed the uniform cause he sure weren't no colonel."

Gettysburg came after my stint in the blues of the Union, but I heard tell of the carnage that unfolded and the ignorance of Lee in his refusal to retreat. I looked down my scope again at the figure of the man, and saw him now in a different light, given my new-found knowledge of his history. I thought, with some certainty, that we could talk, me and him, and would easily find a friendly banter and mutual respect for our shared experiences, but that was not ever going to happen, I knew. That war, despite any good intentions, had only succeeded in widening a gap between two jagged cliffs that stand opposing, as was now, it seemed, the mood of the nation.

"If we're patient, Rosco, he'll be going to get supper soon, then we can slide on down to The Bonner House and get us that hot bath," Marjorie nodded, and like it was already decided, lifted herself off the ground and crouch-crawled back to the horses. I takes another look at Calvin and wonder what might have been, had it not been for my encounter with those Terrible Trowleys. I wouldn't have met Marjorie, for one thing, and that in itself is enough for me to be thankful that I had met those boys, despite the events that came after, and were surely soon to come.

I sit patiently watching Calvin. The sun draws low and the twilight of early evening settles in. Suddenly he's moving, slowly steering his mount from beneath the willow. I stiffen for a moment, hovering my hand over my Sharps, waiting to see which way he's going to ride. I'm hoping he turns left, not right, in my direction, but when I sees him turn and begin trotting my way all hope is lost and knowingly, I move my hand from above my rifled and draw the wide, Bowie blade from its sheath, which hangs at my backside, at the centre of my waist. I turn back and look at Marjorie, just a smudge standing still in the darkened trees. She sees what I see and immediately drops flat the moment my hand beckons her to get down.

I wait. The horse moves slow, and the man lights another smoke as he and his mount meander their way closer to the edge of the trees. My patience grows thin as I'm eager for the kill but can't charge him headlong, as the blade of his sabre is considerably longer then the blade of my Bowie, and the pistol on his hip would draw down on me long before I got within reach to sink my metal. Firing a shot was out of the question, and something I would only commit to if the pressing were dire, meaning life or death hung precariously in the balance. A shot would bring the whole town down this way, and probably end the incredible exploits of Rosco Pitt and Marjorie Trowley. Personally, I wasn't ready to see this story end quite yet, as I was starting to like the plot twist Marjorie had lent to the telling of the tale. So, I waited.

At long last Calvin steered his horse past the edge of the tree line, and I sprang from the ground and raced with careful footfalls to catch him from behind. The man has no idea I'm there until he feels my hand grab the hem of his coat. He looks down, surprised. His eyes grow wide and his mouth grimaced becoming aware, much too late, that the shimmering flash is the blade of my knife which I promptly and forcefully bury deep in his abdomen. I twist the blade and force it up through the meat until I feel the steel strike the sternum. Only then do I pull it out, and the man's guts follow, spilling across the neck of his mount, which bucked and whinnied then bolted, causing Calvin to crumble back on the ground. I hear a crack as the man's neck breaks. 'Don't matter none,' I thought as I step back from the mess that now pools at my feet.

Marjorie rushes through the trees to stand by my side. She looks down at Calvin and gasps, seeing what the man is made of strewn across the ground. I hear her gagging, heaving dry, then the vomit erupts from her mouth to mix with Calvin's entrails. I grimace at the thought that I'm going to have to clean up the mess, lest someone sees it and assumes something's amiss. I lead her to the trees, and I whisper to her ear.

"Real quiet like, sweetie, take the horses round back of the boarding house and settle them in the stable. Be quiet and invisible, as best you can. Let your friend Millie know our plight, see how she responds. Watch her close, Marjorie. Get sense if anything, anything at all seems off, you know?"

Marjorie ceases her retching, long enough to look my way and nod. "Ok Rosco."

"Good girl," I says. "I know you're bright, Marjorie, but don't tells her nothing less you have to, lie if you must. The least she knows the better."

I glance back at the path. The night grows darker by the second, but I can still make out the pile of blood and assorted internals. "I'm gonna clean up that mess, so as no one will notice. Wait for my whistle. I'll whistle once. If all is well, meet me at the back door. If all is not well, and this is so important, don't pay no mind to my call. Stay safe through the night, and I'll see you in the morning."

She nods, we kiss, and I pay no mind to the taste of bile – such is love. She moves off, leading the horses down the path, and quietly slipping behind the house fading in the dark as she neared the stable. I turned to the task at hand and make short work of scooping much of the stinking pile of intestines, stomach, and other vile innards, off of the path. My boots and the hem of my coat are bloodied when I'm finished. A wide, dark splotch still remains on the ground, hidden by the dark of night. My concealment of the kill does not demonstrate thoroughness that some would strive to attain, and I leave the indelible stain of Calvin's death for any detectives, Pinkertons or otherwise, who, by light of day, may be looking to detect.

Fully dark, and now I move with a bit more ease to my thoughts, welcoming the cover of night. I goes around the back of The Bonner House and see the light of the kitchen window illuminating the yard. I see my Marjorie sitting at a table. Her head, like the woman from which she sits across, is bent in deep conversation. Millie Bonner, on my initial assessment, appears a refined woman, dressed for a night on the town as opposed to a neighbourly chat in the kitchen. But her hair is as red as my dear friend McTavish – all hellfire and curls abound in the bob that rose high on top of her head. I see her red head turning to glance out the window, blue eyes peering to see into the dark. I assume Marjorie dismissed my misgivings and had told her of my lurking presence, so I whistled. I don't wait, watching, to see who gets up to respond to my call, but I hurry to the back of the house, drawing my pistol as I mount the porch and press my back against the wall to the left of the door. I level my Colt and cock the hammer so any head, but Marjorie's, which peeks out that door will be caved in from the blast of the barrel.

The door opens, and the golden tresses of Marjorie greets my eyes. Her eyes light up as she sees my face, smiling behind the barrel of my gun. Hastily she swings the door open wide, and with just as much haste I slip inside the sanctuary of The Bonner House – For Tired Eyes 'n Weary Souls.

CHAPTER 7

The Bonner House

As a boy, I was always mindful of my Ma and as such, would never fail, when entering our home, to remove my boots, that were generally caked with the dirt of the farm. But it had been so long since I had entered a home, especially one as elegant as the one I'm in now, that I was taken aback when Millie Bonner's voice rose, just a little in its volume at my, admittedly, disrespectful digression.

The thing is, my Ma, in her wisdom, looked away as I progressed in sprouting to become a youthful manchild. In her neglect, the men, around whom I had often hovered listening hungrily to their adult chatter, had set an example. I stopped removing my boots, as I learned that was not something a man did often. It seems to me that Ma had wisdom Millie lacked.

I did back up, into the shadow of what Millie said was the mud room. Not sure why she called it that, looked as good as any other room to my eyes, and did not seem any less deserving to be free of any soiling.

"I'm sorry, Ma'am," I said. "The startling beauty of your shimmering red locks and your Sapphire eyes startled and aroused my manly nature, making me forget my place." I smiled and removed my hat. Millie's hand fluttered to her chest, her lips drew thin and turned up at the corners in the smallest of ways, but her eyes, which were truly as blue as any sky on the clearest of days, flashed with a sudden brilliance at my gentlemanly words.

"But you see Ma'am, and I say this with the utmost of humble embarrassment, it's been some time since my feet's have been freed from their holsters, and I'm a might bit ashamed to say I wears my boots sockless, and my feet, well, I suspect they'll be in a terrible state."

I saw Marjorie smile quickly, knowingly, her eyes thinned as they darted at mine and her head tilted in the cutest of poses, for one so fair. Millie too tilted her head, and actually flashed some pearly white, but her frown returned quickly when her eyes again fell to my boots.

I sigh a deep sigh, and with hat in hand I gaze at both the ladies who stand before me in this lavish kitchen, that honestly, by itself, was the size of my home on the family farm.

"Tells you what," I finally said, placing the black hat back on my head. "I'll brush and spit and wipe them clean. And I promise, though the task will be foreign to me, I will do the best that I possibly can in order to ensure that not one granulate of soil will be left behind wherever I may wander in your exquisite house for tired eyes and weary souls. That's the best I can offer Ma'am. It's either that, or come along Marjorie," I turned to her quite serious, though I knew my ploy would play and such action would not be necessary, "let's get back on the trail. East is gentle travel, and we can move just fine in the night."

"Don't tell me to come along, Mr. Man!" Something I said had gotten Marjorie riled. "You're gonna drag us out in the dark of night, riding down trails we can't even see, looking for some hole where we can set a camp and try to sleep on the cold ground, all because you don't want to take off your boots?" Marjorie was riled, and I'd admit she had a point, given the dirt that clearly caked high and muddy on my boots and clung to the hem of my pant, but I did not and would not give in to these women, not this time, not regarding this affair.

"I...I can't. I can't take them off." I looked at Marjorie and Millie, in unison it seemed, their arms folded across their ample bosoms, as they waited for my explanation, other than the poor state of my leathery dogs that howled more often than either of these hand-fed hens could ever grasp.

"I follow a creed, and it is one that's stern and can stain a man's legacy if not adhered to. Since I became a man I've followed this pledge, as most men of any mettle will also attest. And I will follow this creed until the day I die, and on that day, I will have my boots firmly, and muddy as hell, on my feet!"

"Oh. Alright then. But please do clean them up some, the help won't be back till Monday," Millie conceded most graciously, and I sincerely nodded my strong gratitude.

"Thank you, Ma'am," I said, tossing my hat on a bench then sitting down beside it to meticulously clean my boots with spit from my mouth and the scaley, little grooves of my fingers and hands.

"Hold on now." Marjorie, and I should have known better, was not quite finished having her say, never missing an opportunity to bemoan the stupidity of men and their foolish ways.

"Are you actually saying what I thinks you're saying?" She shook her head and laughed, throwing a side-eye to Millie, who joined with Marjorie's laughter, their mocking melody reverberates round the room.

"You won't take off your boots cause you're afraid you're gonna die," again Marjorie shakes her head, and shushes out a breath in distaste, "and men of the trail and the saddle must die with their boots on, lest they find themselves lacking in the happy hunting grounds that your sad minds believe come after. Is that why, Rosco?"

"Yes," I said, quiet and resigned, it was pretty much the gist of it, and I knew that these women had bested me, and made a mockery of my manly nature. As I finished cleaning off the last speck of dirt, Marjorie got in her final word, and, I must say, she is quick as the snap of a whip when it comes to her fast mind and skin-stripping humour.

"You took em off last night," she said, with a wink and a smile and a spin towards Millie. Both their mouths fell open, and despite their obvious maturity, which I dared not mention at this moment, they giggled like girls watching boys watching girls.

"Oh my," Millie's southern bell was ringing. "I do declare! This aint fit talk for the kitchen. Come you two," she twirled as she moved to the hallway, which formed a dark passage to the aromas of high-polished wood, soft leather and lingering's of what I believe is pipe tobacco. "Let's move into the parlour where it's more comfortable," she said, as we followed her down said dark passage. "Neville should be along soon."

I turned and shot a look at Marjorie, who just brushed me along with a sweep of her hands, urging me to move down the hallway.

"There's a harvest dance down at the hall tonight," Millie continued, as she opened the door to the expansive room, which was the source of the scents I previously mentioned.

"We was going to go together, Neville and me, being like royalty around here and all, but maybe we'll just stay here tonight. I'd enjoy a heavy cigar, sipping fine brandy, and some pleasant conversation with the two of you, and I'm sure Neville would find that preferable to the dull-witted company that's sure to be far too ripe with rigour in the hootenanny of the entire affair."

We followed her into the room. I heard a pop as she lit the lamp in the corner, then a second one that sat hooded beneath green-tinted glass, on the ink blotter of the large, mahogany desk. It gave a warm, yet somehow dark and ominous glow to the room, and dimly lit the far wall, which was a wall of books, more volumes of various things than I have ever laid eyes on at once, the spines of their bindings spoke of dust and neglect, and their titles were lost and faded from my view across the room. On the wall behind me hung a tapestry of sorts, and my heart turned sickly in my chest when I spied it was no tapestry, but a large Confederate battle flag, the Stars and Bars. My mind flashed to the battlements of that long-ago fort, the cannon, and the fodder we offered.

"Hmmm," I pondered, quite loud, in the muffled warmth of the mahogany room, my eyes asking the question as I stare at the monstrosity that fills them, centered precisely in the white of the wall, framed by dark wainscotting and the thin trim of wood. Marjorie follows my eyes and widens hers when she sees the banner of the south. Her frowning face told me of this flag she was unaware, then she quickly turned to Millie, who brushed away the display like it was some random hanging that was hung with little thought.

"Casper gave that thing to Neville a couple of years back. My apologies Mr. Pitt. I understand you have northern leanings. Me, myself, I couldn't care one way or the next, but Neville says it keeps the boys calm, and Casper, may he rest in peace, was a might pleased when Neville agreed to hang it in the parlour."

"I see," I says, as I ease my ass into one of the fine leather chairs that are positioned around the room. "Well Miss Millie, my mind finds that story leads to questions, of which the answers, I hope, settle my sudden fluttering stomach. How is it you know my proper name, my family name? Not I or Marjorie have mentioned any formal introductions, and if you'd just referred to me as Rosco, then I'd have no misgivings as I've heard Marjorie's sweet voice utter that moniker several times, but unless your one of them swamies or something, the words 'Mr. Pitt' should not be a thing in your mind."

"She knows, Rosco." Marjorie had sat in a smaller, much less comfortable chair than I, at least so it appeared as I assessed its suitability in this luxurious setting, and she slid it lightly across the glistening caramel of the hardwood floor, pulling herself close to where I sat.

"She started asking me about it the moment she saw me." Marjorie glanced at Millie, who nodded her head vigorously.

"I have heard Mr. Pitt. And just let me say, I never from the start gave any weight to the story told by Marjorie's boy Theodore; how you's killed little Trevor with a poisoned bullet and ambushed Casper, shooting him in the back when you sprang from the barn. And especially not the part, well..." Millie's voice trailed off. Her eyes darted frantically around the room.

"Theodore's been telling folk of your deviant, sexual appetite, and he said somethings that you did to his Ma that I could barely listen to, let alone repeat here and now," she continued all a flutter. "And when I saw Marjorie, and then you came to the kitchen door, I knew for certain there was not a spattering of authenticity to Theodore's lies. Shame on your boy, Marjorie."

"Uh hu," I says. I lean back in my chair, which, as I think I've mentioned, is extremely comfortable, and I reach inside my buckskin waist coat and pull out my tobacco.

"Oh. Um, Mr. Pitt," Millie says, looking cross the room like she already regrets what she's planning to say. "Please don't smoke that nasty tobacco in this house." Before I could mount my feeble protest, Millie moves to a box on the corner of the desk, carries it over to stand before me, tilts the box down, flips open the lid and smiles.

"Have a cigar," she says, "thinks I'll join you. Don't mind if I do," Millie singsongs her remarks, as I gratefully pluck a cigar from the box, and I find a fondness for the woman forming in my heart. But the Stars and Bars are burning a brand on the back of my head, and as I watch Millie light and suck wide-eyed on her stogie, I feel the clouds of another storm creeping in.

Suddenly all our heads turned the same way at once as the sound of a horse stirs us from the continued pursuit of our meaningful discussion. By the sounds, the animal approaching is suddenly steered left and its trampling hooves round the house and head to the back to the darkness of the stable. Not too alarmed but not quite at ease either, I rise from my chair and move swiftly down the hall. Behind me I hears Millie letting me know that it's probably just Neville, which to be honest, does little to quiet my serious misgivings. I hear the steps of Marjorie following close behind, and I feel her press against my back as I move into the mud room and peer through the window that affords a good view of the yard. I can see Marjorie had been wise, tucking Mr. Andrews and Jax back in the far corner in the furthest stall from the light of the house, almost invisible to anything but the most attentive eye.

"I'm sorry, Rosco," her arms slip around my waist from behind as I watch the shadow move in the stable. "I didn't know she would know, and that flag in the parlour took me back as well. I don't know much about her brother, only sees him now and then, and have never, in my life, had the opportunity to exchange words with the man, but I'm sure it's like Millie said, that rebel flag hangs without a thought, and is only displayed to ease the temperament of most of the folks in and around these parts."

I did not speak but I reached down and grasped her hand, letting her know I placed no blame. I watch the shadow emerge from the barn and I see the man walk into the light in the yard, a jaundice glow that spills through the window from the illuminated kitchen beyond. At first I see grey, and my hand shoots to the grip of my pistol, but it's just the colour of his long, wool cloak, and not the garb of my enemy. He approaches the door and I push Marjorie back, motioning her to return to the parlour and the company of her friend. She hurries off, doing as I ask, and I pull myself tight to the wall as the mud room door opens and the man steps inside.

It's dark where I stand and he shows me nothing but back, as he removes his coat to hang on the wall and bends to, of all things, take off his boots. Then without even a glance my way, he moves into the kitchen.

"Millie. I have arrived." I hear his voice bellow as he moves through the house. I turn and follow as he enters that darkened hall. "Are you ready to twirl and whirl at the harvest dance, my dear? What a striking couple we will be. A shame you're my sister, or I might be tempted to ravish you before we commence to said celebration. Oh. I'm sorry...I didn't know we had company."

I hears the last part just as he entered the room, and

undoubtedly saw my Marjorie sitting pretty in that fine leather chair in which I made my own ass at home just a few moments passed. I, myself, swing through the door, still unnoticed by the new arrival, who stands with his back to me, staring intently at my Marjorie. Millie sits carefree, butt resting on the edge of the desk. Her dress is hiked up above the knee and she leans in a manner much to casual and unbecoming to a woman of her obvious stature. She still sucks on that stogie. I see the ember glow as she draws, and her eyes watch the scene before her, like she's mesmerized by some operatic performance in the theatres I hears of, in those big towns back east. I clears my throat, not that it was needed, and the man spins startled, surprised by my close proximity and looming figure that stood silently behind him.

"Oh. Hello good sir," he says with the slightest of bow. He turns to his sister and in sincere frustration admonishes her for not alerting him to the fact that they had company.

"My name is Neville, Neville Bonner, the owner of this fine house for tired eyes and weary souls, and pretty much the lord of the land around these parts. And who might you be?"

He walked around the large desk as he spoke, moving casually and unhurried. He sat himself down in a high-backed, equally comfortable-looking chair, and motioned for me to face him across the desk and to a chair on which Millie rested a single foot, showing much of her inner thigh through the slit of her dance-hall dress. I move to sit, and Millie, with a dash of a smile and a flirtatious gleam in her eye, moved her foot to allow me the chair, but barely made space for me to sit down, pressing her hip to my side as I did. I'm sure Marjorie had to notice her friend's attempted corruption of my morals, for in my mind that was her ploy, but my honey-voiced siren said nothing, and remained quiet behind me, in what had been my favourite leather chair.

"A pleasure to meet you, Mr. Bonner. Let me compliment you on this beautiful house, and how suitable it is for tired eyes and weary souls. It's already cleared the dust of the trail from my eyes and has welcomed my weary mind."

I offered my hand across the desk and Neville, without a

moment's hesitation, shook it firm. "As to my name, Mr. Bonner, let me ask you, as I suspect you already know, who do you think I might be?"

Neville laughed, not just a soft chuckle but a full-throated guffaw, throwing his head back like I said the funniest thing he'd ever heard, but I saw nothing jocular about my words.

"Ah, yes Mr. Pitt. You are a shrewd one. No flies on you I'm sure. I do know who you are." Neville leaned back and smiled, pausing to glint his eyes at me and suddenly clapping his hands, but just once.

"Millie," he turned suddenly to his sister. "Perhaps you can go with Marjorie and find the woman something more comfortable to wear." He pauses and looks leeringly over my shoulder at my golden-haired angel, Marjorie, who I can see in my mind, cause I don't turn around, squirming in discomfort at this strange man's gaze. "Don't get me wrong Marjorie," he continues, stretching his neck to ogle some more. "You do look quite delicious in your riding gear, but this man and I here have some business to attend to and I don't think I'm wrong to say you'd be happy to relieve yourself of such constraining garments." His eyes turn to Millie. "I'm sure Millie, or one of the girls has something more womanly to grace such a fine form, upstairs in the rooms where we play? Perhaps, Millie? Do you think? Or you could check down in the cellar. Perhaps one of mother's dresses would be more appropriate."

"Yes. We got plenty of pretty things upstairs that'll suit you just fine Marjorie. C'mon girl, let's go try on some dresses." Millie moved to the door and waited for Marjorie. I glanced back at her then, and my look assured her it would be just fine. She hesitated, but finally followed Millie out of the room, leaving me an audience of one for whatever business Neville had to discuss, which was, at this moment, a mystery to me.

As soon as the womanly footfalls pitter-pattered down the hall, Neville rose and turned from his desk, walked to a tall table standing in the corner, and poured a snifter of brandy, offering me the same, which I declined, never being a man for the drink.

He offered me a cigar, and I showed him the one I already had, and lit it quite promptly, drawing deep on the Cuban leaf, and feeling my head grow light and floppy. He lowered himself back into his chair, sipped his brandy and took a match to a fine cigar of his own, then leaned back staring, like I was some prized bull up for bidding.

"Let's be frank, Mr. Pitt," he said, leaning back also, matching my relaxed disposition.

"You be frank. I'm going to keep being Rosco," I said, knowing full well the weakness of my attempt at humour, but hoping to put him off guard, which it did, but only for a moment.

"Mr. Pitt. May I call you Rosco?" he asked, and I nodded. "Excellent. Rosco, I'm not sure you are fully aware of your perilous situation. To be clear, I have heard the loathsome tale and obvious lies of Ted Trowley, and I know his words for what they are. We are both men of substance, Rosco. Yours would be drawn from experience whereas mine would be, well, great wealth. So, I will be upfront and respectful to you, good sir. You're trail weary and a northern sympathizer in a southern man's county. Pickets, even now as we speak, are being formed to the east, the north, and the south. To the west lies the mountains and even to a man of your substance, the Cascades, though not quite as vast as down Oregon way, can still be a weighty deterrent as a possible route of escape. Your provisions are running low, and winter, my friend, is coming fast. Now, it's not just your wellbeing you have to consider, you've gone and taken this woman to ride at your side, which not only hinders your odds of getting free of this county but puts her life and yours at great peril." He paused to look at me, raising an eyebrow. "How my doing so far?"

"Well Neville, I gotta say, I'm impressed with your abilities to assess, but you assume much in your wise review. Assumptions, my Pa used to say, can be a dangerous thing to a man who moves ahead without checking the conditions of the path he wanders."

This man scares me. He has no gun and no knife I can see, and he's a twig of a man, tall, but with limbs so frail a strong wind could break him in half. But his words flow with a confidence that seems almost the gospel spilling from his lips, and end with a finality that seems to indicate that my fate is in his hands and in his hands only.

"Ha. I know what you're thinking Rosco, and I do respect your mind, good sir, but you cannot shoot me. Such a sound would bring the town all a-running, and just fifty yards away in the community hall at the harvest dance, is the majority of those men who march proud as the Sons of the Confederacy, who's leader you saw fit to kill yesterday."

Truth be told, I wasn't really thinking of shooting him, yet. I open my mouth to speak but a raise of his hand stops my words. "Wait my friend, there's more." He leans forward across the desk, drawing his face closer to me. His eyes shift left then right, like he's looking to make sure no one else is listening, though we're alone in the room, then he drops his voice to a conspirator's tone and whispers what I'd been starting to suspect, but it still hits me hard like a heavyweight pugilist's punch to the gut.

"Casper was buried this morning with much pomp and ceremony. The men truly loved him and were quickly lost without a leader, which they collectively realized, once the man had been returned to the dust from which we all spring.

"With the head of the snake removed, one would have a tendency to believe that the snake would die, but in the case of the Sons, that head grew back amazingly fast and those brave men were quick to choose a new leader. Any guesses as to who that might be?"

Neville leaned back, his face beaming and his mouth grinning so wide it seemed about to bust his high-boned cheeks right through his skin. I knew the answer, as I'm sure you intelligent readers do too. The new leader of the Sons of the Confederacy was him, Neville Bonner. I did not please him and gave no answer to his self-absorbed question.

"I see," was all I said. I knew there was a hitch. This man held all the cards, on my initial assessment. He could easily and surely provide safe passage for both Marjorie and me out of this county, but there was something he wanted that he thought I could do, and that was my point of barter. But I waited. I waited for him to tell it, not giving the scum the satisfaction of hearing my ask.

Footfalls in the hallway turned both our heads at once to see Millie snake her body around the jamb of the open door. She'd changed her dress, but I see no sight of Marjorie, which left my eyes to the moving temptation that Millie had become. Her red hair was loose and free, falling across her shoulders in undulating waves. Her dress was now much shorter and much tighter, and her bosom swelled full beneath the bodice, and she played the vision she knew she was with much abandonment.

"Marjorie will be coming along soon, Rosco," she said, batting her eyes and licking her lips before she turned to her brother. "You were right Neville. One of mother's dresses would suit her shape just fine, so I showed her the cellar and the trunk at the back. You know, the one we use as a table that holds all of mother's things. Marjorie is there now, getting ready."

"Fabulous," Neville replied, rubbing his hands together.

My ears perked and my senses tingled like hot steel was taking swipes at my innards. There was something peculiar about this sister and brother. I had noticed it before but dismissed it as playful siblings, but his remarks when he first entered the house, and the way his eyes moved up and down her posing form that stood amidst the frame of the door, sickened me with its intonations.

"Rosco!" The man suddenly shouted, and I jerked visibly as the sound startled me from my contemplations. "Come my good man. I have something to show you and I know you, of all people, will truly be appreciative of its beauty. Come."

He stood up, and moved to the door, where he paused and turned to Millie. His hands grasped the woman's hips and pulled her waist close to press against his. Neville's hands slipped slowly up her torso, coming to rest, and squeezing gently, on the generous swell of her breasts. Millie tilted her head back against the door jamb and moaned softly. I couldn't believe my eyes – my mind was aghast that a man and a woman, even more so a sister and brother, would put on such a private, if not sickening display in such a public way, with me being the public just looking to get away. Needless to say, I was immensely uncomfortable and was relieved when the sound of the front door opening and the chitter chatter of female voices broke up the incestuous foreplay that was commencing before me.

Like a squall blowing hard down off the mountain, the women poured into the nearby front entrance, full of bluster and chaos, bringing a touch of the cold in with them, but gentled themselves as they turned to the parlour and graced the room with their presence.

"Left the dance a little early girls?" Millie's question spawned a chorus of nods from the three women.

"Mr. Pitt." Neville moved towards the three ladies, placing his arms around two of their waists. "Allow me to introduce Trixie, Sarah and Maddie."

Like Millie's hair had been styled earlier, they each had similar bobs on top of their head. Trixie was a brunette, small and thin, she approached me as I assumed any jezebel at any common whorehouse would. "Hello there," Trixie breathed, low and gravelly, then moved to the side making space for the next.

"Sarah," Neville nodded, urging the coloured woman forward with the hand at her back. "Good evening, kind sir," she said. Her eyes were dark, and they flashed with surprise when she spied the thin stripes set against the blue of my pants. "Whoa sugar man, you'd best be whistling Dixie as opposed to belting out the Battle Cry of Freedom, lest while you're here in Randy River. Did you catch that Neville?" she asked, spinning quick to eye the man who stood smiling with his arm still draping over the last little lady.

He did not respond to Sarah's query but moved on to what appeared to be the final introduction.

"And of course, my personal favourite, Maddie." The woman who stepped forward would not raise her eyes. I saw her face wince and her waist push forward suddenly, as Neville raised his foot and kicked her from behind. "God damn it, Maddie. Look at the man and show some respect. Say hello, for Christ's sake."

"Hello," squeaked a small voice.

Creed I could not tell, but Maddie was to my eye, definitely one of the mountain people. Her cheeks were plump and round, and her eyes, which drifted up quickly to glance at my eyes, showed no signs of weakness but glared with the strength and resilience of her kin, who walked these lands long before any of us was even a thought on the wind.

"Yes." Again, Neville rubbed his hands together, as his eyes danced over the three women, who, like horses being paraded to sell, stood displaying themselves before me.

"Always the bells of the ball, these lovely ladies," Neville said, "and an hour of their time fetches a pretty penny from the boys around here. But for you Rosco, the choice is yours, free of charge. But first, come as I asked. You're gonna like this last little lady, Rosco. I know she's just your huckleberry and I can't wait for you to meet her."

As the man beckons I rise from the chair and follow him down the darkened hallway. He leads me to the stairs, which climb up to an even darker passage, and I follow as he hurries ahead taking each step two by two. I don't fear the dark or the man to my front, but my mind turns to Marjorie, who has been absent for too long and my worry weighs heavily, causing my legs to slow and my mind to scream 'go find her!' But I don't... I mount the stairs and strain my eyes to follow Neville through the dark.

He had said I would like "this last little lady," and as Neville lights the lamp in the room and my eyes fall on her golden sheen, I must admit, the man was right.

"Well, Mr. Pitt, what do you think of that!" Neville was busting the seams with pride, gazing at the gun like it was the most beautiful woman he'd ever had the pleasure to lay his rat-like eyes upon.

She was beautiful, sitting by the corner window on two large-spoked wheels of high-polished steel. The housing of the formidable weapon gleamed a plated gold, warm in colour but cold in its intentions. The barrel, or barrels I should clarify, to be precise about the Gatling Gun, were six dark tubes of demise pointed out the window's direction, and judging by their condition, had never once spun on their central shaft to spit out death at two hundred rounds per minute.

"She's never been fired, not once," Neville said, seeing my appreciation. "Gold plated, the only one, and only one of a handful ever acquired by the Confederacy. A shame it was we lacked the ballistic prowess to defeat the northern horde, but I do confess I was envious of you Union boys when I saw the Gatlings being pulled on parade or growling with menace from the flanks of your navy vessels. Look at the plaque," he said, grin growing. "This gun was awarded to me by Robert E. Lee himself. Go on, look at the inscription."

I turned from the gun to look at him, with full intention of falsely professing my lack of literate abilities, and that's when I felt the crack on the back of my head, and like the hallway we had just followed, everything went dark.

CHAPTER 8

Northern aggression

I open my eyes to a dim, damp room, smelling heavily of mold, earth and stone. This room, which appears more like a cave, as the stone walls sweat and drip with moisture, was lit by the single, haunting glow of a lamp, sat on the floor in one corner. I see the broad, pale, back of a man, shirtless, making himself busy before what I assume is a work bench. My eyes adjust to the dimness of the light, and I see shimmering's of things on the surface of the bench, but I can't make out what they are, as my vision blurs and swims in and out of focus.

I am restrained. Tightly set strips of thick leather clamp my forearms down to the arms of the chair in which I am sitting, and similar restraints served the same purpose around my ankles. The chair, firmly fixed to the floor, is hard and made of iron and I feel three cold rods extending up from the seat to form a backrest of sorts. Overall, it was not the comfortable chair I had come accustomed to within the walls of The Bonner House.

The passage of time is but a blur to my fog-riddled mind. At first I'm confused but slowly my mind clears and my sudden panic erupts with recognition. I clench it down, hard. I sit motionless and quiet, but inside the storm rages. In through the nose and out through the mouth, I control my breaths and focus, calming my anguish and forcing my mind to assess the situation, to become one with the mountain.

I must profess, I am feeling a little unnerved by my inability to move my arms or legs, and though I'd never been subjected to a formal session of torture, I suspected I was about to experience just that. Again, I briefly rage and struggle against the leather restraints.

That big, pale man at the work bench whistles softly, just random notes, paying no mind to my fretful panic, which surged then settled as I accepted the futility of my efforts. Then he finally turns to face me. His quick motion caused a stir in the air, and I caught a whiff of what I can only describe as shit, death, and vomit.

I blinked my eyes, not really understanding what I was seeing. Once, as a boy, me and Allbright, who was, I suppose, my best friend in my youth, had abandoned our chores on one fine day, and snuck off with youthful laughter to a side-road circus that had come to our county and had set their tents not far from our farm, just over the hill and yonder, a quick jaunt for young-boy legs. It was, in my recollection, one of the strangest things I'd seen, as a boy. We spied from a short distance, not having the pennies required to enter the shows, the busy movements of the most bizarre collection of folks I'd ever laid eyes on: bearded women with bulging biceps washing rags in a tub; little people, a man and a woman, not much bigger than Allbright and me, and we was only eight at the time; a strong man, dressed in spotted tights; and the most frightening spectre of all, a grease-paint clown, who only stood staring with a face much too white, eyes framed black, lips fat and red and fire for hair, that only grew on the sides of his bald head. The vision of the clown frightened my boyish self badly, and Allbright, as I recall, didn't seem too comfortable either as we fell under that jester's black-eyed gaze. We ran home quick, never to return.

Well, that's the best way I can describe this man's appearance, who now turned around to face me. Frightening he was, even in my full-grown manhood. His greasy, black hair was cut in a bowl shape at the top of his head. He wore an old, soiled butcher's apron made of heavy, brown canvas, tied behind his neck and around his expansive waist. Beneath the apron he was shirtless, rolls of flesh flopped over the belt loops of his work pants. His eyes were a strange blue, with pinhole pupils dotting the center, and like that clown of my youth, they were framed in thick, black paint, which ran melting beneath his eyes and mixed with the sweat that endlessly flowed down his too-white face. His lips were as red as Sally Green's in the kissing booth. She'd been a child crush of mine, and I never did work up the nerve to spend a penny and plant one. But this fella: all the pennies in the world could not tempt me, nor anyone with the gift of sight, to kiss this gruesome side-show clown.

"Hello Rosco." I hear Neville's voice behind me, but I can't turn my head enough to see him. His greeting is cheerful and almost ripe with eager anticipation. "This startling fellow is my good friend, Herman. Herman Mudgett."

Upon hearing Neville's introduction, Herman proceeded to spread his red lips and gurgled a wet chuckle that welled up and bounced to my ears, escaping from between the empty gums, void of teeth, which framed the darkness of his foul mouth.

"I've known Herman for a long time, but I only call upon him when I have a special task to be undertaken here in my den of iniquities," Neville continued. I heard him snap his fingers and watched helpless, as the large, pale man moved at me fast across the room. Herman leaned in close, his pin-holed pupils dancing before me. I snapped my head to the side and twisted my face in disgust.

"Pee-hew! Mister, I'm not one to cuss much but you fuckin' stink!"

That's when I saw the shimmer of steel he held in his hands. He held what looked like a potato peeler, but smaller, sharper, and specialized. With heavy breaths, increasing in both depth and frequency, Herman's eyes watched mine with intent as he dragged the instrument, one at a time, across the nervy tips of each of my fingers. Herman seemed disappointed in my lack of reaction, I suppose, tossed the peeler aside, which I might mention, had successfully peeled more than one layer of skin from the ends of my appendages, leaving them sufficiently raw and bloodied. Sure, it hurt, but it weren't the worst thing I'd ever felt in my life, and I was jaw-set determined to not give these boys the smallest speck of satisfaction.

I struggled again, briefly, and I thought I felt those leather straps give, just a little, down around my right ankle. I felt the bone gain space and edge away slightly from the press of the chair's cold, iron leg. Herman had gone to the bench and turned to face me again. I wasn't too sure what he had in his hands, now that he'd discarded the peeler, but he had more than one of whatever it was, and he proceeded to jamb sharp slivers of an undetermined nature, deep beneath my fingernails. Needles, I quickly and painfully learned, widen the deeper they plunge.

My mind had been conditioned to endure the horrors of war and the trials of the mountain trails but this was a new form of hell that set my thoughts reeling wildly. 'What the hell,' I thought, this fella sure had a thing for fingers, and I confess I did, at that juncture, open my jaws and gave them more than enough satisfaction then I thought was fair. I screamed bloody murder! It hurt like hell. But I contained myself quickly and turned statuesque in my sitting posture, with ten shiny needles, long and fat at the ends, protruding from the tips of my fingers.

Herman, the grease-paint clown, stared at my pain. His toothless grin filling my vision. Well, I did what any man would do, the only thing I could think: gathered as much spit as I could in my mouth, then propelled it heavily to splash the white face of that twisted clown. Herman raged at the affront. I laughed at him, despite the pain.

Neville was still positioned behind me. He was breathing awful heavy, and I hoped he was having his heart attacked, but I knew that hope to be fleeting when he encouraged his good friend Herman to "better his efforts" and inflict greater pain.

"But yes, my friend. No crippling wounds or broken bones just yet," Neville continued, and I kinda gave up, I must confess, and counted myself dead already, just on account of his words. "The boys are coming over," he claps his hands. "I do like to watch my boys work, Mr. Pitt. I calls them in from time to time. Bones is there specialty."

I hear Neville, but my attention turns with alarm to Herman, who has returned to the workbench and fiddles with his tools of torture. Again, I hear the clinking of metal and the shuffling of feet. His back, I notice now, my mind avoiding what may be coming next, is broad and pimpled badly, long black hairs, single in strands, dot the landscape of his skin.

From behind me Neville emerges in my side-eye to walk and stand beside Herman. Neville's lanky, bone-thin swagger speaks comparatively to his frail mental state, and his hands shake visibly as he implores my torturer with another request. I watch Herman nod his head to Neville's whisper, and I see Neville reach up to grasp the jowls of Herman's face. Pulling the taller man's head down, I watch and grimace in shock and disgust as the men press their lips together, swappin' spit for more than a second. I guess somebody would kiss this grease-paint clown after all.

"Why, that scalpel looks quite efficient, Herman," Neville says to the man on the heels of their kiss, after briefly glancing down at the workbench. He takes the three steps forward to be standing directly in front of me, and turns nonchalantly, making a plucking motion with his hands.

"May I?" he inquires to Herman who has turned to watch. The fat, white clown nods, his hand slips beneath his apron and he rubs himself in a disgusting manner and I'm sickened. Neville bends down and leans close, bringing his eyes close to mine. I feel the beginning of a tingle beneath the nail of my thumb, and I see the small smile playing on Neville's lips as he begins to twist the first needle and scrape side-to-side.

Well, that really riles me, and I starts thinking: first off, Neville forgets himself, obviously, leaning in so close as he does; second, his breath really is the rankest of hot wind ever to blow my way, especially leaning in so close as he does and; third, I'm really getting tired of these boys and their strange finger fetish,

I thinks they calls it. I jerks my head forward hard and Neville, well, like I said, leaning in close like he was, bore the full brunt of my bony forehead and I swear I heard his nose crunch. He flew back fast and crashed heavily into the workbench, taking big Herman and himself both down to the floor.

Herman landed on top, and I swear I heard more bones crack, and my immediate assessment was that things weren't going so well for Neville. Herman had cracked his head with a necksnap, hitting the bench as he found his way down. I could see the blood dripping from his head, as he pulls himself up from Neville's now unconscious form, grabs that scalpel Neville had been talking about, and charges at me meaner that a rutting' bull moose.

As fate would have it, and my good fortunes sometimes never fail to amaze me, as the big man charged I felt the leather around my right ankle tear and snap, and poor Herman's charge, scalpel raised high, ended prematurely as I raised that free leg as fast and hard as I could, and kicked the fat man squarely between his two boiled eggs in a sack.

Again, I am amazed. That scalpel, flew to the air and shimmered, guided by angels wings, and fell softly on the back of my restrained hand. Herman slowly crumpled to a curl on the floor, all the air rushing out of his lungs as he gasped from the force of my blow to his sensitive regions.

Eventually, the man was going to get up, I knew. I also knew that would probably prove badly for me. So, with some haste but maintaining a level of care, I twist my wrist painfully, getting that scalpel between my fingers, and began a furious sawing motion against the restraint. Neville had been right; it was an efficient tool. That scalpel made short work of them leather restraints and before the fat man could regain his legs, my hands are free and I'm making short work at freeing my feet, which as it turns out, really are in a bad state.

Herman's charging again, but he's too late and I am free and meet his charge with the swinging arc of the scalpel, which finds purchase behind his ear, where the neck is soft at the base of the skull. With girlish screams Herman tumbles backwards, tripping over the unconscious lump that was Neville, and smashing the back of his head on the stone wall as he fell.

I stand there and look down at the two fellas. Herman's eyes stare open, head tilted and propped against the base of the wall, a scalpel sticking out the side of his head. Neville remains motionless, dead or alive I can't really tell, but neither is moving so I do. I glance to the floor at the scattered shiny metal things, all grinning sharp in the light of the lamp, and I pick up a large knife. I see my boots standing on the floor in a darkened corner, like they was waiting from my feet to slip inside once again, and for a moment, everything kinda feels right in the world.

I've never seen a room without a door, but, it seems, I'm seeing one now as I look around in the dimness of the single lamp aglow on the floor. I spies some narrow cracks that form thread-thin, straight lines on the wall – which only holds the look of field stones, a common material for a home's foundation. But these cracks, barely visible, are the only things in the entire room that offers the hope of a door. I feel its surface, and though it feels just like the rounded grit of field stones, my hand grasps a loop of rope, hidden to the eye, and I pull it. The door swings open with a whisper of air, I move slowly through, and it closes whispering behind me. I watch it, amazed, pulling the two remaining needles that still protruded from my fingernails, as the hidden door disappears and looks just like the stone walls that encases this cellar in which I find myself. And just a cellar it is, barren and empty but for the several large barrels that stood like short, dark, sentinels in a far corner. Webs dangled from the thick beams that frame the floor of the home above, and I moved to the base of a stairwell, warped, wooden and wobbly. The stairs heaved from the wall and creaked in protest as I mounted them, and with blade held ready, burst through the door at the top.

I exploded into silence, wild and already flailing cold steel in my mind, but the house only whispered of emptiness, the sounds of clocks ticking, ticking from all the rooms.

I felt like an intruder, and guess in some respects I was, as I crept down the hallway to the brightest of rooms, that I knew had the widest of windows and the broadest view of the day. My stealth was less then desirable as it would seem I'm more apt at avoiding the snap of a twig then the creak of the floor, but I eased my way into the room, and assessed what I saw accordingly: A teacup perched at the centre of a side table, precisely in the centre of a crisp, white-laced doily. Its contents appeared a dark, cold brew, which swirled and stained the porcelain inside as I raised it to give it a sniff. Tea. And a cold, extinguished cigar, just a chewed stub sitting in the ashtray beside the abandoned cup of tea.

Proud of my detecting and establishing firmly in my mind that this was Millie's sitting room, I moved carefully to the window and pressed to the frame. I did not touch the draperies, as they proved quite transparent and through them I could see the empty street and the sun rising to the east, leaving plenty of blue between itself and the tree line on the path of its ascent. At the end of the street, I saw the horses and buggies gathered, and for the first time in years I thought of what day it was: Sunday. I sighed, and moved more casually, knowing Millie would not be one to miss the Sunday service, commencing now at the church down at the end of the street.

Feeling as I have the place to myself I turn back and head past the parlour and upstairs and retrace our steps of the previous evening to enter the room with the Gatling. I briefly glanced at the gold menace poised by the window and notice the hoppers, six of them, placed on the floor between the gaps of her wheels. I glance out the window again, and by the light of day, from this second-storey, the view of the street is fair, though at an awkward angle. I move behind the Gatling and bend slightly to look through the sights. Though rudimentary when compared to the fine precisions afforded by the sights of my Sharps, the street pans before my eye and I can sense the damage of which this little lady was capable.

The thought of my Sharps rifle inspires me, and my eyes scan the room seeking my pistol, my hat, and my coat, not in any particular order. I spies my gun in its holster, and I smile at that slap of angular leather and the one-fisted reckoning that's nestled inside. It's hung nicely on a hook, on the back of the door that sits slightly closed having swung a little when I entered. When I move to reach for my gun I trips on my duster and my hat sits beside it, both just tossed to the floor.

Back to my old self, my mind turned to Marjorie and my heart sang a song of sorrow as I wondered where she was and what might have befallen her at the hands of these people who all, and I'm really not one to judge, behave in such evil manners and undertake such hideous things. I had begun to suspect that we, Marjorie and me, were not the first to be lured into this house for tired eyes and weary souls, and toyed with in ways a feral cat, whose belly is full, still finds pleasure in the tormenting of the mouse. I had begun to suspect this whole town, nay, this whole county, was quite a bit wacky and while I'm just a back-woods hick fresh down from the hills, the level of depravity I had seen in such a short time astounded yet saddened me deeply.

I thought with despair on the state of this world, as I moved from one room to the next, seeking for any signs of my blonde-haired beauty with the voice of fresh-rendered honey, who's wellbeing was foremost in my mind. I found nothing in my searching's, least not that would have any attachments to Marjorie. But my eyes did see and my hands did handle objects I could but will not describe, as that, I believe, would be offensive to most, and not anything I'm interested in jabbering about anyways. And besides, there's voices approaching. I can hear them plainly as I move back into the room with the Gatling and once again peer through the transparency of the drapes.

There's seven men approaching, and I'm guessing that's "the boys." Big fellas for sure. I could see, even with them being halfway down the street, how bones could be their specialty. I'm not much one for breaking things, but I'm tempted to break the window right now and open up on them boys with my Colt, but I don't. I think of my Sharps and Winchester on my saddle, and Mr. Andrews, poor fella, been hitched beside big old Jax, with not even a lick of salt between them.

Fast as I can move I turn and I fly down the stairs, barely touching but one, then through the kitchen and mud room. I burst into the yard with more abandonment then I'd recommend, but I was in a bit of a panic. Once inside the stable I grabbed my desired weapons from my saddle, unhitched the horses, and urged them to, "Gitya!"

Mr. Andrews was off like a shot, not sparing me a second look as he rounded the side of the house and charged for the trees; Jax just stood there and snorted. No time for him, I heard the men holler when Mr. Andrews made his dash across the front of the house, and their hurried footfalls now fell clearly to my ears.

Not seeing much choice, and there never had been, I ran back into the house and straight up the stairs, smashed out the window where that Gatling gun perched, and fired off a few quick rounds from my Winchester to kick up the dust at their feet and send them scrambling for cover in the street below. While they was ducking, I reached down to grab me a hopper for the Gatling, when my eye caught the plaque Neville had been so proud of and sparing one eye for a flash out the window, I bent down to read the inscription, seeings how I had a second or two.

To the right honorable Mr. Neville Bonner,

In recognition of your unwavering and valued support for the glory of the Confederacy, it is with an honor and with pleasure that we present you and your cherished family with this gold-plated instrument in the battle for our freedom from the tyranny of Northern aggression.

Muchly heartfelt,

Robert E. Lee

'Well,' I thought, 'she looks pretty. But can she shoot?'

I slammed the hopper into the slot and glided the gun on its axis, left and right. My fire, I assessed, could cover a sweeping patch of ground. In fact, most of the town's only street, which was now growing busy fast as folks wandered out of the church, fell easy within the gun's broad radius. No doubt service cut short when my Winchester hollered. I watched the street fill with God-fearing souls.

The men ducking down below were certainly large men and probably quite skilled at the exercising of their bone-breaking intentions, but they weren't much good at taking cover, as they peeked out from behind one water trough, all seven crouched together in a bunch, heads clearly visible and for the one on the end, asses to boot.

"Neville! Have you been hitting the brandy before noon again, boy? What you shooting at?"

I don't rightly know which of the seven were yelling, but I noticed they all stand up, and stare towards the house. Suddenly Neville, much to my shock, appeared in my view, weaving wobbly up the street, screaming something about somebody getting away and calling for the men to "mount up, arm yourselves," and other shit like that. Up the street, I see more men coming, lots of them, and God bless them for the heavenly men they are, for it appears that's where they want to send me. Each one of them was walking at least one-side heavy, with the weight of a hog strapped to their leg.

As the mob nears I take a quick assessment of my options: I've chased off my horse so running is not an option, and to be clear, that suits me just fine cause I'm tired of running, been doing it all my life it seems, and damn it all to hell, I want my Marjorie; I could start cranking that Gatling and rain hard hell down upon them, and I was seriously leaning that way; or I could go easy and pick off just Neville, and any that decide to stand and make a fuss. I thought on it for a moment and knew I was wasting time as I saw Neville meet up with his boys and point right up to this very window, like he knew, and he did, just where I'd be. Well before they could figure it all out and take up positions I'd made up my mind and figured all's fair in love and war, and it was time for these boys to get a taste of some genuine, southern-raised and battle-fed, Northern aggression.

I turned that crank, and damn if it didn't feel good when that Gatling started spit'n. Though I could have swung its axis broad as I raked the street, I was careful in my motions, and the sequenced cranks required to make the dogs bark. And while my aim was intended to be lethal to some, I kept the line of fire far and away from those down the road, who now scampered like startled marmots seeking their holes. But to those to whom I had intentions, I swept with some abandonment and them 50-cal sought out and found the moist meat of their flesh with such frequency even I was startled.

Neville, like the fox that he had proven to be, evaded the golden gun's fire. I saw him stumbling between that lone standing willow, and the rare, red-bricked structure of 'Willy's Mercantile, Neville Bonner, Proprietor,' the sign said. After about a minute, when the barrels spun empty and the heat and smoke rose from the shimmering metal of the Gatling, I saw several bodies in the street below, at least four big fellas, Neville's boys, and a couple of more to the right side of the street, one still crawling. I let him be.

Now, I don't reckon to see the future as I do not possess one of them seeing balls of crystal, but I'm guessing there may be some historians, or perhaps John Maximillian himself, who will write and spin a tale of courage, filled with inspiring words on behalf of the valiant and courageous men of Randy River, who stood strong to protect their freedoms against the relentless rampage of the murderous villain Rosco Pitt. Far be it from me to tell them what to write, but they weren't here, as far as I can tell, and it sure didn't happen like that in my eyes.

History. Would I be that murderous villain, shot dead through an upper window of the legendary Bonner House? Would history tell of them digging down, years later, beneath that strange "den of inequities" – beneath the place for tired eyes and weary souls? Would they find what I suspects might be the long-dead bones of said weary souls, bones scratched and scraped, revealing the signs of a tortured demise at the hands of a grease-paint clown and a pompous, stick man of the sickest perversions? I had to shake myself from such wonderings. The thoughts made my stomach turn and my heart ache, as I saw Marjorie's eyes, staring and dead in the dark, some where's beneath this very house.

I shuddered and turned my eyes to the street, then remember the side and back of the house were absent of any scrutiny, and I was certain there were men, at this moment, creeping through the yard and through the door of the mud room. I glance quickly up the street, and seeing no movement I spun on my heel and dragged a large, heavy table across the floor, flipped it on its side, and pushed it hard against the door of the room, which I'd swung shut with a bang in my haste. It was feeble cover, at best, I knew, but it would have to do, as the street demanded my attention.

I heard the distant sound of a single horse gallop and stop at the far end of town. Voices shouted from that distance as I eased the drapes aside, for a truly clear picture, and spied the stranger dismounting his horse, then shaking the hands of another and another and another. The men who'd gathered around this new arrival all pointed at my window and expressed themselves with waving arms and furious murmurs. This new arrival, who was wider and taller than any man that had gathered around him, raised his arms, appearing to calm them down, then stepped forward a few yards down the street, standing alone, a tempting target if I been holding my Sharps.

He stared standing motionless, like somehow his eyes could see me, standing here staring back. He wore a white straw hat with a bright, purple band, the hat of a man strolling through his garden in the humidity of more southern climes, I thought. His hair sprung out in crazy ringlets, a dirty brown curl he'd grown long. His cloak was black and shimmered dust free, despite him having just come in off the trail. Beneath the cloak was a shimmering white vest, wool of some expense I imagine, and his trousers appeared pressed, stiff as paperboard and clean as if freshly attended to by a skilled Chinese launderer. I saw his belt hanging crooked across his waist, the grip turned inward towards his frame, speaking of his preference to draw his gun across his body – a draw I'd tried and found inadequate in both efficiency and accuracy, though I knows there are those who would argue this point, that fine looking fellow being one of them.

I was surprised as he began to walk calmly up the street, right in the middle. He flipped his cloak back and put his hands in the pockets of his pants, and kicked the dusty street as he went, seemingly finding the dirt that rose from the scuffle of his boots interesting. I must admit, a part of me watched him with admiration, and that's when I saw the badge pinned to his chest and chuckled at the finest U.S. Marshal my eyes had ever seen.

For a moment I felt optimistic. Here was an outsider, a government man in the service of the highest law enforcement office in the land, and a right bold fellow, which was to my liking and sparked the beginnings of respect. But, as I've been noticing, hope for me seems fleeting and I feel my stomach drop just a tad, as Neville emerges from behind the mercantile and, with furtive glances my way, rushed to shake the hand of the proud pose the Marshal had struck.

Men of the town filtered back on to the street. I shook my head as they too, in a bunch, began to follow the path of that Marshal and move closer to my position. They were just plain stupid, I tell ya. It's like they forgot there was a Gatling gun up here, moving in a mob as they did, not thinking for a moment how I could cut them down like a sweeping scythe mowing down the wheat.

I took the opportunity to tend to the Gatling, and replaced the empty hopper with one that was full, and heavy with two hundred more rounds of certain death ready to proclaim their dominance. I sensed the boys were once again ready for a fight, and if that's what they wanted that's what I'd give them.

As my eye fell level and peered through the gold-plated, iron sight of the gun, I saw that Marshal wave the mob back, Neville included. Dumbfounded, I stared, and I tracked him, as he continued his stroll up the street, stopping only when almost directly below me. He tilts his head back and looks up at my window. His eyes squint and one hand moves to hold his hat on his head, such an angle did he have to crane his neck, and spoke level, not shouting, as he knew that I could here, but the men who hovered back down the street could not.

"Mr. Pitt," he said, not a twang or hint of a southern drawl tainting his crisp pronunciation of my family name. "My name is Quentin, Quentin James Morrison, U.S. Marshal."

A man of the north, my oh my, not since I'd heard Marjorie's honey voice speak my name had I heard such a sound so sweet.

"Yes sir," I spoke through the drapes, which I'm sure gave the Marshal no detail, but would subtly reveal my form to his position out front and below. "I sees what you are. How can I help you on this fine morning, good sir."

At that, the man took off his hat and scratched, turned and looked up the street, visibly laughing at my salutation, then turned back my way, to cause again an awkward strain on his neck.

"Well Mr. Pitt, I sees a lot of men down here who don't look to be in the best of health, what with being shot to hell and all. And last evening I received an urgent wire, pertaining to some concerning events that have taken place in and around these parts as of late. Now I'm not the only one who has word of these things, there's been a bounty issued, Mr. Pitt., dead or alive I'm assuming. And there'll be more men coming shortly, who I'm sure will find you're not worth the trouble and will shoot you dead, not caring about the deduction that will be applied to their renumeration. In addition, Mr. Pitt, as I'm sure you are aware," his arms spread wide like one stating the obvious, "there are a lot of townsfolk down here with guns of their own. A lot of guns, Mr. Pitt. And like those bounty hunters who are sure to arrive, these townsfolk, I'd be willing to bet, care not for the blind countenance of Lady Justice and would shoot you down like the dog they believe you to be. And that's why I'm here Mr. Pitt., which is a good thing for you."

His neck got the better of him, I saw, as he straightened his head and rubbed a hand vigorously, against the muscles that had been so cruelly strained given the duration of his explaining.

"Is that so," I replied. "And what is it about you being here makes my situation any better, Mr. Morrison?" I knew the answer, but I just wanted to see him strain his neck some more explaining that aspect of the here and now. And he did.

"Well, as a U.S. Marshal, Mr. Pitt, it is my job to see that you are treated, as is required under the laws of the United States, as innocent until proven guilty before a jury of your peers, after which time, I imagine you will be found guilty, and as such will inevitably hang from the neck until dead. That is my duty, Mr. Pitt. And believe you me, I take my duty quite seriously."

He rubbed his neck again, and I felt some sympathy for this fella, as a pain in the neck, depending on its frequency and ferocity, can be a torturous thing to endure, as my mother often told me when I was a child. So, I did not continue my ruse and force unnecessary conversations. Nor did I pull my pistol and pop a bullet in his head, though I might have done if he had been a Son of the Confederacy.

"Alright," I said. Then I raised my voice loud so even the women and children hanging back at the sanctuary of the church, at the far end of town, could hear my words.

"And, you'd best be telling those boys downstairs, cause I can hear them, and the ones back in the yard, cause I knows they are there, to clear on out. I'm coming down two-fisted, out through the front, until I come eye to eye with you Mr. Morrison. And I will kill any other man, woman or child, or dog for that matter, who gets in my way. Is that clear, Mr. Morrison? I need to hear you say. Is that clear?"

"Yes, Mr. Pitt," Morrison replied, then like I did mine he raised his voice loud, clear for all to hear. "Gentlemen, withdraw from your positions in the yard and in the house and move back towards the church immediately."

I couldn't see them complying, but I heard the trample of the boots downstairs, and I watched the eyes of Marshal Morrison follow their retreat up the right side of the street, so I assumed they had done as was asked, and the Marshal's nod towards me confirmed my assumption. At that I sighed, and assessed myself, then gathered my weapons and moved downstairs.

I raised both rifles high above my head, pointing nowhere at no one, and walked out the door and down the porch steps to stand almost eye to eye with Marshal Quentin James Morrison. He was taller than me, and at least half a yard wider, thicker and leaner, both at the same time. And though I figured I could whoop him, on my initial assessment, I had no desire to inflict violence on this Marshal. He looked me up and down, making an assessment of his own, then without a word and fast, I might add, he pulled my Colt from its holster and slid it in his waist, reached up and snatched the rifles from my raised arms, and tossed them to the dusty ground. I winced at that, thinking poorly for my Sharps and its delicate sights, while he spun me around with force and brought my hands together roughly, behind my back, and I felt the cold iron of handcuffs snap tight around my wrists.

That is what occurred and brought an end to the storied Standoff at Randy River. And so should the histories say.

CHAPTER 9

Moral instruction and the price of sin

I've always loved horses. The wild ones I've seen are a thing to behold, and certain domestic individuals that allowed me their backs have easily earned my respect and admiration of their melding of power and beauty. I find the pounding of thunder they carry together, or alone, when they race across an open space, hooves hammering the skin of the earth, haunches glistening and rippling with their efforts, to be a thing that quickens my heart, even when just watching. But just watching is starting to wear thin, and the languid trot of a lazy mule, or a tired team pulling a heavy wagon, is dulling my conviction for the creatures I so cherish.

It had been but a couple of hours, at most, since the Marshal and that flat-faced fool Freddy Simmons, the "locally elected" Deputy of Randy River, had escorted me up that dirt street before the scornful eyes of the townsfolk, and already the town was filling up with people. The continuous sounds of their traffic, both man alone and wagon plum-full, that come to me in my bar-striped window is fraying my mind so I can't think quite right. Of course, I've been standing in that window for near just as long, so I'm as much to blame for my scattered thoughts.

I'm sure those bars in that window cast shadows across my

face, the face sought out by the eyes of the folks riding them horses or sitting in their wagons. Some pass by, moving further down the street and out of my view, while others hitch their horses or rest their wagons around and to the side of the church, which stands white, and clean in its judgements across the street, and if I press to one side is visible, from my jailhouse view. They're close enough and I can hear them when they pass. Some speak in whispers that are breathy, pondering their proximity to "the murderous scum," but others speak plainly, level and loud, celebrating the opportunity to see a man hang, and the arguments to be presented before that inevitable outcome arrives, or something to that effect.

I pull myself away from the window, the sounds from outside become random noise as for the first time, I assess my new home. But for the wall now behind me that holds my window, a wall of a stone not unlike one might find beneath the Bonner House, my prison consists of cold bars on three sides, and is the only cell at the Randy River Jailhouse.

The jailhouse, I discover, is but one large room, and the view from this cell sets the stage, which widens before me, the entire expanse of that room. The door through which I had been escorted, by Marshal Morrison and Deputy Freddy, was a normal man-door, appearing flimsy, paneled wood with a square cut high at eye level. To my right there was a table, grey with age and burred with slivers the legs did appear. Its top was a mess of papers and such. Beyond that table, and I almost cried when I sees them, a white-oak box-cabinet with glass doors is mounted on the wall, inside is slotted shotguns and rifles, but there hangs on a hook my pistol and holster, and my rifles lean crooked below. To my left is a desk, and a cabinet of sorts.

At that desk sits Freddy, as happy as can be, basking in his perceived glory as if all the hustle and bustle that has invaded this sleepy town, will somehow provide him the admiration he feels he's denied. And, I guess, that's my initial assessment of Freddy.

I hadn't really given him a second look before, as he and the

Marshal flanked me on my walk of shame up the centre of town. I had other things on my mind at that time. But now, as he sat at that desk, pulled back far, his long legs extended to rest his crossed boots on the desktop, I found more time to examine the man.

"Hey!," Freddy suddenly shouts. "What you eyeing Billy Yank? Sit your ass down on that bunk for a spell. You bout giving me the willies."

I felt sorry for Freddy. I really did. For one thing, I could see he was at the top of his game, right at this moment, and it wouldn't be, nor never had been, any better: yelling at an unarmed man separated by iron bars, sticking out his chest displaying as such. I shook my head, not having the heart to tell him I was a man of southern blood, Missouri born. For another thing, though his legs were long, his measure as a man above the waist was short and stilted, and his back curved in a strange way as he leaned in his chair, leading me to believe the man had some strange affliction of the spine, most likely a defect at birth. This saddened me. I was certain Freddy's life had been nothing but hard, as was also reflected by his tattered cloak, rope-cinched pants, and frayed, dirty hat on his head.

I did as he asked, allowing him his moment, turned and sat on the bunk. Smiling at his desk Freddy rested an unlabeled, glass jug of clear liquid on the back of his bent elbow and tipped the neck to his lips. His Adam's Apple bulged, but not out of fear. He shook his head, just once, and smacked his lips, as he returned the jug to its place on the desk. We both jumped a bit when the door flew open, and the busied sounds of the usually dead-quiet street came flooding inside. Marshal Morrison filled the frame and commenced to move through and was followed by another; a man who some may say represented a higher authority.

"Hey Marshal," Freddy greeted the man. "Things sounding busy out there."

"There's a few folks gathering, Deputy. Nothing of any real concern." Morrison nodded at Freddy and was turning to address me, I assume, when Freddy had more to say.

"Pretty special seeing all these folks come into Randy River." He was excited, as I've said. "Not too surprising though, seeing what's going on and all. Pitt here is probably the best thing to happen to this sleepy town. I hears Bonner's planning a community picnic among other things, on account of all the folks flooding in."

I listened to Freddy, but I watched the Marshal. He didn't turn back to Freddy, right away. He took a spell for a sigh, and a roll of the eyes, then turned back smiling.

"A picnic, you say! Well, that sounds swell, Freddy," the Marshal replied. Then he pulled off his hat and wiped his brow and shrugged in a weary way. "Say, Freddy. How's about you do me a favor and head on out and keep an eye on the town? Me and the reverend here, we got to talk with Mr. Pitt for a spell, and I'd be mighty appreciative if you could keep an eye for me whilst I'm occupied here in the jailhouse."

Well, I won't say Freddy over-expressed his joy in being assigned to do what he'd been wanting to do all day, but he did.

"Yes sir, Mr. Marshal. I'd be honoured to help you sir." Freddy's face damn near split in two, I swear. He shoved an old single action, powder-blasting pistol that looked like it hadn't been fired in my lifetime, into the waist of his pants. As he moved to the door he had an ominous warning for Marshal Quentin James Morrison.

"Watch him Marshal. Watch him real close." Freddy's eyes were slits as he glared at me through the bars, posed gripping the handle of the door. "I've heard tell he can do some things. You-all just holler if he gives you any trouble." He grabbed the end of his antiquated pistol and glared at me as he slipped through the door, closing it behind him.

No sooner had the door shut and the Marshal was pulling up two chairs, offering one to the quiet man who removed his tall, black top hat with a nod of his head in gratitude as he slid quietly into the chair. He observed me with an expression of inquisitive contempt, and judging from his overall black attire, and the peek of white rising a hair above the line of his buttoned-up shirt, I suspected he was a holy man of some sorts, and like many of my suspicions, I was right.

"Mr. Pitt. This is Deacon Beauregard." Seemed to me the Marshal had made an appropriate introduction, but apparently the Deacon was of a different mind.

"Deacon Harold Beauregard the Third, to be precise. I represent the Southern Dioceses of the Episcopal Church." The man must have thought I had a third eye in the middle of my head, cause that's where he stared as he spoke, as opposed to looking me in the eyes as I did him.

"Pleased to meet you, Deacon," I replied with generous politeness. "Beauregard? A Louisiana man no less?"

The Deacon nodded, but still would not look me in the eyes. I glanced at the Marshal, questioning with a look the purpose of this visit. He began to explain, calling me Mr. Pitt, when I held my hand up, stopping his words.

"Marshal," I says, "Please do not call me Mr. Pitt. That was my father's name, and nobody called him that either."

The Marshal chuckled, not noticing the scowl of disapproval to furrow the Deacon's brow. "Rosco," he said, returning to his explanation. He told me of the Deacon visiting with families in and around Randy River, to aid them in their time of grief, and how these visits, which had just been undertaken within the last hour or so, had "led the Deacon to request a visit with you, seeing's how you are the man accused of being the cause of said grief."

The Deacon cleared his throat. "Sir. I can barely contain myself, sitting in such proximity to you," he said, still looking at the third eye I didn't know I had. "I've seen the women and the children of the men you killed this morning and the day prior. You've cut a wide path of sorrow through the Valley of Many Rivers."

I tried to interject, really I did. I pushed forward on my bunk and even opened my mouth, but I guess with him looking up at my third eye and all he didn't notice cause he just kept right on talking.

"But there was one such woman who was so afflicted by your evil, it caused my blood to boil and if I were not a man of the cloth, there would be much more foul words coming from my mouth."

Again, I tried to interrupt, but when I did well, sure as hellfire, brimstone and fury, his eyes found mine and he erupted, growing red in the face and shaking his fist, like God raging thunder on mountain high!

"Don't you interrupt me!" Spit flew from the Deacon's lips. Whoo-hoo, this was one pissed padre, and I was glad I was safe on my bunk, a fair distance away, and not struck by droplets that flew through the air. And he still wasn't done. His thunder had quieted but the storm still brewed.

"I would just as soon spite you to Hell this very second," his righteous rage continued, "but I am a man of God! And as such, I am obligated, which is the only reason I attend here now, to provide to you moral instruction and impress upon you the dear price of sin."

I had dropped my eyes as he ranted, to avoid the flight of spit and not out of shame. Keeping my head bowed I raised my eyes now, peeking at the Deacon from beneath my bushy brows. "Can I speak now?" I asked, and not waiting for permission, I did.

"I want to thank you Beauregard, for coming here today and delivering that eloquent sermon that I did not ask for." I saw him open his mouth and my hand flew up and I lost all composure.

"Don't you interrupt me!" I bellowed, and my bellow proved much louder than his. "You had your say. Now it's my turn."

The Marshal tensed, I saw him, and the Deacon shrank before my eyes as he realized the wrath of God may prove less lethal then the wrath of Rosco Pitt. All of that, and here I was, just getting started. I yelled no more, but my thunder rumbled deep.

"My god is the god of the mountain, and she is beautiful in her majesty, strength and dependable countenance. My god does not judge a man as you do. She does not assume the measure of any man but tests them against her might. Nor does she judge a man by the colour of his skin, or the colour of his coat. My god is the mountain, and under her arbitrary gaze, life gives, and life takes, but it is equal as such to all men who have the mettle in their minds. I spit on your righteousness and tell you I have committed no sin before my god."

I turned to Marshal Morrison. He sat on the edge of his chair, hand on the grip of his pistol. His eyes were wide with wonder. "Get this man out of my face, please," I said.

The Marshal gently took the Deacon by the elbow. The man was dumbfounded, I think, or petrified, and did not look back as the Marshal escorted him to the door. Morrison returned to his chair and sat down quietly. He took off his hat and examined it, thoughtfully, spinning the brim in his hands as he did.

"I could use a drink," he said, "how about you Rosco?"

I shook my head no, never being one for the drink, but beckoned the man to do as he must, not realizing the drink was courage for him to tell me what he had to say. He slid his chair closer to the bars of the cell and tipped the jug of moonshine in the same manner as Freddy, taking a deep swallow, and grimacing as it went down.

"The woman the Deacon was talking about, Rosco," he paused, looking up from the jug and hard into my eyes. "He met her at The Bonner House. It was Millie who brought her into the parlour. It was Marjorie, Rosco."

I couldn't believe my ears. "My Marjorie?" I asked.

The Marshal looked puzzled by that, tilting his head. "Marjorie Trowley. She's not well, Rosco, and folks around here are set on it being your doing. I've only heard the murmurs and the stories third hand, and have nothing directly stating your involvement, but I don't blame the Deacon for his anger over the state of that woman and what was obviously done to her to cause such an affliction. She's battered and doctors say catatonic. Your just like folks say, Rosco, a murderous villain, if you're the type a man to inflict such savagery on the gentlest among us. But you know something? I don't think you are."

I laid back on my bunk then put my arms over my eyes so Marshal Quentin James Morrison would not see me cry. I heard his words again in my mind and the sobs came to me, which I stifled some, but I know sounds escaped and Morrison could hear me.

"Well, I...I'm going to head out for bit, Rosco." Only my suppressed sobs replied. "I'll send Freddy back with some supper for you. Feeling a bit starved myself," he said. "Millie, I hear makes a great stew. Thinking I'll head down to The Bonner House and fetch me some."

I wanted to warn him to watch himself in that Bonner House. I wanted to advise him to take a close look at that stew and consider what kinda meat it might contain. I wanted to thank him for believing my innocence in relation to my Marjorie. I wanted to say all these things but as I heard the door close only my sobs filled the air, and that's all that would for the remainder of the day.

CHAPTER 10

When the Sons come home

I'd never thought a man's head could hold so much water, but I remembered Ma's lessons, back on the farm, that for the longest time left me and Allbright scratching our heads. She'd been explaining "the human anatomy," and while conceding it was a beautiful, complex creation of God, she also professed, her words carrying the strength of fact, that Allbright, Nickle, Fanny and me, sitting proper and straight at our desks as instructed, were mostly made of the eyes' most precious dew: water. Now, even at the tender age that I was, nine or ten at the time, I was tempted to point out to my Ma that I'd seen a man's skin open a few times and what pours out, much like water I agree, is what we folks have always called blood, but I kept my thoughts to myself and had still, until this very moment, doubted those long-ago lessons my Ma so astutely provided. Turns out, I thought, as I raised my head from the damp, soggy spot I'd left on the cloth of the mattress, that Ma was right after all, as the depths of my sorrow for my Marjorie had spent the bright hours of the day proving.

My sorrow and longing continued to weigh on me. I sat up in my bunk, in the dark, nothing but Freddy's snoring making a sound. He'd brought me supper earlier, and I never even turned on my bunk to see what he'd brung. Now, as I sat in the cell, the lingering aroma of stew drifted through the jailhouse and though I had not eaten, my stomach flipped with revulsion as I figured that stew was courtesy of The Bonner House. That same house where the memory of Marjorie looking back at me, as she followed Millie to try on some dresses, and me nodding to her assuredly that everything would be alright, played in my mind's eye over and over again. That had been the last time I'd seen her, and I'd barely spared her a glance.

Battered, cata...cata something. These were the words Marshal Morrison had used to describe my Marjorie, whom he had seen the morning just passed, and I had no reason to doubt the man as I consider him to be an honourable one. I wasn't sure, I will admit, to what cat-a-tonic was, but I thought it might be some poisonous brew she'd been given, that somehow had stricken her mind.

My anguish, I'm sure, showed on my face, though I made not a sound in the dark. But I could feel my face pull, the corners of my mouth drawn down, all on their own, and I fought hard to keep more water from streaming down my cheeks.

I had left her there. Left her! Even though I'd known, or suspected, the wickedness that walks in the walls of that house. I'd been in that cellar and sat in that chair and looked in the unfeeling eyes of that fat, grease-paint clown. And still, I'd left her there. Had she been down in that cellar somewhere, sat down in that chair and had the same done to her as was done to me? And what of that door? That hidden, whispering door? As undetectable it was, like the stones of the walls it had appeared, had there been more hidden doors in that cold, empty cellar? My mind imagined all things, and I can't stop the images I see in the dark.

I feel my head getting punched, at the same time on both sides, and I realize it's my own fists doing the punching. I glance over at Freddy, turned on his side, knees curled up as he snores on a stretcher of canvas bridged between two wooden chairs. I can just makes out his shadow, and the rise and fall of his log-sawing breaths. I stand up and pace my cell. The silence is peaceful yet somehow it whispers of doom, and the darkness of my jail-cell window spills a strange glow. I moved to peer out and found the night also hung a heavy head, as I watched the thick fog roll through the town, the white of the church barely visible in the woeful waves of the midnight mist that plumed and twisted, thin then thicker, enveloping the world. I stared down the street through the thinning mist that drifted low, and I saw a grey wall, full of curls and swirls and wispy tendrils, writhing and swelling and swallowing the road. Beyond that wall of mist there was nothing but grey.

They say that the fog has a way of muffling the sound, much like a heavy but soft fall of snow; fat flakes, I calls them, which I had caught on my tongue often, when I wandered the shoulders of the mountain. Well, whoever first noticed the quiet of the mist was right, cause as I peered through the bars of my window at the curling wall of fog, the yellow of their torches tainted the night, long before the trampling of their horses hooves ever reached my ears. They exploded from the wall of mist, like ministers of death on riled beasts of burden. The huffing of their horses and the drum of their approach was a delayed accompaniment of sound to the frightful vision of their stormy arrival. They wore sacks on their heads to hide who they was, I gathered, with holes cut for eyes. They whooped and hollered and rebel-yelled, horses rearing up and screaming of hell's fury; some drew their pistols and fired shots in the air, as they gathered their mob before the front of the jailhouse.

From behind me, I heard Freddy fall from his cot and crash heavily. I turned from my window and saw him hurriedly lift himself off the floor and run to the door, opening and peeking through the trap to observe the sudden gathering of men, men with hoods and bad intentions.

Freddy lit the lamp on the desk, filling the jailhouse with a dangerous light. I ducked away from the window, just in case, as I watched Freddy grab his antiquated pistol and strolled to the gun case at the end of the room. He plucked out a shotgun of the double-barreled sort, slipped two shells in the tubes then moved to the door.

"I don't recommend you open that door, Freddy," I said, from my shadowed position against the stone wall of my cell. Freddy turned and looked at me and that son of a bitch had a grin on his face.

"But Mr. Pitt," he replied, mocking me with a drip of sincerity to his tone, "these men rode a long way just to see you. Wouldn't be right to send them away disappointed." He cackled, not a laugh or a chuckle, but like the tales of witches all seem to contain. He cackled and flung the door open wide, stepping out on the porch and greeting the men who now appeared, from what I can see through the door, to be dismounting their rides and filling their hands with clubs, chains, knives, and one of them, running a looped length of rope through his hands.

"Good evening, boys." I heard Freddy greet them. "Bout time you-all arrived. I'd waited but my eyes got heavy, and I must have dosed off."

"Shut up, Freddy." I heard the voice and did not know who said it, but it struck me as harsh, seeing how Freddy was being so cordial and all. I saw Freddy's form get pushed aside and the hooded men crowded the door, three at the front stepped right inside, and came to stand at the bars of the cell. Menace danced in their postures and hooded staring eyes.

To them, I imagine, I appeared a dark streak of misery leaning back on the stone wall of the cell, arms folded over my chest and ankles crossed casually. I said nothing but stared at the three figures who stood as judge, jury and executioner in the dim flicker from the lamp on the desk. My eyes moved slowly over the men as I made my initial assessments. I scrutinized all three at once, as their similarities were to bold to dismiss. Though hard, wide men, appearing chiseled from stone, I couldn't unsee those damnable hoods they had on their heads. Any man, in my assessment, who is so fearful of eyes seeing his face is not one to be afforded respect and lacks any honourable qualities that exist in the most common of man. And that was my initial assessment.

"Howdy boys," I said. "Neville letting you-all off the lines? I'm betting you boys were manning those pickets I'd heard were out in the hills waiting on me. Well, I am sorry to disappoint. Waiting can be a thorn in the mind, I know, and I was all set to ride on out to meet ya but some damn Marshal showed up in town and figured I might be a bit more comfortable in here. But I'm glad you could all stop by. How can I be of assistance, on this woefully foggy night?"

"You a funny man, Billy Yank." The man in the middle, the jury I'm guessing, announced his verdict with a gravelly voice that scraped my mind like carpenters' nails on a board of slate.

I chuckled, smiled and replied, "Guilty as charged, Johnny Reb."

"We gonna drag you outta town and stretch your neck," said the man on my right, the executioner, I assumed.

"Freddy!" belted the man on the left, who can now only be the judge. "Get in here with them keys and open them bars. Let's get this lynching done. My arse is sore from the saddle and my back cries out for its bed."

Freddy came bounding through the door, like a dog left out in the rain, finally allowed a dry respite on the floor by the hearth of the fire. The keys rattled loudly as he rushed to the barred door of the cell and jabbered endlessly as he fumbled with the lock.

"Yes sir, Mr. Renfield. One thick neck, ready to be stretched, coming right up!" Again, he cackled.

Mr. Renfield's hood wrinkled when he snapped his head to glare at Freddy. "Shut your mouth Freddy. Fool that you are, saying my name!" I saw his boot rise off the floor and thrust at the small of Freddy's back. The Deputy slammed hard against the bars of the cell, and the door he was trying to open. He dropped the keys and they fell to the ground right where the bars met the floor. I saw them flashing in the light of the lamp. And while the hooded men were occupied in their continued admonishments of Freddy, I dashed from the wall at the back of my cell and sprang to those keys, grabbing them quick and jumping back, dangling them proudly from my fingers for all to see.

They stood there for a moment, stupid like, the judge, jury and executioner, as I dangled them keys. And the executioner, but of course for who else would it be, pulled his pistol slowly. He aimed it at me.

"Keys!" yelled the judge. I heard the executioner cock that pistol.

"Hold on boys," the hooded juror drawled. "You got another set, Freddy?"

Freddy, who was staring at them keys in my fingers like a raven eyes a shiny thing, did not respond to the jury's request, at least, not in an adequate time to satisfy the judge who then bellowed, red-faced.

"Freddy!"

This caused Freddy to jump, and I thought as I watched his sudden, startled expression invade his generally droopy face, that the Deputy had come close to soiling himself at the barking of the hooded magistrate.

I heard the rowdy rumours that had been rumbling in the background, just outside the door the whole time. Those grumblings grow quiet suddenly and I see another representative of the court stroll in like sunshine burning through the mist. I put my hands on my hips and tilted my head, like he was a caller come late who I'd thought was not coming, but his appearance was a pleasant surprise.

Despite the unpleasant hour, as I would think in the luxurious Bonner House he would have found much comfort in one of them fine, wide beds, Marshal Quentin James Morrison appeared fresh as a daisy on a lump of earth just recently turned. He was dressed much the same, not surprising for a common-sense man in these times, but he looked a might pale to my assessing eyes.

"Don't worry about them keys none, Deputy Simmons." He did not draw on them boys backs but he had his hand firmly on the grip. They spun at his sudden sounds. "Good evening gentlemen," said the Marshal, his hand slipping off his gun. "My name is Marshal Quentin James Morrison, and it is my duty to inform you that you are presently in the process of violating the law as I have assessed you are attempting to break this man out of jail."

There was a pause in the moment. Even the mob had grown quiet. I looked around and nobody was saying nothing and seeing how these fellas appeared not to have an attorney, I spoke up on their behalf.

"Well, hold on there, Marshal. That's not what these boys were up to at all," I offered, explaining to him how they had appeared in the fog, hooded phantoms on horseback howling at the night. I told him of the executioner's threat, to drag me and "stretch your neck." Then I expressed my genuine summation, that these boys were part of a lynch mob, here to do the hangman's job. "And that fella's gonna get paid anyway, so, in a reach-behind sort of way, they'd be robbing the county of the wages was due."

I aint no lawyer but it sounded pretty good to me. And the funny thing is, the whole time I'm testifying those boys in the hoods, heck, even their friends outside, joined the fog in its silence, and listened to my litigation-like words. Marshal Morrison listened too, and I saw that smile stretch his lips and I knew then I had at least one possible ally mixed amidst this mess I stumbled across in this Valley of Many Rivers.

"Is that so," he said, his head leaning back and looking at the three hooded men, the judge, the jury and the executioner. Then he glanced over his shoulder at the men crowding the door of the jailhouse and pronounced the letter of the law. Now, I know this man speaks eloquently, though I would advise him, being a bit of an orator myself, to try for more conciseness in his words, and it is not necessary to repeat his honoured title as a representative of the court. But the Marshal went ahead with his name and all, telling those boys that if what I claimed is in fact the case, then he was duty bound and obligated to inform them that lynching a man before his case is weighed before a judge and jury of his peers, is also against the law, and is, in fact, the Marshal said, punishable by, you guessed it, hanging.

I sat on my bunk listening to him, such a beautiful man speaking beautifully, and he turned his back to the judge, jury and executioner and faced the men on the street who were pressed in the doorway clamouring to see and hear what was going on inside.

"Of course," the Marshal continued, addressing the mob whilst showing the men inside his back, "I could never arrest you all, being strong in numbers and spirit, but I could easily detain these three men," he said, spinning to face the three leaders, "and lock them up in that cell with Mr. Pitt here, and see who comes out, just for sport. Then drag them beaten and bruised before a judge for conspiracy to lynch a man accused, and only accused I stress, of crimes against the United States of America."

He drew his pistol then, and before the judge, jury or executioner could object, he ordered those three men, and only those three men, to drop their belts and raise their hands. To the men outside, he turned his head just an inch. "The rest of you boys go on home now... go on!" Marshal Morrison fixed his eyes sideways, and kept his gun glued to the three men, who had commenced to unclasping their buckles and letting their heavy holsters fall to the floor with a thud. "Freddy," he said quietly, "shut that door, please."

Freddy did as was asked, a quick wave to the mob as he swung the door shut. The Marshal eyed the three men.

"Take off your hoods, gentlemen." He moved slowly, keeping square to the men who grumbled and slipped the sacks from their heads, revealing the most sullen looks I've ever seen three faces all show at once.

The Marshal positioned himself between the men and the cell, in which I sat captivated by the drama unfolding on the stage before me. I saw his fingers wiggling between the bars.

"Keys," he said simply, and without a second thought I slid those keys to those fingers.

The Marshal, without turning, inserted the key in the lock and swung the cell door open, moving with its easy sway to maintain a position facing the men through the bars, gun pointing, he motioned for them to enter the cell.

From my bunk, I saw three Adam's Apples bulge as I rose and took my stance, eager for the dance the Marshal seemed ready to call, but not a man moved an inch. They just stood there, the judge, jury and executioner, heads staring down at the three crumpled hoods now woefully cast to the floor.

"Get out." The Marshal growled at the men, his eyes stabbing them with sharp points of disgust. They bent down, attempting to collect what they'd dropped. "Leave the guns," the Marshal instructed. And with that, the men walked out the door like boys that had been caught stealing their grandad's whiskey.

The mob had waited, and their questions murmured, and disappointments expressed echoed as they collectively mounted their horses. One man dashed forward, eyes blazing through the open door of the jailhouse from beneath the sack on his head, his horse rearing up at the last second, damn near riding straight into the room.

"This aint the last you seen of the Sons, you sons a bitches. The Sons are home. The Sons are strong. And the Sons…" The Marshal slammed the door then turned to look at me.

"You alright, Rosco?"

"Well," I said, "I'm a might bit parched. I could use a drink of water."

CHAPTER 11

Freddy's redemption

It was a miraculous conception, and birth for that matter, as sometime in the foggy night, the same fog from which the phantoms came charging, that lily-white church across the way spawned white tents with little white tops, posts sticking out the middle and banners of different colours flapping in the breeze. I had paid no mind and did not look until long after my eyes had been open, so full of the events of the days gone by my mind raced wide awake while my body lay weary.

When my eyes finally followed my ears, I eased myself from my bunk, which I should point out, looked a might better than that meagre, old cot on which Freddy snored once again, having been forgiven of his "treason to the badge," Marshal Morrison had scolded. And, I guess, after thoughtful consideration, and the Marshal's eyes shooting thoughts in my head, I forgave poor Freddy too. But we'll get back to last night in a moment.

Across the road, as I was just saying about the church giving birth to tents, I shook my head at the sight as it appeared the circus had come to town. In the field beside these tents, which were a fair size and were meant for shows, were three of them tiny houses on wheels, and the horses to pull them. The folks who lived in them wagons were moving around the field making themselves at home, setting camp like they planned to stay for a spell.

To be clear, these aren't your average, every day, Randy River folk, but I'm guessing Neville, and probably a few choice others in and around these parts, would fit right in with that bunch. There were some washing their clothes in basins or sipping coffee and cooking by their fires. Others are practicing their juggling and acting the fool, and a few are dancing with each other, then stopping, then doing the same dance again, then stopping, and carrying on like that, but here's the things: I don't hear any music.

These folks aint your average lookin' folks either: a long-necked lady and her three-foot husband; a mime wearing dark glasses tapping a cane and bumping into invisible walls every time he took but two steps; and of course, the bearded lady, the strong man, and the infamous dog-faced boy. Yes indeed, it was fixing to be quite the shindig after all, and the best thing to happen to Randy River.

I turned my head from the window and mumbled to Freddy when he rolled out of his cot. He rubbed sleep from his eyes and gave me a nod, and rubbed his stomach which, like mine, was rumbling with hunger. I took that as a good sign, and directly related to the resurrection of Marjorie Trowley, which was a miraculous thing and felt my steps lighter by that thought. Though I was yet to see for my own eyes, I trusted the words of Marshal Morrison. Yes, it was still, just a thought, but on this sunny morning it was a sweet one!

As I recalled how Freddy manage to keep his job last night, I watched him move through the warm morning light of the room, to the stove against the far wall and "get fixin' fixin's for mornin' coffee."

He had no place else to go, he had told us last night, not ashamed of the fact but just stating what it was. The cot, on which he slept, was his, but not the two chairs between which it perched, he was careful to clarify.

After firing a few quick questions at him, mostly me cause

when it comes to detecting I got that Marshal beat, we was able to determine some things that I kinda figured, and seemed of keen interest to Quentin James Morrison, U.S. Marshal.

Freddy, as it turns out, had been allowed to reside in the jailhouse, not long after the thing was built. Neville Bonner himself, Freddy had said, was generous in his ways with the folks who had endured the harsh, long journey from the south. And while I pondered that demonstration of kindness from Neville Bonner, I weighed it beside the cruelty I knew, and felt the scales of justice crash quickly to one side, heavied with the load of the latter.

I asked Freddy if Bonner let him eat from the kitchen at The Bonner House, and he nodded, a pleasant thought in his mind. I asked him if he gave fair trade for wages at the mercantile.

"Well, yeah," Freddy says, starting to stare at the toes of his feet.

"And liquor, he provides you with that too. Don't he Freddy?" I prompted him, and he nodded, his hands sliding into his pockets.

"He give you that badge and that gun, Freddy?"

Well, now he jumps in, taking over my line of questioning and thinking he's some kinda detective. The Marshal already knew the answer anyway, but to have a man testify to it being so was mud of a different matter to a Marshal's mind.

And that's why Freddy kept his job and that flimsy, tin badge. That and the fact that I recruited him, with some threats of legalities that, true or not, the Marshal confirmed with much expression and great concern.

Now, Freddy was still not to be trusted and both the Marshal and me knew that. But, as the old saying goes, some rule of war written by some China-man I think, translates into "Keep your friends close and your enemies closer." And now, that's why Freddy kept his job.

The coffee smelled awfully good, better than the dirt I carry. I turned back to my window and watched the circus across the road and listened to Freddy making brew, and I leaned my head back on my neck, shut my eyes and just drifted in the solace of a peaceful morning. My drifting dissolved quickly when Marshal Morrison walked through the door. His sudden entrance made me jump, and I realized those hooded phantoms had gotten to me more than I'd thought. I turned to him with my hand on my heart, "Mercy man! Don't walk up on my back."

Marshal Morrison apologized, sincerely I might add, then turned to Freddy and made him jump too.

"Freddy! How about some coffee." He did it on purpose, yelling loud Freddy's name, then saying the rest real quiet like. And I was about to admonish him for being so cruel to poor Freddy, but then I thought, nah, and I hollered too. Well Freddy bout jumped through the roof and spilled some of that fresh hot coffee onto his hand. Be damned if that didn't get him hollering louder than a hillbilly at a hootenanny, but I was surprised he could feel it, given the thick of the dirt on his hands.

The Marshal laughed and I turned back to the window to watch the circus folk, but I heard him behind me, sliding chairs across the floor. Then I heard the sounds of papers being rustled and tossed, and I felt a slight movement at my back, as I am capable of, sometimes, and I spun around, and my jaw fell open wide.

I'm sure I looked a sight to go join that there circus: the Gaping Mouthed Man, come one come all!, cause the Marshal was grinning, like that cat-in-that story bout that girl who fell down that rabbit hole, and he held that cell door wide open.

"I got breakfast outside," he tossed back his head, still smiling. "I'll go out and get it." He moved towards the door. "Have a seat at the table and we'll all have breakfast."

I moved slowly at first, glancing at Freddy who was staring at me, gripping that pot of coffee like his life depended on it. Then I smelled what the Marshal had balanced on his arms, three hot plates on a padded cloth and the prettiest pile of eggs and sliced baked-ham I've ever seen, almost too pretty to eat! Well, I moved to a spot at the table then, faster than I moved across those Carolina sands so long ago. I sat down and yelled at Freddy again, telling him to get over here with the coffee and bring three mugs to match.

For the next two minutes or so, there was nothing to hear, and nothing I want to describe, but I'm gonna.

Like pigs at the trough we fed, and the noises we made were much the same, and I wished I'd had me some bread, but I was thankful for what I'd been given and I burped, as was polite, and the others did too, and we had formed a fine breakfast chorus, filling the jailhouse with sounds of gluttony and satiation.

"See the circus?" I asked Marshal Morrison, as we sat back enjoying our coffee. Freddy had made a good brew, I'd give the man that, and he'd paid a dear price for his efforts, as was shown by the burn on the back of his hand.

"Circus!" Freddy exclaimed, and he was up and out like a shot. I looked at the Marshal who was shaking his head, and I said, "Maybe he'll join them."

Marshal Morrison remarked on the town and the people that were flooding in: people from all across the territory, some travelling at least a full day to get here. The Bonner House, he said, was booked to capacity, and there were people in the county renting out spots in their yards for visitors to park their wagons and rest their horses and camp while they stay for the hanging.

"Business is good around these parts right now, Rosco. Bonner hasn't stopped grinning since he's seen the crowds arriving and his mercantile is doing a strong and steady business. He was busy this morning making arrangements to send wagons south, in haste, to acquire full re-supplies for the stores of his shop and the boarding house. He's restocking his shelfs and filling the pantries at the house, and he's smart cause this whole affair might take a while, and he's aiming to make a killing."

"Hmmm," I said. "Happy coincidence." I sipped my coffee and eyed the Marshal. He received my meaning and put his cup down, asking why it is, I thought, that he let me out of that cell.

"Cause you're a damn nice fella and a mighty good Marshal and it was the humane thing to do." And I meant it. But I knew what he was getting at. He told me he'd been looking closer at things, "here in town, and around a bouts.

"There's a strange feel to these parts, Rosco. I've been getting a feeling people want to say something, want to tell me something, whenever I givem' a nod as I pass them on the street or stop for a chat if I sees them in their yards or feeding their chickens. They're friendly enough and all, but it's like there's something they need to say and can only say it with their eyes." He raised his cup and took a sip.

"Well now, Marshal, I've been all across and damn near the length of this land, and I can tell you what you're talking about aint unusual. I've rode through many a places, and usually I just kept on riding, where people were strange, their looks were strange, and the parts in general have a strange feel."

I reached into my waist coat seeking tobacco, found none. Frustrated, I continued.

"But having said that, you are right good sir, this place is strange, and If I was you I'd be taking a look down in the cellar of that Bonner House. There are things I'd like to tell you Marshal, but the fact that everything I say can and will be used against me in the court of law, I hesitate to say too much. But why do you think I was there in that house rattling vengeance from that Gatling gun? – by the way, did you get a look at her? Aint she a beaut?"

Marshal Morrison agreed with my assessment of that Gatling gun.

"A fine instrument of death, to be certain. But as to you being at that house cranking that gun, that's to the point that I'm getting. I'm leaning to be of mind, Rosco, that shooting that gun and killing the men you've killed around here was very likely justified. And, as you know, that would leave your only charge the terrible tragedy that is the widow Trowley, and I am certain beyond any doubt that you are not a man who would commit such acts."

He raised a hand to stop me from speaking and took a moment to look contemplative and all deep in thought, his eyes seemed to glaze for a moment, but a blink brought him back.

"There's not much I can do about the charges and the trial, or the hanging. I'm sorry for that Rosco."

And I knew that he was.

"That trial is coming," he continued. "There is no stopping that. And I've heard, though I can't confirm, that the judge is a fine southern gentlemen who is good friends of the Governor's, and as my inquiries have discovered, the Governor is a good friend of none other than Neville Bonner, whose town you shot up with his own gold-plated, never-been fired Gatling gun. And you should know, the prosecuting attorney who has been assigned the case, a man by the name of Percy Rawlins, was once a judge on the circuit in the state of Missouri, back when that war was still raging ripe. Oh, and the jury, well, they're not exactly a jury of your peers; a jury of Freddy's peers, yes, but not yours."

"Hmmm. Is that so," I said. "Well hell Marshal! Here I was having a pretty good morning: sun shining, a wonderful breakfast, and the circus is in town. And you come in here all doomy and gloomy not only reminding me of my dire situation but impressing on me that its much worse than I thought, though how that can be is beyond me!"

I was truly distraught. That man, as kind and respectable as he was, had taken my sweet morning and turned it sour.

"I'm sorry, Rosco. It pains me to be your constant bearer of bad news. I'll take a look around The Bonner House, but I'll have to be discreet, that place is a bustling."

Marshal Morrison started turning for the door when one word stopped him dead in his motion. "Quentin," I said. "You be careful. There's doors down there in that cellar you can't see, and only appear when they open, then disappear again once they swing shut. You be careful, Marshal."

He nodded, and started to turn to the door again, then stopped and looked back. "But I do have some good news, Rosco."

Why he pauses now, right there in his words, is beyond me. He's getting to be like one of them needles good old Herman shoved up my nails. I know, the man brought me breakfast and all, but why is he tormenting me so?

"I met a man who just checked in at The Bonner House this morning. He was fortunate to get the last room. Said he was a barrister and had come as he heard there was a man in the jail in need of representation as he was told there was none fair around here to be found."

"A lawyering man." I said. That was good news, and my countenance brightened somewhat.

"Yes," Marshal Morrison replied. "He said he would stop by the jail this afternoon to meet with you. Sorry Rosco, I didn't get his name, but he seemed quite competent to me, and you know what they say Rosco: 'beggars can't be choosers.'"

They do say that, too much to my mind, and it made no sense anyway. Who's to say a beggar can't choose? Why I'm quite certain there are those who chose the life of a beggar. I would guess, depending on the locale, begging could be quite profitable. I did not argue with him about this but accepted his use of such a tired cliché. That's French I hear. I think it means tired.

The Marshal stood up just as Freddy came back in, all excited with the characters he had met across the road.

"I've got to head out for a bit," he said, like we hadn't already figured that out. He tilted his head to say get inside, and I begrudgingly obliged his request, returned to my cell and mostly swung the door shut behind me.

"Shut it," he said, standing in the door. So, I did and with the clunk of heavy iron he was moving to leave when he turns and remembers something he forgot.

"Oh, If I'm not back when that lawyer gets here, but I should be, just so you know he's a little, thick Scottish fella with fiery red hair. Quite the character," he said and finally, he walked out the door.

'Get on,' I thought. 'Couldn't be.' But I smiled, cause I'm thinking it is.

I sees Freddy eyeing me, and I know he's wondering why a man considered already to be condemned, such is the situation in which I find myself, would be looking so chipper and lighthearted.

"Mr. Pitt," Freddy says, sitting down at his spot by his desk, "I don't think a lawyer's gonna help you much, not around these parts. And, I'm sorry to say that sir, cause, well, you and the Marshal have treated me fairly and that's a rare thing, and I've grown to like you both very much."

I had always suspected Freddy was a good man down deep inside, that his heart just needed a nudging, I guess you could say, back to a path of morality. But when the hand that feeds you is a wicked one, a person can easily wander from that path. It was quite evident that the entire Valley of Many Rivers, particularly the settlement known as Randy River, was fed collectively from one wicked hand, which was now looking to wrench my neck.

"Well thanks Freddy. I appreciate the kind words and I'm sure the Marshal would too. Be sure to tell him that when he comes back." I smiled at Freddy. His words fell warmly across my heart and lightened my step even more.

"Say Freddy, would you happen to have any tobacco?" I knows my breath comes easier since I've been going without, but I crave to burn my lungs just the same, while I ponder the prospect of Lachey actually coming down.

"I got your toe-backy," Freddy drawls with a nod and a smile my way. He shuffles in the drawer of the desk and pulls out a crumpled bail and some papers for rolling. "I'll even roll it up for ya, Mr. Pitt."

Well, I'm much obliged, and I tell Freddy so as I stand at the bars, watching and waiting. My mouth starts to water at the prospect of a smoke and my mind returns to the lawyer in town. I'm pulled in the hope that it is my old friend, if for nothing else to say our goodbyes, but I'm equally pulled with the doubt that it is, as I recall he had once adamantly professed he would never go down from the mountain. "Not on your life," Lachey had plainly said the one time I had asked.

I paced the cell. The finely rolled smoke, by Freddy's skilled fingers, glowed an ember bright at its end as my hauls were deep and long. But Freddy would roll me a dozen or more, as I smoked and pondered with the one I had, and stacked them neatly between the bars with several wooden matches to set them a blaze when I so desired. So when the first smoke was gone I immediately lit another, and partook in a more casual fashion, enjoying the activity and its therapeutic value it had on my thoughts.

To the window, again, I returned. The bustle had quieted as the day had commenced and the street had grown sparse of the steady flow of traffic that greeted the morning. The circus folk had settled, it seemed, and were gathered together around one fire, talking about whatever circus folk talk about. The church was still white, much like MissT, the structure's countenance was unchanging. The part of the livery that was visible to my awkward angle looked much like it had all day, but two fellas, one perched on the top rail of the fence and the other with his back to me, looked deep in discussion.

I wouldn't have spared them a notice but for their similar dress, and the man on the fence sparkled in places where the metal of his holster and the hilt of his blade caught the morning sun. The man with his back to me held a rifle in is hands, and both men wore dusters of the same design and colour.

The man on the fence, who was broad of shoulder, as was his faceless friend, kept nodding as he spoke, in the direction of the jailhouse, then he turned his head and spoke to another who I could not see. Suddenly, well at least it appeared sudden to me, the man showing me his back turned and walked to enter the church, as the man on the fence dropped to stand on the ground and swung the sawed-off from beneath his cloak.

"Freddy. I strongly recommend you get me a gun."

"The hell I will," Freddy said not looking, and laughing as he focused on pushing a broom.

"Freddy," I turned from the window and moved to the bars, placing my hands between them in a pleading gesture. "There are two, maybe more, men coming here right now, armed, one, at least, has a shotgun. Please, give me a gun."

Freddy looked up alarmed, rushing to the desk to grab and push his old gun into the rope for a belt that was cinched around his waist. I returned to the window, keeping low and peaking over the sill. The man still stood by the fence but his eyes were watching something – some movement occurring out of my view.

I shot my eyes to the church, where the other man had gone, but he was not a sight to be found. Then I spied the barrel of the rifle, poking out like a thin, dark line against the whitewash steeple at the top of the house of God.

I heard a noise on the bars of my cell and much to my surprise, Freddy had placed my pistol and holster between the bars beside the smokes. He now stood at an angle to the door, a look of determination on his droopy face, a shotgun leveled at the jailhouse's only entrance.

Quick as I could move my hands I loaded that Colt and strapped the holster to my waist. I fastened it down out of habit though I doubted any quick drawing was gonna be required. I moved back to the window: the man was still by the fence and the rifle was still in the steeple.

The pounding on the door spun me around and I leveled my pistol at the trap near the top, dead centre, right between the eyes. I didn't wait for a demand or a shouted threat, I squeezed that trigger and watched the wood splinter outwards as the bullet tore a hole through the door. I heard the distinct thud of whoever was dumb enough to come a-knockin' then spun back to glance out the window. The man at the fence was gone.

"Another coming Freddy!" I shouted, "cover the door." Then the bullet whizzed past my head before I heard the shot of the rifle from up there in the church steeple. I dropped to the floor and watched as Freddy did the same when the jailhouse door imploded, the blast leaving a head-sized hole in the flimsy timber. The man who once had leaned on the fence had rallied his shotgun to join the action. He sported a single-barreled sawed-off, that much I knew, so he would not be effective from any distance and would have had to come close to effect such a shot.

Another bullet zipped in through the window behind me and found the boards of the floor at the foot of my bunk. That fella in the church was a patient man, and one I could not contend with at this juncture. With Freddy and I both aiming at the door, that shot-gun man would be a fool to make any attempts, but damned if he didn't and damned if he's not dead.

It was Freddy who let him have what's coming, for being so bold as to attack his home, and he pronounced just that, "My home!" when his shot's ring grew quiet, and his voice echoed in the silence that came.

"Freddy," I whispered, still hugging the floor. "You gotta get me my Sharps."

I saw his feet moving and then they returned. Through the bars he slid the gun across the floor, and a box of my shells as was needed. The steeple man fired another shot, guessing he saw our movements somehow, to ping off the bars and rattle harmlessly in a corner.

I rolled to my back and loaded the Sharps, mumbling profanities defaming the man's mother, who I declared had probably never entered a church given the bastard status of her son who was now shooting at me. I slid across the floor to find myself sitting below the window. Freddy, the good man that he had become, had again took up position to cover the entrance.

Now, I had spent much of my life in solitude and while I have spent some time with and met some fine people, I was never really one to chummy up to folks and form any real attachments, which, in retrospect, was probably the advisable path to take through life given how my presence in the lives of others seems to inspire misfortune, current events definitely included. However, what happens next has led me to express my belief in a common phrase I hear is spoken at times among close acquaintances: 'it's good to have friends when you need them.'

You see. That man in that steeple who insisted on taking pot shots threw my cell window, well, he kept on shooting but either his aim got bad or he found something else to aim at more dire, cause I keep hearing his gun go off but no other rounds come through my window or even any where's near this jailhouse which is not exactly the size of a barn but would be a sight bit difficult to miss, to anyone whose sober that is.

I hear return fire, and I knows its return fire cause I can hear it hitting the church. My ears, which possess an acute sense of hearing, can also identify the direction and source of the gunshots: a pistol, moving up the close side of the street, and a repeater of sorts, firing off in quick succession pelting the steeple with blemishes, and moving up the opposite side of the street. Both shooters advance steadily and with purpose.

I rise at these sounds and look through the window at that steeple and not wanting to feel left out I set the Sharps aside and I emptied my Colt at the top of God's house. After several seconds of some serious suppressing fire, the silence grows the loudest and I look to the church and see no rifle's barrel poking out up high.

"It's the Marshal. I'm coming in. Don't shoot me, Freddy." His voice tumbled through the holes in the door.

Freddy and I both stand and turn to the door and in walks the Marshal. His fine coat is now dusty and his pants are no longer pressed smooth as paperboard. His white straw hat sits askew on his head, and he appears rather winded, red-faced, and still gripping his pistol, smoke lingering from the gun's black void. Behind him, and my face must have split, is a familiar face, but that's about it as the rest of the man, I swear, I would not recognize had he not looked me in the eyes as he entered.

"Well now, Pitt, what have you gotten yourself into the noo?" Lachey smiled his infectious smirk, rushed to the bars and thrust his arm through to grasp mine.

Yes sir, it was good to have friends.

CHAPTER 12

Southern sensibilities

Have you ever stood on the precipice and watched an angry storm roll across the land, like a bruise on the world swirling purple and flushed; a raging mass of energy contained by the grip of God, some might say. If you have you may have noticed the calm that follows its passing, and the quiet heaviness of the air left in the wake of the storm.

Well, on this morning a storm had raged in Randy River, the second in as many days, and like those wonderous whirlwinds so mesmerizing that one might view on the precipice, the wake of this storm rolled thick and heavy with tension through the town, which once again filled with the ogling eyes and excited voices of those who had travelled to watch the show.

It didn't take long for the looksie-loos to gather, and for the Marshal to relieve me of the weapons I'd obtained, which I saw him admiring as he returned them to their places in the gun case on the wall. On the heels of the gunplay, McTavish was assigned to keep his eye on me, while Marshal and Freddy stacked the bodies of the two that lay dead in the street and retrieved the body of the man in the steeple, which I noticed was gonna need more than just a coat of paint, the steeple that is.

Freddy fetched the undertaker, a smooth young man named

Reggie Burrell; smelled like caramel and every line of the man was straight and edged. The white cuffs of his shirt, which peeked out from beneath the sleeves of his fine woolen waist coat, were equal in measure of whiteness displayed, just a crisp line beneath the black wool of the coat. His hair was slick, streaming back flat and wet on his head, and his eyes gleamed a piercing grey from either side of his hawk-like nose. He was a silver-spoon vulture, circling the town, and just me being here, such as I was, provided an unending buffet for this caretaker of carrion.

His daddy had most likely been an undertaker, and probably his daddy before that, as it seemed to be the way in the pursuit of such a livelihood; a thing to be kept in the family and one, trying not to judge, I've always found revolting.

Reggie, not only being an undertaker, built the boxes too, so the Marshal being the smart man that he is, commissioned the coffins for those fallen assassins, and commissioned the man to build a new door for the jailhouse. The door, of course, was top priority.

"Make it thick and heavy," I instructed Reggie with a raise to my voice as he commenced to measuring the frame of the door required. "So, it don't implode and splinter the next time they comes and start shooting bullets," I concluded. He glanced at me nervously, not feeling too easy about being so close to one so many seem so eager to kill. Can't say that I blames him.

Lachey had pulled a chair into my cell and had planted himself across from me sitting on my bunk, both of us sipping some fresh coffee Freddy had just brewed. The Scotsman smacked his lips, appreciative of Freddy's skills with the beans. He flipped his head at the Marshal, who'd been hovering around the empty jailhouse door for the better part of an hour, tapping his pistol with his finger and sticking his head out to gawk up and down the road, and glare at the craned necks who still wandered by, not wanting to miss the chance to glimpse the murderous villain Rosco Pitt, and the courageous lawmen who guard his unworthy soul.

"Oy. Is he always like that?" Lachey whispered, watching the back of Marshal Morrison's silhouette angled in the light of the empty door frame. "He's giving me the willies. Like a man waiting for the 'pale horse,' so he is." McTavish shivered at his own reference to death.

I told him the Marshal, from what I've seen of the man, is usually quite composed and had not demonstrated himself to be a man easily rattled. This town, I explained to the Scotsman, has proven to be full of surprises, and given the frequency and ferocity demonstrated by those who ride under the banner of the Sons of the Confederacy, the Marshal's uneasiness was completely warranted.

When all three of the dead men had been loaded onto a wagon, Reggie climbed up on the buckboard and told the Marshal he was heading to his shop to get working on the jailhouse door. He promised he'd be back with the new door as quick as he could, flicked the reigns and urged his mules forward, steering his rig slowly up the street and out of town. As the Marshal stood in the doorway watching the man leave, he looked to Lachey and me, sitting in my cell sipping coffee.

"Those men were not with the Sons," the Marshal said quietly. "They was professionals brought in to do a job. Them dusters they were wearing, I've seen them before in these parts and further south, all three of them the same; a common coat of preference for a bunch of boys who work with the Cahill Cattle Company, which happens to be both a vendor and a customer of Mr. Neville Bonner."

Lachey turned his head from the Marshal to look at me with serious concern. His red hair was now slicked back city-style and his beard had been ran-through with a comb. He wore a fine suit of clothes, acquired, he said, at Willie's Mercantile, where Neville had insisted Lachey's credit was good. Which made me chuckle, knowing Neville would have a hell of a time collecting once Lachey heads back to the mountain and disappears in the folds of MissT's skirt.

"What have you done, in such a short measure of time, to

deserve such attention Pitt? I knows you're a man set in his ways, as are most who choose to dwell up high, but you've only been doon a few days and already your scalp is in more peril here than after many years on the mountain."

I shrugged, not really having an answer to his question, other than my sunny disposition seemed to have rubbed the wrong people the wrong way, and my penchant for wearing my Union hat put a target on me as soon as the ground became level beneath my feet.

I explained to my friend, who squinted his eyes as he listened, a lawyer's mind being attentive I realized, that had I known this valley was the home to the Sons of the Confederacy, "me and Mr. Andrews would have steered far and wide of Randy River. You know me Lachey, I'm not one who goes looking for trouble."

"Ha." Freddy guffawed from his seat at the desk. "Seems to me, Mr. Pitt, with all due respect, that trouble is always hot on your scent and you need not make an effort of looking, it'll always find you in due time."

Freddy was right. I agreed with a nod of reluctant acceptance. "Since I'd come down from the hill the prevailing winds had shifted, and blew a constant cold from the north, and on that wind travelled trouble, and it seems to have found a comfy place to settle, clinging to my back."

"Aye," Lachey agreed with my assessment. "Well then, it's a good thing you have obtained the litigation skills of Lauchlin McTavish." With a wink and a smile, he made plain his boastfulness, and added. "With words alone I will wipe that trouble from your back, and when all is said and done my friend, we'll ride back up together, and leave this godforsaken place down low, to rot in its own pestilence."

I thought of Marjorie, spoke how I was determined I would not leave her behind again if fate were to smile upon me and give me but one more chance to have her by my side. All three men, even Freddy, listened to my words, and lowered their eyes knowing, as did I deep down inside, that the likelihood of me getting out of this jam is about as slim as the smoke that now hung loosely from my lips. I struck a match and brought the flame to the end, drawing deeply as I became filled with melancholy over my Marjorie.

"You'll see her tomorrow, Rosco," the Marshal said, from a chair he pulled close to the door out of which he still watched for anyone approaching. "She's on the list of witnesses for the preliminary tomorrow. It's just a formality, but the widow will be there, Rosco…"

His words were interrupted as he rose from his chair, alarm flashing in his eyes. "Bonner's heading this way. He and three rather large and heavily armed men." He moved his chair aside and stepped out the door to meet them.

I glanced at Lachey, who raised both brows at the Marshal's announcement, and we both stood and moved to the bars to watch as Neville arrived outside on the street, flanked by three of "the boys" I'm guessing – the only three to survive the bite of the Gatling gun.

Freddy, unable to resist, moved to stand beside the door, keeping out of eye shot, not wanting Neville to see him. I'm guessing Freddy still held some misguided loyalties for the man and could not yet face his benefactor.

"Mr. Bonner," we listened to the Marshal greet the man on the street. I could not see Neville, as he stood directly facing the Marshal, but the three men standing guard behind him were clearly visible to me and Lachey. "What can I do for you on this fine, clear morning, sir?" the Marshal asked.

Again, I could not see Neville but his voice, sounding like he was speaking the gospel as it always did, fell clearly to my ears.

"Why Marshal, my goodness, it seems you are missing a door." The sound of his voice took me back to the cellar, to Herman's pinhole eyes, and my fingers ached at the memory.

"We heard about the trouble this morning Marshal, and me and the boys thought we'd come by and see if there was anything we could do to help."

"Help who?" I shouted, and watched Neville's head appear over the Marshal's shoulder to smile at me standing at the bars of my cell. "The boys from the Cahill Cattle Company?"

The Marshal shot me an admonishing glance and I felt Lachey bump my shoulder, beckoning for me to stay quiet.

"Oh. Mr. Pitt, there you are. Relieved to see you are still among the living after all that gunfire." Neville moved out from behind the Marshal and moved towards the open door. The Marshal moved aside to let the man enter, but returned to his stance, barring the way, when the three large men tried to follow. The Marshal just shook his head, fingered his pistol, and stared at them.

I felt my knuckles scream white, as my hands went to the bars of my cell and gripped them with such anger the bones pushed tight against the skin. I watched Neville move close to the bars, but not close enough where I could reach out and grab him, which I would have done if he'd just came a couple of inches further. I guess Neville had learned his lesson about leaning in close, as was evident by the two black eyes that were starting to fade, and the once straight but now crooked nose that swelled angrily in the middle of his face.

"Sorry bout your nose Neville," I grinned. "How's Hermie doing?" I must confess, I was finding myself becoming an expert in the art of sarcasm, but Neville's blank stare told me he did not share my enthusiasm for my ever-evolving linguistic prowess. Even Lachey, dropping his lawyerly countenance for just a second, chuckled quietly at my barbed jab. I had told him, being my lawyer and all, the entire affair of what happened in the cellar of The Bonner House, so he grasped my reference to Herman's wellbeing and the battered look to Neville's face.

Neville opened his mouth to respond, but my lawyer informed him that addressing his client, that's me, Mr. Rosco Pitt, would be a violation of procedure and would be equated to witness tampering, in the eyes of the court.

I was amazed as I watched my friend's familiar countenance transition before my eyes. Though he had always possessed the look of a knowledgeable man, he addressed Neville Bonner with the glint of authority and the steady tone of omniscience, which my Ma had taught me meant "all knowing," and that I should use it often when describing her to others.

"However," Lachey continued, having the full attention of Mr. Neville Bonner, "if you feel so inclined to engage with my client I would be happy to file a motion to dismiss, and with a Marshal and a Deputy as witnesses, I'm sure the judge would see fit to grant my motion on the grounds which I just rightly mentioned. You sir could be held in contempt of court and I'm sure the judge would correctly advise the good Marshal to take you immediately into custody on charges of, like I said, witness tampering. But, Mr. Neville, the choice is yours. Proceed at your own discretion."

Bonner stood keeping his eyes on me. His shit-eating grin wavered, and I took great satisfaction at seeing his face turn sombre at the words of my litigator. He turned to Lachey and let his eyes grow hooded, malevolent in their glow.

"Ah yes, Mr. McTavish. Had I known you were here in town to provide your legal representation to this blue-belly scum, I would have thought more than twice about giving you lodgings at my house and credit at my store. But we do what we do and hindsight always provides clarity to what was a cloudy situation." Neville paused for a moment, glancing over at Freddy and scowling. Freddy caught his look and his head dropped in shame. Neville turned back to Lachey and me, his words were meant for the Scotsman, but it seemed he only had eyes for me.

"Very well Mr. McTavish, I will not engage with your client. Such a shame. Me and Mr. Pitt have always had such engaging conversations." He tapped a finger to his lips, contemplating his next words.

"Your motion would be denied, Mr. McTavish. This case will not be dismissed, not here in this county and not by the presiding judge, who I have had the pleasure of conversing with earlier this morning, before all the gunfire disrupted the day. But I will oblige and not engage with Mr. Pitt, henceforth.

"The judge is the Right Honourable Francis Henry," Bonner continued, "a fairly common name in the south, but not a common judge. This man has been a stalwart member of our community and while maintaining his judiciary appointment under the dominant gaze of our Northern masters, he still manages to personify, in both spirit and actions, our Southern sensibilities."

Lachey nodded at the man's words, thanked him for the update, and offered some biting words in response. "I'll no stand in a jailhouse arguing my case, Mr. Bonner. But I will take into consideration the new-found knowledge of this Judge Henry, and his apparent 'Southern sensibilities.' Perhaps it will be prudent to remind the man, and yourself as well, Mr. Bonner, that as I recall the South lost that war, and as such, perhaps Northern sensibilities should be the order of the day."

Well, that riled Neville plenty. I could see it in his posture. His stance stiffened, his shoulders tensed and his neck strained with taught tendons. His hands, just like when he grasped Herman by the jowls, quivered momentarily.

Bonner's smile, which had been faltering ever since he had walked through that door, was wiped clean off by Lachey's words. The Marshal, sensing something, shifted uneasy in the daylight void that was the frame of the door, half turning to keep one eye on the bruisers who still stood outside, and the other on the back of Neville, on which, if he had them, hackles would be raised.

"Yes. Hmm. I see," mumbled Neville, staring with fresh malice at my fine Scottish friend. "In light of things, Mr. McTavish, it would be best if you removed your things from The Bonner House and found some other accommodations more in line with your sensibilities." He turned then, abruptly, and stared at Freddy who still hung his head low, staring at the floor.

"Freddy," he commanded, "I will need you to accompany me to The Bonner House." He turned back to look again at McTavish. "Mr. McTavish, I believe, would benefit greatly, as would his client, if they could spend as much time in consultation as possible. As such, I need you to gather and retrieve Mr. McTavish's things, he will not be residing at The Bonner House anymore."

Neville paused, his eyes moving over the jail cell, up the bars and across the ceiling, then back to settle on my face. "Besides, it appears there is plenty of room in this here cell for two, and I'm sure Mr. McTavish would be quite comfortable sharing these accommodations with his client until the proceedings here in Randy River have been completed."

With that, Neville spun on his heels and moved to the door, where he paused and eyed Freddy, who had not budged and inch from his chair.

"Freddy," Neville breathed, "are your ears thick with wax, boy. Come along!"

Freddy got up from his chair and moved to the door slowly. He glanced back at me and McTavish, tossing a slight nod our way, then paused as he looked to the Marshal, who had sided himself out of the door and met Freddy's questioning eyes.

"It's okay, Freddy," the Marshal said. "Do as Mr. Bonner asks. Oh, and Freddy, if you could collect my things while your there and bring them up this way as well, I think that would be advisable. Take the buckboard from the livery, that'll make the hauling easier."

Freddy nodded to the Marshal then followed Neville out the door. We watched them move out into the street, and dissolve like a mirage in the bright, afternoon sun. I returned to my bunk and rested my chin on my fists, elbows propped on my knees.

Neville had painted a gloomy portrait of the days ahead, of a trial filled with 'Southern sensibilities,' and the sudden depth of my worry struck home. Lachey, sensing my sudden onslaught of despair, pulled his chair closer and patted my shoulder. He offered words of reassurance but his eyes were dark with doubt and foreboding, as a storm seen from a precipice.

The Marshal pulled up a chair just outside the cell, and sat to face Lachey and me, his eyes finding us between those cold bars of iron.

"One day at a time. That's the best advice I've got." Morrison said.

"Aye," McTavish agreed, raising his eyes to meet mine. "Maybe best rest up Pitt," he said, "you and me both. The heavy lifting is about to begin and I fear we will need to ensure all our sensibilities are firmly intact."

I laid back in my bunk and closed my eyes and let my mind drift to the one thing that still lightened my heart: Marjorie's chestnut eyes. I would see her tomorrow; my thoughts were eager and filled with longing.

'But would she see me?'

'Cat-a-tonic.'

CHAPTER 13

A writer of chronicles

Another monstrosity had appeared in the night, but for the first night since my arrival to the Randy River jailhouse, my sleep had been uninterrupted, soothed by the rumbling chorus of sleeping men, and by the weight and bulge of my heavy holster strapped firmly to my side.

The Marshal, with the support of both Freddy and McTavish, had once again demonstrated his wisdom and left my cell door open in the night, and allowed me my guns, which also contributed to my blissful slumber.

The monstrosity of which I speak, had been erected right beside the jailhouse, and like the tents of the circus that appeared in the night, this grey behemoth of a tent now stood as the last structure before the road stretched barren and desolate to the distant trees to the south.

It was this mammoth of canvas, flapping in the breeze, that first greets my eyes on this morning, as I take a gaze out my window at the circus folk who busy themselves in preparation for the day.

Randy River County Courthouse: my eyes had to squint some but that's what the sign said, swinging and swaying in the same breeze that rumpled the tent on which the sign was hung.

The flaps of the entrance, which faced the window of my cell, had been pinned open to allow the men I saw carry in the chairs, tables and necessary accoutrements for a functioning courthouse.

There were already people arriving, lining up to get inside. What space there was remaining between the church and the roadside circus, was filling up fast with fine, black wagons and beat-up old buckboards. Already the buzz of the murmurs begun to ring in the air even though the sun had just begun its ascent. Behind me, my newly acquired roommates continued their low rumbling symphony of sleep, which growled deep in the dimness of the day's early light.

After waking and watching by the window for a bit, I fulfilled my promise and did as was asked. I retrieved my guns from beneath my bunk and returned them to the gun case once again, locking the glass door – the glass door – and leaving the key in the lock. Then I returned to my cell in the still gloomy room, letting the cell door swing shut behind me. Freddy, Quentin and Lauchlin never stirred.

I thought of escape and how easy it would be. I could've ran right now and none would be the wiser if things remained as is and the slumber of these men was not disturbed. I'd have me about an hour's lead and could make good ground in an hour, with a decent horse and a determined charge. A horse like Mr. Andrews, for example.

Freddy had informed me Mr. Andrews was also dealing with incarceration across the road at the livery stable. I could see him being an uncooperative prisoner, which caused my mind some concern, but Freddy assured me Mr. Andrews was well cared for, and from what he can tell appeared healthy and full of spirit. I knew Mr. Andrews would be okay. He was and has always proven to be a resourceful and adaptive creature, and given my present circumstances, I had to convince myself that my own reassurances were true.

Escape. Yes, it came to my mind often, but there was one thing stopping me, and only one thing. I will not leave my Marjorie again.

Just like on the mountain, I cherish this time in the morning, when things are just so quiet, and all things are muffled yet carry so clear.

My mind is clearest in the morning, unless I'm being shot at, arrested, tortured, or otherwise somehow preoccupied. But here in this jailcell the quiet speaks plainly to my meditative state, which rises from my toes to my head as a warm wave of calmness and an acceptance of the reckoning to come, whatever it may be.

I'm at peace once again with the mountain, and will accept her judgement on me, and as she not only expects but demands, I will rage against my foe, even if it be the mountain herself. And as all struggles should be, must be, the conflict will be brutal, and what will be, shall be and was meant to be.

In my mind's wanderings I settle myself, and become like a stream on a mountain slope, flowing undeterred by barriers of rock and deadfall, but bending to their immobility and continue on my winding wander, determined and unyielding in my advance.

It is in this place of peace where my mind rests as the pounding on the door startles my roommates from their sleep, while I turn my head on my pillow, slowly to look, and calmly swing my legs to the floor to sit on my bunk. The pounding comes again, and Freddy, rubbing sleep from his droopy eyes and wearing nothing but dirty long-ones, shuffled to the new and improved jailhouse door, and opened the trap to see who's knocking.

"Hello." A voice, quiet and defined drifts in through the trap. The Marshal is just pulling on his britches, hopping on one foot, and McTavish sits on the edge of his cot, raising his short, thick arms above his head and opening wide for a gaping yawn.

"I'm hoping I could speak with…" there's a pause and a rustling of paper. "A Marshal Quentin J. Morrison, U.S. Marshal. My name is John Maximillian. Expecting you might have heard of me."

Well, I'll be... it truly is a small world after all. "Let the man in, Freddy!" I slapped my knee in pure delight at the hearing of that name. "John Maximillian!" I said to both Lachey and Marshal Morrison, who continued their hurried dressing and rising to the day.

"That man will make you all famous," I said. "Aint that right, Mr. Maximillian?" I raised my voice slightly so he could hears. I heard a soft laugh as Freddy unlocked the three deadbolts that now secured the door.

"Well," the soft voice of Maximillian replied through the wood, "I'll do my best."

McTavish turned to look at me, now mostly dressed and standing staunchly with his hands on his hips. His hair, rising and shooting up in crazy waves, was truly like flames upon his head. "Who's John Maximillian?"

Right then the door swung open, and I'll tell you, the man did not disappoint.

"That," I said, "is John Maximillian."

He gleamed in the morning light, like from somewhere above a lantern was forever shining down. Trust me. I am exaggerating.

He was not the celebrity I had imagined. His eyebrows were not penciled on and he had no moustache at all, but a pleasantly round face with a healthy lustre and cheeks demonstrative of a man well fed. He was wider than he was tall, and his suit was not a shimmering white, finely tailored affair, but a neutral grey, cotton, I'm guessing, that looked like it would be itchy against the skin. His hat was a derby, I think they calls them. It appeared to be too small for his very large head, and reminded me of Boston, though I've never been, a town to the east I might someday visit if I ever get out of here.

His face glowed with a friendly smile and nothing but good intentions, and I won't deny I was disappointed he was not the slinky, slithery snake in the grass I thought he would be.

"Hello," he said again, taking off his hat exposing his mostly bald head and meeting all our eyes with a nod. "As I was saying.

I'm John Maximillian, a writer and…"

"A writer of what?" McTavish interrupted, but the question was fair.

"Um…I write chronicles of the wild west, and the proud, brave men like you fellows, who live their lives determined to tame it." Maximillian's face was beaming. It was like he was just as taken by meeting us as I was of meeting him.

"Chronicles? Are you a newsie?" McTavish seemed full of questions, and I'm guessing he was just getting warmed up for the morning's proceedings.

"Well, not exactly," the man started to explain, but then the Marshal, who seemed thin on patience first thing out of bed, interrupted again.

"We know who you are, Mr. Maximillian. Lachey," he addressed the Scotsman quickly, "we'll tell you later. Mr. Maximillian, I'm Marshal Quentin James Morrison. I'm assuming you wish some time to speak with Mr. Pitt." He pointed at me, and Maximillian's eyes followed his finger. I smiled at the man and gave him a wink. The bars cast vertical shadows across my face. I told him I'd be happy to speak with him, but perhaps at another time, "we've got a previous engagement, or haven't you heard?"

"Well, of course I've heard. Yes. The trial of course," as he spoke he moved closer to the bars, but not too close, and pulled out a pencil and pad of parchment, "but the judge doesn't convene for what…" he checked his pocket watch, a gold watch too fancy for the man's plain suit, "another three hours. Why Mr. Pitt, I would require but a fraction of that. Thirty minutes? That's all I ask."

Suddenly Barrister Laughlin McTavish appeared, gliding between Maximillian and the bars, and me.

"No the noo," he said, simple and plain, staring dull at Maximillian's blank uncertainty. I could see the man's mind turning, his eyes flickering as he considered his options and then, much to my disappointment but surprised amusement, he chose the wrong one and ignored the response from my wise and assertive attorney.

"No the..." Maximillian mumbled, gave his head a quick shake, then looked at me, pleading his case. "But Mr. Pitt," he began, "If I could even get..."

"No the noo." McTavish had moved closer and shifted his position to stand between the writer of chronicles and his legal client. He said those three words much slower than he'd previously expressed, and the threat that carried with them was evident to all, even Mr. Maximillian it seemed, who took a step back and averted his eyes.

"Mr. Maximillian," I said, hoping to remove the tension from the air. "This is my attorney, Lauchlin McTavish. He and I do have some preparation to attend to prior to the start of this morning's proceedings. I promise, you come back tonight... Wait. Do you have a room at The Bonner House?"

Maximilian glanced around unsure of the question's intent. "Yes. I do."

"Ok then. Tell you what. Like I was saying, you come back tonight. But you gotta bring us all supper from the kitchen. You tell Millie, or whoever, you got some friends to feed, she'll fix you five plates, assuming you'll be eating too, and we can all have supper together and I'll fill your notepad with the entire tale of the frightful events in the Valley of Many Rivers. Fair enough?"

The man thought for all of a second and agreed with a vigorous nod. "Thank you, Mr. Pitt. Thank you." And he bowed and nodded at all of us, as he made his way back through the door.

"John Maximillian, you say?" McTavish said.

"Yes sir," I smiled at them all. "A writer of chronicles."

* * *

The morning seemed to pass slowly and I could've sat with Maximillian after all, as the preparation for the proceedings to come took all of one minute with McTavish repeatedly telling me to just "sit there, sit still, and shut up. It's just a preliminary thing, neither you nor I have nothing to say at this point, accept 'Not guilty, your honour,'" McTavish explained. Though I interjected often, with a "but" or "what-if," he was clear, "sit there, sit still and shut up."

After that brief consultation, Freddy fetched me some water in a bucket, soap and a rag, with which I washed my face and hands and the stinky parts of my body. I had lost three fingernails thanks to Herman and Neville, and the water, though cold, got the nerves in those fingers screaming in protest.

As the time drew near, I returned to the window in my cell and looked out at the crowds standing outside the court tent. There were men holding them back and I heard a voice inform the crowd that seating inside was full "to capacity." But they had gathered on the street just the same, some sitting, some standing, and some just walking and talking excitedly.

A female voice, a mountain voice, drew my eyes downward in the window's view, and there was Maddie. Either she had gotten shorter than I remembered since meeting her at the Bonner's, or my cell window was much higher from the ground than I had thought. She stood directly below the window, flashing eyes staring up, wearing a hooded cloak and a typical court-day dress, much like Sunday's dress I'm guessing. I stuck my hand through the bars and wiggled my fingers to let her know I was there, as I figured she could not see me as result of the severe angle.

"Pitt," she whispered. "The widow sends her love."

Suddenly, some in the crowd noticed Maddie near the jailhouse and like looksie-loos do, began to drift in our direction. Without another word Maddie moved from my view toward the road but the people meandering kept drifting my way.

'Marjorie. The Widow Trowley herself!

My hope and heart both flew at once with the thought. I have spent much of my hours over these last few days lamenting the loss of my Marjorie, but at the same time there were moments where hopeful anticipations would elevate my energies, these moments were rare and fleeting. From a valley to a summit, I seemed to ascend in my emotional wanderings.

I turned from my window and looked at the Marshal and McTavish, both dressed in their own Sunday best, and me, riding hard still in the dusty rags I've had on since I left the mountain.

"Lachey," I nodded at the man, who turned to me as he buttoned up his vest. I jabbed my chin at him then the Marshal. "You fellas look great. Very impressive," I said. "How do I look?"

They stared at me, both seemed to freeze at the asking of my question. I knew what I looked like. I didn't need their eyes to tell me. Then finally after several seconds they understood my meaning.

Marshal Morrison was looking sharp, as one would expect of a U.S. Marshal going to court, but despite the formality of the circumstance, the black and white of his complete attire gave his solid form sharp angles and a gunfighter's edge. His badge shimmered, a morning star in the dimness of the Randy River Jailhouse.

"Say Freddy, what do you say we find Mr. Pitt some decent clothes in town here? Go down to the mercantile…" he paused when he saw Freddy's reluctance spread across his already reluctant face, then the Marshal finished his thought. "If they give you a hard time for a proper suit a clothes, come and get me." At that Freddy nodded and headed for the door.

My thoughts were racing and my body was screaming at me to walk, pace, so I did, at first, then I sat on my bunk. Slowly I lay back and close my eyes, again I become like a stream on a mountain slope and tether my drifting thoughts. It didn't take long for Freddy to arrive, with a shirt and pants that were modest but far better than the kit I was donning right now. So, I changed my clothes and dampened my head as best I could and when all was said and done I'd say I look fit for the harvest dance on a Saturday night. McTavish was telling me just that, when the Marshal appeared at the door and gave us a nod.

"Going to go check our route. We can't go in through that crowd at the front so we'll use the small entrance at the back. The one the judge uses. That means," Morrison sighed as he continued, "that we gotta walk all the way up the street. As you all know, we aint exactly a dominating force around here so I'm gonna go see if I can find a few accountable fellas to help keep the crowd back when we make the walk."

There goes my Adam's Apple, and yes, it was due to fear.

As I'm sure you've all figured out, I'm not one to really appreciate the social aspects of life, the mingling and cavorting with others for the sake of pure entertainment. I've always been and still am, I think, more of a transactional-based fellow in regard to my ways of thinking, and generally, do not like people on a whole. Not to say I dismiss any man, woman or child individually, as individually is how each person should be judged, but I've often found humanity in general to be a stain on the world, a parasitical infection feeding on and devouring all that it finds.

So, what I'm saying is, I don't like crowds. But that is a common trait and one I know is shared by McTavish and many folk who choose a life on the mountain.

After what seemed like mere moments the Marshal returned. With just a nod he indicated our route was ready, then he moved to the wall behind the desk and I heard the clinking of metal and the shuffling of feet. The jailhouse door opened and Freddy came back in. He was huffing and puffing and out of breath, flushed with excitement, the sounds of which streamed through the door when he'd opened it. The circus beside the church was beckoning the crowd with whimsical music that carried on the air, and scents of roasting meats and baked treats found their way inside the jailhouse.

In his hands Marshal Morrison held the handcuffs and shackles.

"Sorry Rosco," he said, opening the door and motioning me to step out. Lachey stood waiting, hands clasped at his waist, a face flushed like a fairy-tale gnome, orange hair slicked back on his head.

"Today's not the hanging is it?" I asked, knowing full well it was not. They all just looked so doom and gloom. "Not guilty, your honour. That's it for today. I'll say it. That's it. We'll leave. Now let's go get it done."

The cuffs weren't so bad but the shackles were a burden, both physically, limiting my stride to barely two feet, and mentally; being so inhibited in my movements stirred little surges of panic to churn in my stomach.

The walk was relatively uneventful. There were a few men with outstretched arms keeping folks standing "a safe distance away," they were explaining. Some folks spit, as was to be expected, and others shouted profanities and descriptions of the unbearable temperatures I would have to endure when I arrive in Hell.

"YOU GONNA HANG!" was my personal favourite, as it was shouted with such bravado and confidence that I actually looked for its source with some admiration.

Inside the court tent, as we entered the rear and walked slowly around the Judge's lofty pulpit that had been erected with fresh white lumber, every voice in the tent, and there were many, grew silent, and all eyes watched our progression.

Freddy, as the officer of the court, remained by the Judge's entrance. The Marshal escorted Barrister Lauchlin McTavish and defendant Rosco Pitt to the defendant table and small wooden chairs that seemed to lack both comfort and function, low to the ground and barely a hair's thick padding on the seats. So bad they was, I opted to stand, as did my attorney.

Freddy took a step forward, being careful not to catch any eyes, and loud enough to be heard announced, "Hear ye, hear ye. All rise. Honourable Judge Francis Henry presiding. Today's hearing in the District of the Valley of Many Rivers, Randy River County is now in session. Please be seated."

In a flapping flurry of black fabric, much like a crow to my eye, the Judge made his way to his chair and stared down at me immediately from his perch upon the bench. His eyebrows bushed a furious bristle and spiked equally above his cold, colourless eyes. His hair was thick and full, but as white as the peaks of the higher ranges. The murmurs of the crowd seemed to rise for a second then dropped fast as they settled into their seats.

I begin to feel the flitter-flutter of panicky swirls in my stomach again. I look around, craning my neck to gaze through the gallery of the court and quickly I find her. Her head is down and her eyes stare at the back of the seat in front of her. She does not look up and her face is pale, drawn and carried the droop of prolonged exhaustion.

I stare at her. Her hair falls loose around her face to splash upon her shoulders and her lips no longer pout in that natural way they did but are drawn tight and thin. My heart aches for my Marjorie.

I continue to stare at her, ignoring the grinning spectre of Neville Bonner, who flanked her on one side, with sister Millie flanking her on the other. Behind them floated the face of Ted, Terrible Ted Trowley, who also appeared to have been dragged through the dry bed of a rocky creek in the last few days. But I ignored them all and had only eyes for Marjorie. My panic increased.

"Good morning ladies and gentlemen," the Judge began, but then my hearing begins to buzz and my face feels flush and my mind's all a-spin inside my head. I struggle to focus but find my feet and plant them firmly on the ground, easing myself down into the second most uncomfortable chair I'd sat in since my arrival in Randy River.

I close my eyes and slow my breathing and MissT flashes in my mind's eye. After a few seconds, breathing steady and even, seeing her unchanging countenance clearly, I'm at peace once again with the mountain, and will accept her judgement on me, and as she not only expects but demands, I will rage against my foe, even if it be the mountain herself.

And so, the trial of that murderous villain Rosco Pitt began.

CHAPTER 14

Crazy Appaloosa

There always came thunder when the man spoke, at least it seemed that way after a while. The canvas that served as a courtroom rumbles and snaps in the gusts and breezes of the open field where the road winds away from the town. His explanation of today's proceedings is simple and clear: "the charges will be read one by one and to each charge the defendant, or his legal representative, shall enter a plea of guilty or not guilty." Judge Henry paused and glanced at McTavish, who smiled and nodded at the man on the bench.

"Today is neither a day for arguments nor objections. The purpose of the day is to ensure that the state and the defence are both aware of the charges and are ready to proceed. Based upon the entry of a plea, it shall be assumed that the defence is prepared?" Again, Judge Henry paused, lowering his silver, wire-rimmed glasses to the end of his nose and staring down hawk-like at McTavish.

"Aye... I mean yes your honour, we are prepared," McTavish said, looking to me not like the confident man of the mountain I knew, but a tad timid before the bench where the Judge sat peering down.

"Very well," said the Judge, turning to face Freddy. Judge

Henry extended his arm and fluttered a paper over the edge of the bench and Freddy stood stone still, frozen in uncertainty. He looked around nervously and the gallery, which stretched seated all the way to the double-flapped entrance and lined the walls standing half-way round on each side, started to chuckle and murmur. For the first time, but sure not to be the last, the Judge brought his gavel down.

"Bailiff," he said, "please read the charges," looking Freddy hard in the eye.

Freddy rushed forward and scurried to the bench, reaching up tentatively to take the paper from the Judge's fingers, he paused and said something to the Judge, but I couldn't make out what he said. Judge Henry looked annoyed, a slight grimace wrinkling his brow. His eyes shot up from Freddy's face and darted around the courtroom looking for something. Then I guess he found it because he immediately started shouting at Marshal Morrison.

"Marshal," bellowed Judge Henry, projecting his voice so Morrison could hear him where he stood at the far end of the tent. "Please assist the court if you would. We require a bailiff who can read." Judge Francis Henry looked down at Freddy in disgust.

The gallery began their muffled pleasure at Freddy's embarrassment, and the man turned red as a ripe tomato fresh off the vine. Again, I feel sorry for Freddy, forgetting for a moment of my own dire straits. It occurred to me briefly, odds were that most of those making a mockery of Freddy's literacy shared a similar lack of reading skills.

Marshal Morrison strode to the bench and took the paper from Freddy's trembling fingers, who once free of his burden, turned and walked straight out of the tent, the same way he'd come in. Without hesitation Morrison turned to the gallery.

McTavish, my lawyer, stood up and told me to do the same, so I did.

"Mr. Rosco Pitt. You stand accused of several charges, violations of both State and Federal law," the Marshal said. "I will now read to you these charges, stating the victim's name, and ask that you or your attorney please enter a plea of guilty or not guilty after each charge read. Do you understand my instructions?" Though the statement itself was somewhat redundant, given the Judge had just said all that, I thought Morrison did a pretty good job, being the soft-spoken person that he is.

"We do," McTavish responded.

"Very well," the Marshal continued to read and McTavish, with darting eyes and a motion of his hand, signaled me to remain standing. "I shall now read the name of the victims and the crimes against them, of which the defendant Mr. Rosco Pitt, stands accused:

Trevor Jason Trowley, murder."

"Not guilty," McTavish said, as he did for the next six names and charges read. Casper and Calvin and some fella named Jean, damnedest thing I ever heard, on and on the list seemed to go, then the Marshal paused, glancing at me over the edge of the paper.

"Mrs. Marjorie Trowley, rape and battery."

The tent literally gasped. A large gust of wind hit hard, just as those charges were read, and the people gathered inside joined the canvas in its verbal reproach. I grabbed McTavish's arm before he could proclaim what I myself was determined to say. I turned my back to Judge Francis Henry and gazed back at the gallery, once again, only having eyes for Marjorie.

"Not guilty, your honour," I said, plainly and clear, then just kept right on staring at her and nothing else.

I did not hear the prosecuting attorney, Mr. Percy Rawlins the dreaded Percy Rawlins, to hear Neville talk. But apparently the man was bellowing his objection to my "blatant intimidation of a witness" while Judge Henry slammed the hammer repeatedly, loudly ordering me to turn and face the bench.

Finally, after ignoring him for at least the count of ten, he said: "Mr. Pitt! If you do not turn and face the bench immediately I will find you in contempt of court. Do you understand Mr. Pitt?" the Judge pounded the gavel again.

That's when I turn around.

Marjorie, I'm sorry to say, still sat slumped between the family ties of Neville and Millie, still suffering from what I guess they call cat-a-tonic, and McTavish was furiously tugging at the cuff of my shirt, staring in exasperation at Judge Francis Henry. So, yeah, I thought, I'll turn around.

"Um, your honour? What is the penalty for contempt of court?" I tilted my head, truly bemused and eager for his response, but not eager enough to allow him to speak.

McTavish opened his eyes wide and clenched his pearly whites, begging me to shut up with a hissing whisper. I continued with my questions, leaving the Judge staring in disbelief with his mouth hanging wide.

"Are you going to…throw me in jail?" I spun around and faced the gallery and threw my hands in the air. "Or wait, maybe you'll hang me."

My eyes rested on Marjorie again and as sure as my mouth was getting dry fast, she was looking at me without raising her head, those chestnuts glimmering and that pouty-smile look, just for a second, playing on her lips. The smile that spread across my face was the broadest I'd ever felt that skin stretch, and I swear it hurt me for at least an hour after.

Well, almost forgot about the Judge and that forever pounding-thumping gavel but combined with the gusts of wind throttling the tent and the growing murmurs from the crowd, it started to grate on me in a very short time, so I once again turned around, gracing Judge Francis Henry with the face-splitting grin I just couldn't wipe clean. I noticed McTavish had sat back down, slumped and dejected.

"My apologies your honour," I said. "But these here proceedings are a bunch of…poppycock," I said, coming close to cursing but stopping myself short and feeling good about that accomplishment.

Judge Henry was either not aware of my demonstration of verbal restraint or didn't care about the measures I had taken to avoid insult, because he just started yelling at the Marshal.

"Remove him from my court!" The Marshal, at the sound of old Francis's voice turning all gurgled with the shouting, jumped and did as was asked, swiftly escorting me and McTavish towards the exit.

"Mr. McTavish. Marshal Morrison," Judge Henry delayed our departure, "I will see both of you in my quarters at The Bonner House, this afternoon. Is that clear?"

"Yes your honour," they said in unison, like a two-man choir, then looked at each other in disgust for their sudden harmonization.

We got to the flap and had to wait for the Judge to adjourn for the day, but the Marshal had gotten us out of the judge's eye, which seemed to me was the source of the Judge's annoyance.

Judge Henry dismissed the jury. "We are to reconvene tomorrow morning at 9 a.m., at which time the prosecution shall present its case. Thank you, you are dismissed for the day."

The gavel came down.

"All rise." Marshal Morrison's voice called the gallery to their feet. Without ceremony Judge Francis Henry rose from the bench and exited the court. His flowing, black robe fluttered and flurried – a murder of crows – as he rushed passed us. The day's proceedings were over.

As soon as we exited the tent flap, after the Judge and the jury had made their departure, it was apparent that our relatively peaceful route we had taken to arrive at court was now a gauntlet of faces and an unrestrained crowd, all eager to hear what happened inside. Adding to the steady flow of human traffic were those from the gallery exiting at the front, flowing into the road to mingle with the looksie-loos. Even the circus had ceased its antics. Staring back as we passed were the faces previously mentioned, the bearded lady and the dog-faced boy, mother and son I realized, as our eyes met and we all shared a smile.

Freddy, poor fella, was nowhere to be found, so with just the Marshal and McTavish as escorts, I shimmy my way up the street, shackled and cuffed, enjoying the sun on my face but cautious and leery of all those staring faces we pass.

My eyes scan the street from side to side. I can see the jailhouse, my jailcell's window, and across the road is the livery, and I can see the corral out back and this Appaloosa running crazy in circles, 'U S' stamped on his front flank. I nudged McTavish and nodded in the direction and he too saw the object of my gaze. Without thinking I whistled and be damned if Mr. Andrews didn't spare a moments glance in my direction when he jumped the corral's highest rail and casually trotted across the street, the crowd parting before him, to ease up beside me and give me a shove with his spotted snout.

He brayed, like I knew he would, and I teared up a bit as I showed him my cuffs and my shackles. I stroked his chin and ruffled his mane. I was absorbed in my attentiveness to my much-missed friend, Mr. Andrews, and I told him of my sadness with soft whispers meaningless to human ears, and he rumbled his lips and shook his head, which I took as a sharing in sentiments.

So absorbed I had become that I failed to notice the gathering of folks that had stood peacefully observing. They did not shout vulgarities or damn me to hell. Many looked solemn and respectful. Doe-eyed women tilted their heads and watched, some hugging children, appreciative of such displays of affection between a man and his horse.

Marshal Morrison and McTavish stood close by quiet and respectful as Mr. Andrews and I had our moment. I whispered to him, again, meaningless to human ears, and he perked and danced for a moment, shoved me hard with his spotted snout, turned and bounded back to the corral behind the livery, back to running circles – crazy Appaloosa.

We continued our slow walk down the road to the jailhouse, a hallway of living portraits, faces frozen in expressions of all sorts. My assessments ranged from fear to loathing, sympathy to malice, to just plain curiosity, which after all is the mother of invention, and I'm sure those curious minds were inventing all sorts of tales about the day the man and his horse bid their goodbyes on the road through Randy River.

Speaking of tales, coincidently enough, my eyes spot John Maximillian, pencil and paper in hand, no doubt describing the scene after the first uneventful day of the trial of Rosco Pitt. I'm sure he of all people had a strong sense of the literary value that could be weighted upon the scene just played out between myself and Mr. Andrews. His nod and beaming smile affirmed this thought when I caught his eyes with a nod of my own.

I'm glad the people that line the road as we walk are peaceful. My eyes scan the faces for the pale face of Marjorie, but neither she nor her escorts, Millie and Neville, are anywhere in sight.

As we neared the jailhouse door I was suddenly taken a back, when a small, delicate-looking woman and her chubby-legged, curly-haired child, girl or boy I could not tell to be honest, but cute as a shiny button on a brand-new coat, stepped forward onto the road.

In the morning sun the pair glimmered like a blissful scene on a stained-glass window, both fair in hair and complexion, cheeks like cherubs and warm, caring eyes.

"God bless you, Mr. Pitt," the mother said, lifting and hugging her child close. Then the sentiment echoed, and more voices whispered. Of course, as before, rose the usual taunts of "Hang him!" But, one has to take such criticisms in stride, I surmise, feeling the warmth of the good tidings that had been sent my way.

As I shuffle my feet through the jailhouse door, my good friend McTavish stabs me with a not so friendly look. I knew I would be getting an earful, probably from the Marshal as well, but I simply could not sit there and stand accused of inflicting pain of any kind on Marjorie. I was compelled to answer to that charge in my own voice with my eyes firmly looking into the woman who was the target of such atrocities. I offered them both that explanation as I moved and sat down at the table.

"But that is not a common position for one to find oneself in," I continued, "so, I understand why you do not understand, having never stood where I now stand. Do you understand?"

"What are you jabbering on aboot, man! I told you… did I not tell you… 'sit still and shut up.' Do you forget they've got a rope ready to go round your neck, Pitt. For Christ sakes!"

McTavish paced back and forth before me. His obvious animation was a clear indication of his agitated state. Behind him, the Marshal moved to the desk at the far end and lit the lamp. Though it was a bright sunny day outside, things were a might dark and stormy inside the Randy River jailhouse. I saw Morrison's face looking at me over the light from the lamp. He looked a haunted ghost, his face floating at the far end of the room, eyes gleaming.

"Judge Henry is no man to toy with, Rosco," Marshal Morrison declared. "He's apt to hang you for just doing that."

Morrison moved and began making coffee. "Do you want me to do that?" I offered, raising my still-cuffed wrists and kicking out my shackled ankles from beneath my chair. He tossed the keys and McTavish caught them without even looking, like his hand tracked their movement through the air. He freed me from my restraints grumbling, "Got-a good mind to leave you chained."

Now, I'm sure he had a mind to, but was it a good mind? I was tempted to tell him the jury is still out on that one but thought better of tempting McTavish's anger with my new-found mastery of sarcasm. Instead, I looked down humbled, and told the man I was sorry, "but you knows I wasn't just gonna sit there. You had to know that, Lachey."

I motioned him to a chair and asked him to sit down. The Marshal, carrying three mugs and a fresh pot of coffee, joined us making a circle of three.

In the dimness of the jailhouse, we sat silent for a moment, sipping the brew and, at least from my perspective, assessing the events of the morning and their overall meaning as applied to my neck, the rope, and the end of Rosco Pitt.

Though I said nothing, I had long since made up my mind that I had no intention of hanging. I'm sure McTavish was keenly aware of my intent on this matter, and the Marshal was too sharp to guess otherwise. To think I would just sit here and wait for the hangman's noose is not a thought that had ever entered my mind. Though I was lacking in planning I knew when the time came I would know it and come hell or high water I would make my escape, or get shot all to hell trying, but hanging? No sir.

※ ※ ※

The remainder of the morning was spent in silence. I took the opportunity to attend to my journals, these very words which you are reading now. I had planned to present them to John Maximillian for future publicizing in one of them there chronicles of which he professed to be the writer. I had never read a word of Maximillian's writings, but he seemed to me a moral man, an ethical man, and one whose word I would take at face value.

I thought on the night ahead and remembered we're having company for dinner. From beneath my bunk, I gather my quill and parchment, and secure a bottle of ink from inside the Marshal's desk. I feel McTavish's eyes on me and look up somewhat sheepish.

"John Maxmillian is coming tonight," I said. "Thinking I'm gonna give him my journals... you know, just in case..."

McTavish stared at the papers on the desk. After a few seconds, his eyes darted up to mine. "Are you telling fibs aboot me in your scribblings?" He smiled as he asked, his face brightening just a bit, chasing away any thoughts of this morning's proceedings.

I nodded to his response and changed out of the suit of clothes and redressed in my well-worn Union trousers and my favourite deer-skinned waist coat.

The Marshal had freshened himself and told us he was going to go and look for Freddy. I could see the worry of a brother in his eyes and once again was pleased to call this good man a friend.

McTavish claimed ownership of my bunk, and in no time was sawing logs soft enough to easily mix in with the sound from the street, but I relished my friend's sounds of sleep and took comfort in his rumbles.

It is in this setting that I once again turned my focus back to the blank page before me. The writing comes easy now, in the peaceful hum of the morning. The people still lingered outside and the mixed sounds of laughter, the distant sounds of carnival music, a steady flow of voices, and my friend's sounds of slumber, all drifted to my ears, but I ignored the chaos of sounds. I do not feel the hour pass, but the sun in the sky can tell no lies and at least that much sky had been traversed when a soft knock came to the door. This knock, though barely audible in the drone of the day, was but the first interruption.

I moved to the door and peered through the trap. Freddy stood on the porch looking down at his feet but still somehow requesting to enter without uttering a word. I made quick work of the deadbolts and Freddy stepped inside. He walked across the room in silence and sat in his chair, assuming his leaned-back position with his feet crossed before him on the desk.

"Sorry Rosco," he finally whispered and met my gaze as I shut the door.

"The Marshal's gone looking for you. We was worried, Freddy," I said, sitting back down at the table, keeping my eyes on my journal.

"I'm sorry," he repeated his remorse. "I...I've just never been in a real court before and...and with Judge Henry glaring down at me...my...my reading is no good. I can read some... and I know I could-a read the charges, I could-a, but I got real edgy and hot...I just couldn't think straight on anything."

I lifted my head from my journals, just for a second. "It's okay Freddy. We're your friends here, the Marshal, Lachey and me. You'll do better tomorrow during the trial. You're a good man Freddy. Don't forget that."

That seemed to settle him down as I returned my focus to my journals and heard him shift in his creaky chair and take a long pull from the jug of shine in the drawer of the desk. Quiet returned, though the occasional ruckus would carry in from the street, it weren't too excessive and permitted me to focus once again on these here words. Another hour passed.

The Marshal rushed in, and for the second time that morning, an interruption pulled me from the page.

He said nothing when he first entered. He hurried in, spared a smile and a nod to the sight of Freddy reclining at the desk, left the door wide open, and indicated with a tilt of his head and the glance of his eyes that I should take a look at something outside.

The commotion brought an end to McTavish's slumber and with a couple of snorts and a sudden start, he jumped from the bunk and joined me and the Marshal out on the porch. Freddy, less eager to see, hovered behind us, watching. Not one of us spoke. We just watched and assessed what our eyes were seeing.

They'd come in from the south. Riding in formation, four horses wide, the Sons of the Confederacy and the duster-donning boys of the Cahill Cattle Company. They drove their horses at full gallop. A militia of sorts, the Marshal noted.

"I ran into Millie when I was looking for Freddy," Morrison said. "She told me Neville rode south this morning to meet up with some fellas from the Cahill Cattle Company. Pickets are again positioned around the town, and they'll be reinforced now that these boys are in town. The way I see it," Morrison continued, pulling his gaze from the approaching riders and the rising cloud of devil-dust behind them. "Neville's of the opinion that your gonna try and escape. I'd say Neville's opinion is a pretty damn good one."

The riders' advance slowed as they drew closer to town proper. The men were a mixture of cattle company dusters and Confederacy greys as they trotted past the jailhouse and made there way towards The Bonner House. Neville led the charge and spared us all a grin as he trotted by.

"Aboot thirty men, I'd say." McTavish's estimate was accurate by my assessment, and each of them were armed better than any Confederate ever was.

It occurred to me immediately that at least one possible method of escape had just been made all the more complicated, and, as if to add an exclamation point to my assessment, at the rear of the parade came a covered wagon. As it passed our vantage point we saw the golden glint of Neville's Gatling gun, which pulled up in front of the livery and pointed its barrels directly at the jailhouse door. A small contingent of men dismounted and settled in and around the wagon, making busy with their weaponry and prepping their position.

Other riders broke off from the group and took up various positions as they continued down the street. The people and the looksie-loos all made way as the procession passed and finally came to rest directly in front of The Bonner House.

"Check," said McTavish, making reference to that board game I could never understand, what with the Kings and Queens and Pawns and such.

"The entire town is now your prison, Rosco," Marshal Morrison shut the door as we all moved inside once again. "I think its best if we all hang low, keep to the jailhouse."

There were utterings of agreement all around. My stomach, though empty and void but for this morning's coffee, suddenly felt like it was gonna flip, twist, and get all tied up in knots. I glanced at my journals and realized I had little more to say. I will make record of this evenings dinner with Mr. Maximillian, but as that was yet to occur at the time of this writing, that will come later. So, I turned to my bunk with full intention of becoming one with the mountain and drifting into a deep slumber, Miss T's countenance soon filled my slipping thoughts... I poured down her slopes, smooth and flowing like a spring-time mountain stream, finally coming to rest: a calm, gentle, peaceful pool. Sleep had found me.

CHAPTER 15

Banjo Billy

The third interruption came as the sun climbed high. Since Neville's militia had moved into town, the sounds of the looksie-loos and the circus, and the general murmuring of passing voices, had been replaced with an eerie silence.

As I rose from my nap I noticed the Marshal, who sat close to the door, which he had again opened wide, reading one of them dime-store novels written by none other than John Maximillian, the esteemed writer of chronicles. I glanced at the title on the booklets cover page:

The dastardly deeds of Terrible Ted and Twelve-Shot Trevor.

There was a picture – a drawing – of what I guessed to be Ted and Trevor committing some dastardly deed. I chuckled to myself.

McTavish sat at the table playing with a ragged, old deck of cards, and Freddy, having overcome his shame from the events of this morning, was blissfully and drunkenly passed out in his chair behind the desk.

I moved to the door and stepped out onto the porch. The Marshal started his warning, but I shrugged him off with a wave of my hand. "I need some fresh air," I said, patting my Colt strapped firmly to my side as I stepped out onto the porch and the afternoon sun.

The air was crisp and carried promise of a coming snow. I looked north, towards where I knew but could not see the stoic stance of MissT rising up from the earth. Tilting my head, I let my nostrils suck the air. The cold tickles as I breathe deeply and fill my mind with the scents of the world. My eyes finally come to rest on the golden glint of that Gatling gun. It stands in the back of the wagon, six dark chambers whisper threats my way, promising to empty their contents into my yielding flesh.

There's the shape of a man moving behind the gun, gently rocking the wagon with his motions, but he is not the one who decided to catch my full attention. No. He was but a shadow, a faint, undulating form, but the man that emerged from behind the wagon was clear and well defined, playing a woeful tune on a beat-up old banjo – strumming and grinning as he looked my way.

He wore the duster and the hat of the Cahill Cattle Company, but unlike most of the others, he wore his hat in a comical way, set firmly yet crooked and sideways on his head. I didn't know the tune he was playing – just a slow plucking twang of different notes that seemed to tell a sad tale of some unlucky wanderer's demise.

His dark hair hung matted and messed from beneath his hat, and as his grin broadened with every step of his approach, darkness revealed a mouth with just a few crooked, yellowed tombstones that were what was left of his teeth.

He moved halfway cross the dusty street and came to a stop but continued his plucking and grinning. I stared at him, drawing full on one of Freddy's finely rolled smokes, until the strumming finally stopped and the grin became a straight line across his face. The man extended one arm, the banjo dangling from his fisted hand, the other hand he placed across his stomach and honored his audience of one with a deep, I'd imagine what one would call, theatrical bow. He straightened his posture with an unnecessary flailing of the arms, stringing the banjo over his back.

"Howdy," he said, his mouth curling again to that grin. "Folks who know me call me Banjo Billy; on accounts of the banjo I carry wherever I go. Expect you might have heard of me."

Well, I hadn't, to be honest, and as I did to both Terrible Ted and 12-Shot Trevor, I went straight to feigning the recognition of his admittedly fanciful name.

"Banjo Billy you say?" I replied, taking a long draw on one of Freddy's finely rolled smokes. "Hmm...wait a minute." I pointed at him, stretching my face in a grin of my own. "Didn't I hear tell of your exploits in one of them dime-store novels written by the respected chronicler John Maximillian?"

I hadn't noticed, so focused was I on the fella standing before me, that a crowd had started to pay attention. Though they kept their distance, the looksie-loos had crawled back out of wherever they'd been hiding. The Marshal and McTavish had moved to stand behind me on the porch and both cattle company and Confederate boys, Neville among them, had and continued to move their way closer, casually ambling up the street. Even Mr. Andrews, I noticed, had come close to the corral's fence. Quite the audience indeed.

Now Banjo Billy, well I thought his face was gonna split in two, his grin grew so wide at the mention of John Maximillian. He nodded vigorously.

"Yup," he confirmed. "John Maximillian! Nice fella I'm guessing. Never met him, not sure where he gets his stories from, but he surely has made me famous."

"Why, he's right over there Billy," I said, matter of fact, pointing to the round, short man with the derby on his head, notepad in hand, standing amongst the still-growing crowd. "That right there, that's John Maximillian."

Banjo Billy turned to look. Without hesitation he threw all his attention on Mr. Maximillian and hurried to fill the writers ears with words of worship and heavy praise. The name Maximillian was carried on whispers throughout the crowd, and as I swiftly, yet imperceptibly, cocked the hammer on my holstered Colt, I noticed John looked somewhat embarrassed by all the sudden attention.

I smoked my smoke and watched, motioning to Lachey and the Marshal to remain calm and, with a few flicks of my fingers, to stand back. Finally, after the moment of admiration had passed, Banjo Billy spun back my way, moved back to have the Gatling's menacing stare hovering over his shoulder When he found his mark, where he wanted to stand, he took another second to admire the crowd which now circled us.

Behind me was the jailhouse, behind Billy, a wagon of imminent death. Everywhere else was now a moving mass of men, waiting with bated breath. I remained in my casual stance, a slight smile played on my lips as I once again partook of Freddy's fine craftmanship in creating a pleasurable smoking experience. I notice a frown flash across Billy's face and immediately expressed my concern.

"I'm sorry Billy... may I call you Billy? Or should I address you as Mr. Banjo?"

"I'm a pistoleer, Mr. Pitt. Don't be fooled by my youthful exuberance and carefree countenance. I, good sir, am in the business of killing, and when I plays my banjo for a fella, well, I've begun to do my business."

I considered his response for less than a second. "Is my smoking bothering you?" I leaned forward slightly, widening my eyes with sincerity.

"As a matter of fact, Mr. Pitt..."

The gun was back in before anyone even knew it was out. If not for the sound of the shot people would have been wondering why poor Billy fell flat and dead on his back, the top half of his head clean blown off. Again, I was a little closer than I thought. But still, that was fast. I'm not trying to be boastful but I've never felt the pistol pull as smooth and fast as it just did, and its been pulled plenty over the years.

A collective gasp. The Marshal and McTavish were both suddenly by my side, guns drawn, covering the crowd. I spun towards the Gatling and watched the shadow raise its hands.

As quick as we could we backed into the jailhouse and slammed the door behind us. Still in his chair, Freddy remained blissfully oblivious to all that had occurred, still deep in the shine's slumber.

That was the end of Banjo Billy.

CHAPTER 16

Millie's Chili

I gave little thought to Banjo Billy as the rest of the day meandered by. In the same breath, I can honestly say I thought very little of anything for the remainder of the day, but for one thing: the swiftly approaching supper hour and our special visit from John Maximillian.

Ever-present in my heart now was that calming peaceful pool, filled by the ever-flowing progress of a mountain stream. I was one with the mountain.

I had commandeered my bunk once again, much to the grumbling protests of McTavish who resigned himself to the comforts of his canvas cot. The silence continued outside, possibly because of the lifeless lump of Banjo Billy, which still remained lying on the street, buzzards beginning to circle overhead.

Marshal Morrison could not believe someone had not fetched the undertaker. Both I and McTavish had advised against taking such action ourselves. Outside of this jailhouse was no place for anyone of us to be right now and in the death of Banjo Billy, it should be on the Cahill Cattle Company to take care of their own. Besides, neither Marshal Morrison nor McTavish had the time, on this day, to go fetch Reggie Burell. They had to go face the wrath of Judge Francis Henry because of my unconscionable behaviour in the court this morning.

Freddy was awake when they departed, but he was badly in need of the hair of the dog that bit him. Poor Freddy, there was no more shine to be found. I suggested he just drink lots of coffee, straight out of the pot, but Freddy failed to see the humour in my words. Can't say I blames him.

The door to the jailhouse remained open providing an afternoon view of the street, and our eyes constantly drifted to the glimmering gold of that Gatling. Slowly, life came back to Randy River proper. Some activity had commenced once again, despite the dead body on the street. More people drifted into town, what with the trial to commence on the day to come, but amongst the sporadic clunking and clopping of the occasional passing wagon, a fainter sound came to my ears and drew me, once again, out onto the porch.

The boys manning the Gatling tensed visibly as they watched me emerge, one of them gave a sharp whistle. I paid them no mind as my focus and eyes were drawn to the distant sounds of several wagons emerging from the tree line, just beyond the Bonner House at the far end of town.

They drew closer, moving agonizingly slow. In the lead wagon I recognized Reggie Burell, the undertaker, and I assumed Banjo Billy was what the man was here for, but as the procession of wagons pulled up near the jailhouse, I realized Reggie's presence served a whole different purpose.

He nodded my way as he pulled up to a stop, and tilted his head back towards the procession of wagons that followed: three wagons in all, each loaded up with two men and plenty of lumber.

"Well hello there Reggie. Guessing you're here to deal with that lump over yonder?" I nodded towards the corpse that was Banjo Billy, but Reggie appeared surprised by my suggestion, pointed a thumb at the loaded wagons, and shook his head.

"Geez. No. I didn't even know my services were required in that regard Mr. Pitt." He took off his hat, rubbed his head, and looked at me without meeting my eyes. "I've been commissioned to build... um... I'm sorry Mr. Pitt, but I'm here to construct... for tomorrow's..." Reggie trailed off and turned his face from my direction.

"It's alright Reggie," I said, seeing the man truly felt bad about the task he was to undertake. "The hanging. Your building the gallows for the hanging. I'll say it for you, Reggie. Didn't know it was planned for tomorrow but I'm okay with that. I am one with the mountain, my friend."

Reggie climbed down from the wagon. With a quick shout and a couple of hand signals, the accompanying wagons circled round Reggie's buckboard and parked their loads next to the space of land between the jailhouse and the courthouse tent. Immediately the men commenced to unloading the lumber and Reggie moved up onto the porch to stand beside me. I offered him one of Freddy's finely crafted smokes which he politely declined, then lit one of my own, drawing deep. I looked up for a moment and saw the first hint of clouds rolling in from the west, bruised and bottom heavy.

"Looks like weather's coming in." I pointed at the approaching sky and Reggie's eyes followed my finger. He turned to me then, looked me right in the eyes for the first time since he climbed down from the wagon.

"I am sorry Mr. Pitt," he said, his eyes almost pleading for understanding. "It's a damnable thing, having a condemned man watch the building of what will be the instrument of his death. It sickens me, Mr. Pitt."

Reggie paused and glanced around town. His face twisted in a moment of anguish, then smooth and controlled once again, as he returned his gaze to my eyes. "These fellas," his face crinkled in disgust, "these hired guns and fools clinging to a war long over, a fading past; these are not the people of Randy River that I know, Mr. Pitt. I just want you to know that sir."

He paused again as I nodded, and placed a hand on his shoulder, telling him I hold no ill will toward the folks of Randy River. "It seems to be their Sons is with whom I have a problem,"

I spat.

"Mr. Pitt. You gotta know there are plenty of good folks in these parts that don't agree with what's happening here, to you. You gotta know that Mr. Pitt, and I am deeply sorry."

I accepted his apology and shook his hand. Seems my original assessment of Reggie Burell was a might harsh and I found my heart had warmed to him swiftly. We continued to converse as the men in his company kept busy unloading lumber. We spoke of the weather, as I previously had mentioned, and how that might affect the project.

Reggie told me weather would be of no concern, unless the wind picks up considerably, then raising the large, squared cross-beam could be a challenge. The cross-beam, Reggie explained, must not only be a strong chunk of timber, but must be placed with great care, considering a multitude of factors all dependent on physics, which Reggie tried to explain but I could not understand.

I looked at the cross-beam, gleaming white and thick, a squared log of sturdy oak, and wondered aloud why they didn't simply make use of the old hanging tree, also an oak, on the other side of the jailhouse. Reggie, who had moved down to his buckboard to gather up his tools, heard my question and again paused to reply.

"There you are! Right where I found myself – wondering the exact same damn thing. Well, Mr. Bonner sees this whole thing – much like that circus over yonder – like some kind of side-show attraction. He wants it 'done right' and he wants it 'done big. Clean, fresh, white oak,' he says, 'build it high and wide,' he demanded, 'with a far enough drop to snap a neck clean.'"

I'll admit I squirmed: '...to snap a neck clean...' The words were like a serpent slithering up my spine. But, given Reggie's observing eyes, I maintained my composure, nodded, and professed how much them words seemed to suit the vile mouth of a vile man named Neville Bonner. Reggie agreed. Then I had one last question for the man, who I believed I could now call a friend. Though Reggie was surprised by my question, his answer had me damn near whistling Dixie. We parted with smiles, and yes, I had confirmed, Reggie was no friend to the Sons of the Confederacy.

* * *

The day grew longer, and I'm not saying I was nervous for the wellbeing of my friends but how long could it take for a judge to admonish a defendant's bad behaviour?

Freddy, who had finally found his sober senses, brewed up magic once again with his flavourful coffee, and settled his shakes by rolling me a dozen fine smokes to be had at my leisure.

We had shut the front door about an hour ago. By late afternoon them dark clouds rolled in and with them came that cold, damp wind. By my estimates fat snow would be a topic of discussion during our dinner hours, and by the depth of them clouds, stretching off to the horizon as they do, I'm betting there's a chance we could be walking knee deep come the morrow.

A knock on the door got Freddy hopping, and he lifted the trap to see who was who.

"It's the squaw," Freddy said staring through the flap, and I was quick and stern to admonish his slander of the woman I assumed to be Maddie. I pushed Freddy roughly aside, so disgusted I was by his degrading comment, and I gazed through the slat myself. My assumption was correct.

"Maddie my dear," I opened the door and beckoned her to enter, glancing up at the boys in the wagon across the way and giving them a wave to be friendly. "Freddy," I said, swinging the door to a close, "we've got company. Get Maddie a cup of your fine brew."

I helped her with her cloak and pulled out a chair at the table. She sat, just as Freddy placed the steaming cup before her.

Her eyes were the shade of sun-dried mud, and they swirled with flecks of green and a rusty orange striping. They were strange eyes, to say the least, rare among all and not just her mountain people.

She seemed to sense my thoughts and smiled and said, "My mother's eyes. She was special to my people, yeah. She could see the Great Communion and knew when to move and when to stay. Foresight, yeah. I can not see the Great Communion, but I am much like her." Maddie had stared at her coffee as she'd spoke these words. Finally she turned her eyes to mine and said simply, "Pitt, how are you?"

I had leaned forward in my chair so intent I was on listening, at her simple question I had to sit back for a second and think. "I am one with the mountain, Maddie. I have hope you are the same?"

"I am, Pitt. To be one with the mountain is good, yeah." She glanced at Freddy, sitting at his desk in the shadows, far across the room. She smiled again, a quick, slanted, knowing smile. "Peckerwood! Come over here and join us, yeah." She laughed at her slight but I just watched Freddy's shadow slowly rise and move over to the table.

"How are you, Miss Maddie?" Like Maddie had done, Freddy just stared at his cup as he spoke.

"Like Pitt said: one with the mountain," Maddie looked at me and smiled with her eyes – a subtle glint of light in just one. "Nothing more need be said, yeah," she concluded with a wink.

It seemed like an eternity. I stared at her uncertain, for just a moment. As a youth, my Ma had once taught me about a man in someplace called Austreea, or something, a doctor of sorts who talked about magnets and forces that control animals, like a rabbit froze in the light of a torch, I think. Franz Mesmer was his name, as I recall, and he came up with the word mesmerized. Maddie had me mesmerized. She sipped her coffee, her eyes, always seemingly smiling, never left mine.

"The widow sends her words," she simply stated between sips.

"Marjorie!" My smile was broad, and it seemed that Maddie's spell had been broken as my mind raced with all the things I wanted to say. Then Maddie raised her hand, compelling me to remain quiet, and allow her to finish.

"I've been sent to inform you that supper will be served at 6 p.m. Miss Millie was pleased to prepare her prize-winning chili, the best damn chili north of Abelene. She told me to say that." Maddie nodded, having delivered her message. "You make good brew, Peckerwood," she concluded, smiling at Freddy.

"Why you call him that?" I was afraid to ask but I was unfamiliar of the term. My curiosity got the better of me. Maddie just smiled and giggled to herself. Freddy, suddenly saw the need to brew a fresh pot and quickly left the table. After a moment of watching Maddie chortle, her cheeks round and glistening; black, straight hair dangling down her face, I realized she weren't going to answer so I posed a different question.

"Maddie. Tell me, how is the Widow? Is she one with the mountain? I've heard tell of her cat-a-tonic state. How is Marjorie?"

She glanced over at Freddy making more brew and dropped her voice to a whisper.

"Ask her yourself. She's coming for supper." At that Maddie grinned, rose from the chair and slipped her cloak back on. "Thanks for the coffee Peckerwood," she grinned at Freddy. "Don't be a stranger, yeah. Drop by the house some time." She laughed out loud as she moved to the door.

I sat dumbfounded, then seeing her at the door I rose to see her out. I thanked her profusely. Her words meant more than she could know, I told her.

She stepped out on the porch and gave the boys in the wagon a wave herself, then she turned and said, "Oh, and don't eat the chili, ok Pitt. Millie said Neville put something nasty in it. She said something about 'the trots,' and I don't think she was talking about horses."

※ ※ ※

It was the sound of the horses that drew us to the door once again. Freddy was pacing in anticipation of Millie's chili, and though I told him what Maddie had said, he waved me off with a fluttering hand declaring Millie's chili always gave him the trots. He rushed outside, unable to contain his anticipation, and I ambered out behind him to watch the wagon approach.

The Marshal and McTavish walked beside the wagon on which two figures rode, John Maximillian and, much to my disappointment, Maddie, with her hood drawn tight to shield from the cold. She waved to the boys manning the Gatling, once again, then climbed down from the wagon and retrieved a platter of fresh baked bread and slabs of butter. She walked past Freddy and I with barely a nod and proceeded to enter the jailhouse.

"What took you so long?" I mutter the question to either one, Morrison or McTavish.

"Ah, yes," Morrison responded, "Judge Henry holds a lot of wind, and I had to send a wire south to the fort. During my official actions as U.S. Marshal and in direct relation to my investigation of the accused, Rosco Pitt, I have received statements from various witnesses of a possible sedition conspiracy in this area." He smiled as he followed McTavish into the warm light of the jailhouse door, adding it might take a couple of days for the calvary to arrive, as will be the result given the involvement and presence of a "Confederate militia."

I must say, his words gave wings to my emerging hope, and it was with a broad smile that I turned to meet the writer of chronicles. John Maximillian lowered his round self down from the buckboard and turned quickly, all chubby smiles, to shake my hand.

"Evening Mr. Pitt," he said. "Thank you again for this opportunity."

"Well you sir are quite welcome, and I'm honoured to have you here to take supper with us. And thank you again for that as well."

"Ah. No sir. No sir," he replied, still shaking my hand. "It is my honour to be in the presence of the man who shot Banjo Billy!"

"Well thank you," I said, adding, "I got something else for you John. I'll give it to you a little later – a little surprise I think you might like. Now go on, get yourself inside."

I watched as McTavish and Marshal Morrison walked past, each grinning and each grabbing the handles on either side of a rather large pot sat at the back of the wagon. They carefully moved back inside with Freddy bringing up the rear, arms hugging a stack of bowls and two bottles of scotch.

I felt my eyes growing moist as I lingered on the porch, staring intently up the road to the Bonner House. The darkness was descending and the wind blew hard, but that wasn't what was bringing these tears to my eyes. I must confess I sobbed, loud enough to hear. I brought my hands to my face and wiped away the wet. I gasped and vocalized some incoherent denial and was on the brink of blubbering when her voice took me from behind, "Are you coming in, or what?"

It was a voice I would never forget and had been longing to hear. It was the voice that dripped in my ears, sweet as a batch of fresh-rendered honey. I spun, and there in the door wearing Maddie's cloak, hood pulled down, stood Marjorie Trowley, with her smiling, chestnut eyes, her blonde, flowing locks cascading freely across her shoulders, and not a cat-a-tonic in sight. My a

* * *

Marjorie and I had lingered as one for a brief time out on the porch, but the catcalls of the boys in the wagon, who were obviously watching our tender embrace, drove us to the confines of the jailhouse. Given the company we would be keeping, this was not such a bad alternative, and that's my assessment.

I had one once. I have heard others speak about theirs. The years that had passed since my days on the farm had dulled my memory, but as I looked around the table at my friends, who were smiling and laughing and sharing in the warmth of the stoves at either end of the room, the word 'family' popped up in my mind.

I knew the word was a manifestation from my heart, for it was as warm as those stoves and had me basking in the love I felt for the people who had joined me here this evening. It was a feeling I knew I shared in the moment, with each and every person in the room. Their eyes told me so.

It became quickly apparent that I had been elected the master of ceremonies, so with out further delay, I informed our guests, much to the chagrin of Freddy, that Maddie had been explicit in her instructions to not eat Millie's chili.

This news disturbed John Maximillian greatly, as it had been he, a respected guest at The Bonner House – For Tired Eyes N' Weary Souls, who had requested the dinner and had paid a fair and negotiated price for the extra service, something Neville was adamant would be required.

"Well. I won't be returning to their accommodations any time soon," he said in good humour, passing on the chili, as did everyone, but Freddy.

"What should we do with the rest of the pot?" Marjorie asked. As Freddy finished off one heaping bowl and started on another.

"Well," I replied, "If we can ever get Freddy's face out of the pot we could offer some to them boys across the street in the wagon. By the way John, did you have a look at that Gatlin' in the wagon? It's a beaut!"

Maximillian looked at me in wonder. "No...I haven't seen the gun... but wait. You'd share that pot of chili with the same men who are camped across the street just itching to kill you?"

"Well, I confess I wish it would give them more than just the trots, but yeah...yeah, I would."

My reply sent Maximillian to a scribbling flurry, scratching in his notepad as he was seen to do the entire time. Then he started off firing questions: what drove me to the mountain? What brought me down from the mountain? What really happened to 12-Shot Trevor? What really happened that night at The Bonner House? Who is Rosco Pitt, where did I come from? Tell him about the duel with Casper Trowley?

"Whoa, whoa, whoa there little dog. Excuse me for one moment." I pulled the reigns and moved away but did not answer his questions. Maximillian looked confused by my sudden departure, but everyone else smiled knowing my ploy, all but Marjorie, who just kind of guessed I was being my mischievous self and having some fun with John Maximillian, the writer of chronicles. I gave her hand a squeeze as I rose to fetch my journals. John jumped when I snuck up behind him on my return, and dropped the stacked pages on the table before him…

❋ ❋ ❋

…I looked at the first page: 'Best get back down' it reads across the top. I gasped, and looked up at him in disbelief.

"Is this…is this ..?" Speechless. I'll admit, it happens rarely as far as my days-to-days go, but at that very moment I was speechless. Rosco Pitt had handed me his hand-written journals chronicling his time here in Randy River. This was pure gold, and I knew it. Quickly I flicked through the pages, counting in my head.

"Yes," Rosco replied. His voice sounded youthful, emerging from a beard that looked as old as the mountain he'd descended. I heard him.

"Yes it is. The entire tale of my time here in the Valley of Many Rivers, specifically the county and town of Randy River. And there's a glimpse of my upbringing as it fit with the story told." He turned and squeezed the hand of the Widow Trowley, Miss Marjorie Trowley, as she now prefers.

Rosco paused at that moment, and when I pulled my eyes from the pages of his journals, he was looking straight at me.

"I've got something else for you John." He stood up, for some reason. It was the second time I'd met the man, face to face, but now, seeing him in this small room, out from behind the bars, unshackled and armed, I marvelled at his true physical presence.

His size tall, a posture often hard as stone and one that dripped of complete confidence, was an intimidating sight, but was softened by the tanned, weathered face and his calm, hazel eyes, framed by a dusty brown, unkept mane, both round his face and on his head. He topped it off with a Union cap, which I'm sure was a rare symbol to be seen in these parts.

He reached down into his buckskinned waist coat, to a pocket hidden inside, and pulled out yet another piece of paper, this one folded in squares. He passed it to me, his face a docile giant looking down.

While here in Randy River he'd seemed to earn the moniker, 'The Murderous Villain Rosco Pitt,' the man I was meeting on the eve of his trial was not a man one would consider to be "villainous," never mind "murderous." In fact, in the assessment of this writer, he was the exact opposite.

I unfolded the page. A map. I spread it flat on the table, allowing all to see. Marshal Quentin James Morrison seemed the most attentive. He'd removed the often-worn white straw hat and leaned forward for a better look.

"That there is a map of the whereabouts of every other journal I've hidden along my life's journey," Rosco explained, sitting back down beside Marjorie, each of them shuffling closer until their arm brushed the arm of the other. A glimpse beneath the table, we'd see them holding hands.

"That spot right there," Lauchlin McTavish jammed his finger onto the map, leaning halfway across the table and pointing to one of three spots. His head rose sharply, bringing his eyes level and inches from mine.

"If you want to go to that spot there, on the veil of MissT, I can help you. As a matter of fact, I could go there myself and get them for you, but I've got a funny feeling I won't have to. Neither will you!"

Apparently, as was evident by the toxic fumes that were released with his words, McTavish, as Scotsman are said to be prone to do, had found at least one of the bottles of scotch.

"Do you want to know why," the Scotsman continued, blue

eyes in a winter sky, red nose and flaming red hair, a wiry beard to savour his soup, though intimidating, McTavish spoke with assuredness and of course, a thick Scottish drawl. "I'll tell you why. Because Rosco Pitt is gonna go there and get them himself."

He began to sway and was about to play topsy-turvy with the small, round table when Rosco and the Marshal rushed to his side and steadied the man. But drunk or not, McTavish had a point. The trial was still yet to begin, but somehow, this gathering had turned into a premature wake.

"Freddy, get Lachey some of that coffee and hide that bottle of scotch," Rosco said, as he and Marshal Morrison steered the man back to the safety of his chair.

"I'm sorry," McTavish offered once back in his seat. He stared at his friend Rosco, tears welling up in his eyes. "Your not hanging tomorrow. Your riding out of this place weh me. Tell me what you need old friend. I know better. Your not hanging the morrow. No bloody way."

There was a silence in the room, all but from the man himself. Rosco leaned back in his chair and grasped the belt of his holster with both hands. His laughter started as a smile, which slowly spread wide and allowed his mirth to escape.

"Your right my friend," Rosco replied, his laughter subsiding but his smile standing strong. Infectious indeed, as it swiftly spread to each of us across the room.

Marjorie's smile, I noticed, was the most beaming of the bunch. It made her look like a girl once again, and showed the world why Rosco Pitt loved her so.

"What do you need us to do, Mr. Pitt," Marjorie asked, once again grasping Rosco's left hand. A good fit indeed, seeing how possibly the fastest gun in the west pulled his pistol with his right.

He looked around the room at the faces, asked Freddy to fetch five glasses and that bottle of scotch – "None for my friend here. I think he's had enough."

And then... he told us.

CHAPTER 17

The trial of Rosco Pitt

What follows is this writer's version of the trial of Rosco Pitt. A man of the mountains who's violence and anger, fueled by the love for a woman, and driven by the mistreatment of that same woman at the hands of sadists unknown, wreaked havoc on the community of Randy River, leaving a trail of dead bodies in his wake. The defendant stands accused of multiple counts of murder, and the rape and battery of the woman he professes to love. My name is John Maximillian. I expect you might have heard of me, and I was there.

I awoke to a muffled world. Sounds drifted to my waking mind, sounds of voices and morning wagons, shouts and whistles. The sounds were dulled, like the world was wrapped in fabric, thick and dampening the senses. I rose to look out my window and was greeted by the snow, fat snow in the air and a smooth, white bed blanketed the ground, just as Rosco had said there would be.

Outside on the street, I wrap my coat tight as the wind is a whip, whirling and twisting in all directions. The snow still falls, fat and thick, adding to the knee-high depth that discourages my steps. Just like Rosco said there would be.

I feel my derby pulled from my head – like my shout of surprise it's lost to the wind. I trudge on, feeling urgency. I plow my legs through the snow as I move up the street.

Men in small groups sit huddled over fires on either side, equally spaced as the street progressed, at a distance of about thirty feet. These positions watch the jailhouse through the snow, like gazing through a snow globe, one of those new-fangled transparent paper weights that depict wintery scenes when you shake them. I'd imagine the men's eyes blur at the vision of God's high tower faltering amongst the endlessly white menagerie that fills their view.

Finally I reach my destination and knock on the jailhouse door. I spy the nearly completed gallows, just the cross-beam need be raised and it would be fully functional, but the work was stopped when the wind blew hard, and that wind still blew, delaying the final stage of construction, just like Rosco said it would.

Across the street, in the open field beside the shimmering white church, the circus sits quiet, but for one solemn figure. Even from a distance I could see the oversized shoes and the red nose on his face – a clown without a parade. He stood by a fire, alone.

I knock again, louder. The wind and snow suddenly whip in a frenzy, and I shield my eyes to see wagons trudging through the snow, not weighted they slipped side to side, wheels barely turning but sliding instead.

On the lead wagon sat Reggie Burell, the undertaker for Randy River County and the carpenter tasked with building the gallows, returning to finish the job. We exchanged pleasantries, but like my hat our words were lost in the wind. A wave of the hands proved sufficient. My fingers were numb and my ears were starting to burn. Winter, it seemed had arrived in one night, just like Rosco said it would.

I turned again to the door. This time I pounded the wood, as the whirlwind whistled and mocked my efforts. Suddenly the door swung open. Freddy, dressed in dirty long-one's, quickly ushered me inside.

The room is dark and smells of smoked tobacco and liquor. McTavish, undoubtedly the source of the latter scent, lays sprawled on his back on a small canvas cot, his racoon-skinned hat covering one eye, angry wind grumbling from his gaping mouth, yesterdays clothes twisted and creased, scream of discomfort.

Marshal Morrison is crisp and fresh in his chair, he nods at my gaze as he sips his coffee, to which Freddy is forever tending on the stove behind the desk.

Rosco sits on his bunk, head in his hands. He seems a shell of the man who spoke with such confidence just the evening past. The hour for him approaches, so I leave him to his apprehension and trust he will find himself, "one with the mountain," so his mantra seems to state. Court begins in just over an hour.

I remove my coat and draped it over a chair, as I joined the Marshal at the table. Suddenly Freddy rushes to the door and dashes outside. The Marshal shrugs.

"Trots," he said. "He's been running to the livery all morning. Him and the boys on the gun across the street. We sent them some chili to warm their innards. They seemed to appreciate it last night. This morning, I'm guessing not so much."

I pulled out my watch from my waist coat. Saying nothing, I show the Marshal the time. He looked at the watch and shrugged, returning his attention to the coffee.

"Well there John, good morning. Did you see Marjorie safe to her box of sticks last night?" Rosco had risen from his bunk. Like Freddy, he too wore a pair of long-ones, but unlike Freddy, Rosco's undergarments were clean.

"Yes Rosco. Delivered her myself safe and sound. I must say, I was quite amazed to meet your friend Mr. Andrews. He came promptly, bounding out of the corral when Marjorie whistled, and followed us all the way to Plitter-Plop Crick. The animal seemed quite pleased to see that massive beast Jax, and to find a comfy corner in Marjorie's barn."

He nodded as he emerged from the cell, approached to place a hand on my shoulder, then moved to the stove to fetch a cup of coffee. "John. You wanting?"

I turned to see Rosco raise the pot of coffee. I lift my watch and politely decline with a shake of my head. Inside I'm shaking too. I can feel a lump in my stomach as I'm anxious for the day.

Yet the men in this room seem unperturbed by the unknown that awaits. Death could be hours away for anyone of them, or all of them, yet here they lounge, Rosco included, going about a normal routine on a normal morning on a typical day.

"Um... gentlemen. You do realize this is not a normal day."

My words seemed loud in the quiet dark, and Rosco froze in mid-pour, staring at me and overflowing his cup, spilling coffee on the stove and floor. Just then Freddy came rushing back in, shivering and quivering and bringing the cold in with him. He spied the mess that Rosco had made and immediately proceeded to clean it up. Rosco sat down at the table, nodded at the Marshal then lifting his finger to his lips he turned to me.

"Shhhh," he hushed. "For now, Mr. Maximillian, for now, today is a normal day. Why don't you head on over to that tent. Get yourself a good seat. You got my horse and my woman to safety. That's all that I asked. I thank you Mr. Maximillian. But today is not a day for a man who writes chronicles. Today is a day of definitive action. We've got some killing to do today, and right now we're just getting in our game. You best hang low, do what you do best: observe, record and report. Tell the people what really happens here today, regardless of what happens here today. Tell the truth, John. Don't spin no fanciful dime-store story. Can you do that Mr. Maximillian?"

"I can and I will Mr. Pitt. You have my word."

"Good enough then. On you get. Perhaps when all is said and done, we'll see you on the other side. Either way John, find my journals. Tell this story – tell them all my story. Maybe there's something in my words that might be of value someday... you know... like them philosophical fellas, Playdo and Socrateasey."

I stood up and retrieved my coat. Rosco stood and shook my hand, as did the Marshal. I looked them in the eyes, nodded back in the dark to Freddy, glanced down at the sleeping Scotsman, and with a sincerity that pulled tears from my heart to pool in my eyes, I wished them all good luck.

"Carpe Diem," I added, shutting the door behind me as I turned into the wind and, head down, waded through a world of white and made my way to court.

* * *

"All rise. The Right Honourable Judge Francis Henry presiding."

In unison, the sliding of chairs, the shuffling of feet, and the cacophony of collective anticipation vibrate the chilled air inside the courthouse tent. Plumes of condensation fill the air with small clouds from the exhalation of so many gathered in the confines of the canvas. It was full to capacity inside, where the wind was a constant barrage against the fabric of the structure which was to host this days most serious proceedings.

A murder of crows, so the judge appeared, black robes flapping and streaming behind him as he entered the court and took his place on the bench.

"You may be seated," Marshal Morrison instructed all those in attendance.

Freddy had wanted to return to court and redeem himself after yesterday's events, but the symptom's of Millie's chili still more than lingered, and, in truth, as was mentioned during last night's gathering, he had some additional tasks to which to attend while all the eyes of Randy River fixated on the behemoth of canvas that served as a buttress against the pelting snow and steady winter wind.

Murmurs lingered, louder than the judge assessed was needed, so he brought the hammer down.

"Order in the court," Judge Henry said forcefully. "This court is now in session. As a matter of instruction for all in attendance," he paused to glare at the defendant, Rosco Pitt, "I will let it be known that I do not and will not tolerate any such tomfoolery such as what occurred here yesterday. Let the record show a warning has been issued and no further warnings will be given."

He paused again, a lengthy pause as Judge Henry took the time to meet the eyes of almost everyone, finally coming to rest once again on the accused, Rosco Pitt.

The judge looked even more hawkish than the day before, his eyes glared at the defendant as Marshal Morrison read the opening statement on behalf of the court. The Marshal was efficient in his recitation of the charges and the statutes, much to the relief of the gallery who seemed pleased for Freddy's absence, and were eager to get to the meat of the matter.

"Is the state ready to proceed?" the Marshal asked.

"The state is ready." Percy Rawlins, the dreaded Percy Rawlins, as he's known in legal circles, stood and faced the judge and bowed his head as he gave his answer.

Readers of my chronicles may recognize his name, as he played a prominent role in the marathon trial of Davie Crenshaw, the straight-razor rapist who waged a war of atrocities on the Christian settlers of a small outpost in a westerly valley of the Cascades, but that's not the tale being told here today.

Judge Henry turned his eyes to the defendant's table. Barrister Lauchlin McTavish hurried to his feet, as did Rosco. Despite my earlier visit to the jailhouse, both were alert and sharp, clean and crisply dressed.

"Is the defence ready to proceed?"

"Aye. The defence is ready," McTavish replied.

Judge Henry instructed the Marshal to call in the jury. The flap at the back of the large tent was pulled open, and in walked the twelve, shivering, snow-dusted jurors, each one brushing off their coats and placing them over the chairs in the jury box, before sitting and staring at the man who stands accused. From the perspective of an interested spectator, it appeared the minds of the four women and eight men had already been made.

After a few minutes of the judge conferring with the Marshal, Morrison retrieved a stack of papers from the bailiff's table and handing them to the bench, Judge Henry announced the prosecution would present its case first, followed by the defence and ending with the closing arguments. Judge Henry then instructed the jury with a rambling speech that dove deep and detailed what they should consider as evidence, and what they should not consider as evidence.

"I object, your honour," Rosco raised his hand.

Judge Henry looked down at the defence, his glasses slipping to the end of his nose.

"Mr. McTavish, please inform your client that he can not make objections in this court when he has legal representation. That sir is your job. And, before you go and start objecting, understand: you can not object to a judge's jury instructions. That would be dealt with after the trial in what we legal-types commonly call the appeals process. Mr. Rawlins," Judge Henry spun to face Percy, who was quick to remove the smirk from his face. "You may call your first witness."

"Thank you, your Honour. The State calls Theodore Trowley."

Murmurs. They flew around the courtroom. A low rumble of collective whispers blending with the sporadic woosh of the canvas walls. Their murmurs dissolved as all eyes followed Ted, who stood from the back and made his way slowly up the centre isle to the witness box, the wind beating the canvas, whistling a mournful wail.

His face was drawn and pale, eyes sunk deep beneath his black, bushy brows. Faded bruises yellowed on his forehead and beneath one eye. He walked with a stutter, a wounded gait. He did not meet the eyes of the accused as he made his way, but he did spare a wave for his mother, the Widow Trowley, the woman both a victim, and an object of great affection in the case to be heard today.

Ted's wave was a sheepish gesture quickly withdrawn when no reciprocation was offered. In the moment, he was a sad tragedy of a man, and sympathies hung heavy in the air. His hand visibly shook as he placed it on the Bible and stated his name: "Theodore Edward Trowley," swearing to tell the truth, the whole truth and nothing but the truth.

"I object your Honour," again Rosco raised his hand.

The gallery chuckled. Judge Henry stabbed his eyes at Rosco, but addressed his counsel with his words. "Please tell your client the defence can not object to a witness being sworn in."

"Aye your honour," McTavish remained seated, arms folded, and visibly yawned as he replied.

Judge Henry stared at the bristly Scotsman, gavel hovering for just a moment, then dismissed his agitation with the defence and turned back to Percy Rawlins. "You may proceed good sir."

"Yes. Thank you again your honour," Percy replied, not looking at the judge, but thoughtfully at the witness, hands palmed together beneath his chin, fingers triangled in prayer. His eyes glistened pencil black, the eyes of a rodent it has been said, and they shimmered now as he slowly approached Theodore Trowley, finally asking his first question, which turned out not to be a question.

"Good morning Theodore. I hope you are doing well."

"Yes sir. I am." Theodore nodded, he kept his head bowed. His black hair was slicked back wet and shiny. The fading bruise on his forehead drew the eye.

"You've been through quite a lot as of late, haven't you Teddy? May I call you Teddy?"

Ted raised his eyes, glanced furtively at the accused, then smiled at Percy Rawlins. "Yes. Yes I have. It's been a challenging time." He nodded.

Rawlins placed his hands on his hips and spun to face the jury. Even straight on the man's face was all angles: a jagged nose badly bumped with a jaw that protruded much further then a face requires; and cheek bones far too high and ghastly in their prominence – like a skeleton with a living face. His eyes were dark, so dark to seem void of life and colour. Percy's pupils were pencil points: tiny, black and piercing. His hair was thin and wispy white, exposing a startling scalp, one he had no fear of losing if he were to ever encounter the "savages," or any other scoundrels who were fond of hanging such keepsakes. Percy kept his eyes on the jury, smiling at each and every one, as he posed his next question to the witness.

"Teddy, tell us about the day you encountered the accused

Rosco Pitt. In your words, tell our friends here in the jury, what happened that day?"

Teddy's response was lengthy. Between the stutters and stops and the pauses and mumbles, before the "can't quite remembers" and after the "now, I aint all that certain," his version of the day's events were finally unwound and uninterrupted by any objections from the defence.

Ted said he and Trevor had left Plitter-Plop Crick early that morning, as they'd set fresh traps a day's prior and were hoping for a late season rabbit or two. Though he "couldn't be certain," Ted believed he and Trevor were on the northwest trail on the far side of Bailey's Pass, when the accused charged out from the trees "with murderous, thieving intentions."

In summary, the accused, Rosco Pitt, "attacked" poor Trevor without cause, shooting him in the knee and wounding his brother badly – a wound that proved fatal, despite the hurried race back to his mother's shack, and the medical treatment he received to fight "a fection," Ted said, a fever that had raged and led to the young man's death.

Both the judge and the prosecution paused for a moment, glancing at the table of the defence, where McTavish still looked bored and Rosco just stared at the squirming Ted on the witness stand, but no objections were raised, much to their surprise.

"And now I know this might be difficult Teddy, but after it was determined that Trevor had succumb to his wounds, what did Mr. Pitt do then?" Percival had found a perch. He moved back to the prosecutor's table and rested his rear on the edge, leaning back and relaxed, awaiting Teddy's response.

Below is the exact transcription of Teddy's account of the murder of Casper Trowley, and the kidnapping of his mother, the Widow Marjorie Trowley:

"I woke up the next morning, and after I retrieved more bark of the willow, as my Ma had asked, I went into the barn, where Trevor convalesced, and…I, I discover him dead."

The witness sobs. Muffled crying and deep breaths.

"I hurried in to tell Ma and saw that scoundrel camping down by the Widow's Wailing Willow, camping on our land with out our permission. Well, after seeing what he'd done to Trevor I got scared, I will admit, so I hopped on my horse and rode out fast to go and fetch my Uncle Casper. See, I figured being a former Pinkerton and all, Uncle Casper would be better to deal with a murderous scum like Rosco Pitt then I ever would be.

T'werent gone all that long and when we got back we hurried first into the shack to make sure Ma was all right. Well no sooner did Casper walk through the door when that bastard back shoots him, pistol whips me to the floor, snatches my Ma and drags her out. By the time I got off the floor, Casper was dead and I saw Ma on his horse, Jax, being pulled behind Rosco and that crazed Appaloosa that he rides. Then I rode into town as fast as I could and told the deputy what happened and he rushed off to tell Mr. Bonner. He and my uncle were good friends. And that's about it. The days since have been a might blurry, I must confess."

Percy Rawlins remained watching the jury. He studied them as they absorbed the testimony of Theodore Trowley then simply said, without turning to face him, "Thank you Teddy. I have no further questions, your Honour." A smile played on the corners of his mouth.

The gallery's murmurs again rose to the point where the rumbles inspired the judge's gavel, which he swiftly brought down with force.

"Order! Order in the court. Another outburst like that and I will have the Marshal clear the court. Mr. McTavish," he said, turning to the Scotsman after he admonished the gallery, "you may cross examine the witness."

"Thank you, your Honour," McTavish said, staring intently at Teddy who started to squirm like his bladder was busting.

"Are you alright, Mr. Trowley?" McTavish asked with much sincerity, as he approached the witness box. "Do you need a wee break? Should I request that the judge fetch you a chamber pot? You're wiggling aboot like a boy in need of a piss."

Laughter filled the courtroom. McTavish turned to the gallery smiling, and bowing to his appreciative audience. Judge Henry was not amused. The gavel came down. McTavish was warned. "Witness intimidation will not be tolerated, Mr. McTavish," scorned the judge.

"I apologize, your Honour. And I apologize to you, Teddy. I was wrong to mock the obvious imposition, which is placed on you, due to your evident incontinence." McTavish paused, half turning to the gallery, but no applause was forthcoming. Rosco, on the other hand, continued to split a gut seated at the table for the defence.

And… the gavel came down.

"I'd like to go back to the beginning of your testimony Ted. If that would be all right?" McTavish began pacing the courtroom, studying the floor as he went back in his testimony to the morning of the day. He did not wait for Ted to give his consent.

"You stated you and Trevor, 12-Shot Trevor, as he was known, set out early that morning to check your traps. You mentioned Bailey's Pass as your approximate location. Is that correct?"

"Yes. Yes sir," Ted replied.

"Where is that pass that you mentioned? I mean, in terms of how many miles from your Ma's shack and in relation to say, here, Randy River proper? I'm just not too familiar with the geography in and aroon these parts, so enlighten me if you could."

"Um, well, I couldn't be precise in my reply… I'm really not sure how far that might be… but its quite the jaunt," Ted said.

"Ah. Understood, understood. Well, what time did you leave Plitter-Plop Crick and at approximately what time did you arrive at your trap lines?"

"Again, I'm sorry Mr. McTavish but I'm not sure what time we arrived, but it was early when we left my Ma's cabin."

"Early. I see," McTavish had stopped his pacing and now stood still, glaring at Ted. "How early, Mr. Trowley? Surely you have some idea when you and your brother departed. Was the sun up? How high in the sky? Was it still dark? Did you rise with the rooster or did you just jump out of bed and declare it was early?"

"Objection, your Honour. He's badgering the witness." Percy

stood in protest.

"Sustained. Mr. McTavish, you have established the witness's uncertainty to the precise time of the occurrence. Please, move on in your questioning."

"Yes your Honour," McTavish replied, turning quickly back to Ted. "So just to be clear," he dashed a furtive glance at the judge, "you have no idea as to the times you departed or arrived at…where was it again," he flipped through his notes, "ah, yes, Bailey's Pass?"

"No sir." Ted replied, starting to squirm again.

McTavish moved slowly closer to Ted on the stand. Jumping forward in the testimony, he asked Ted to describe the attack again, the gunfight that occurred between "yourselves and Mr. Pitt? You were scant on some details in your initial testimony."

Ted looked around the room, everywhere but at the defendant's table, where sat the man he claimed committed this unprovoked attack.

"He came charging, that man Pitt. Charging right out of the trees, guns blazing hitting everywhere and everything. I was lucky to duck and dodge but Trevor took a shot to the knee and fell to the ground. Course, I jumped off my horse to tend to my kin, what with him bleeding and all, and Rosco Pitt cracked them reigns on his horse's flank and charged off through the trees. Left poor Trevor dying. Murdering scum."

"Your Honour!" McTavish objected.

"Mr. Trowley, please refrain from defamatory comments."

"Yes sir."

"So," McTavish ploughed ahead with his questioning, slowing his pace as he surmised Teddy's situation. "there you are, alone with a wounded brother, at Bailey's Pass, a fair jaunt, as you've so stated. Is that correct?"

"Yes."

"In the name of the wee man! You must have been distraught. Your brother lay their bleeding. There's a madman in the woods and he could come back at any moment. You can't let your brother die, you had to do everything you did to get him home.

And you did it! You got your brother home, didn't you Ted?"

A quiet clearing of the throat put a stop to Ted's reply. Percy Rawlins appeared standing, fingers splayed on the prosecutor's table. "Objection your Honour. No relevance to the case being tried, and simply considering the known facts of present day that question has been answered."

"Sustained." Judge Henry ruled instantly asking no questions of the defence.

McTavish almost spun where he stood in frustration, his hands noticeably clenched into fists. Someone in the gallery yelled, "Let him answer!" and a few other voices joined them. The judge brought the gavel down, repeatedly, but the chants did not subside:

"Let him Answer!" The voices of many. The gallery spoke. Rosco stood and turned to face them. His smile was broad and his eyes appeared moist. Judge Henry was frozen, apparently in shock. Percy observed the crowd in wonder. McTavish stood quietly, his hands clasped in front, staring at the judge.

Finally, after repeated pounds of the gavel, "order in the court!" became "enough, enough! Marshal Morrison, please clear the court for a fifteen-minute recess!"

"All rise," Morrison called out over the chorus of voices. "Fifteen-minute recess." Judge Henry flew from the bench and out the tent's flap.

"Let him answer! Let him answer!" the crowd chased out the murder of crows.

* * *

Fifteen minutes quickly became thirty. Thankfully, the wind had subsided and the heavy fall of snow had become but a few fluttering flakes.

The day was growing warmer and the blast of winter turned to mush as the feet of the many had trampled many paths into and around the courthouse tent.

I flee the mob who have stepped out for fresh air during the brief recess. Their voices filled the morning as those who were inside shared the events with those who were not.

As I gazed down the street of the town, rutted and muddy as the wheels of wagons had furrowed the damp ground to blend with the snow, creating a sloppy, brown path of slush, I notice a man moving behind the mercantile at the very end of Randy River proper.

I knew immediately Freddy was completing one of the two tasks Rosco had given him, while all attentions were fixed to the proceedings in the court. The mob behind me does not notice. They are too busy, deep in discussions, focused on debates. The mob, so far, had been thoroughly entertained.

Finally, the tent flaps were flung open and we're ushered back inside. Marshal Morrison caught my eye as I entered and I nodded, tapping the tip of my finger against my chin. The Marshal tapped a finger against the brim of his white, straw hat and continued his bailiff duties. I moved back to my original chair.

"All rise. This court will now reconvene. Judge Francis Henry presiding." Again the crows entered. "You may be seated," the Marshal concluded.

After Ted was sworn in again, the judge instructed McTavish to resume his questioning. "Tread carefully," he warned.

"I'm sure you'll let me know," McTavish stated quickly, dismissively, not even sparing a glance for the bench, instead, he moved directly to the witness.

"Hello again Ted." McTavish smiled as he approached the stand. "Where did I leave off? Nope... sorry, don't tell me...oh yes. How did you get Trevor home?"

Percy shot up from his chair. His mouth opened then closed abruptly as the judge gave the wide-eyes and shook his head quick.

McTavish stared at Ted. The silence in the court was complete and only the rhythmic rustle of air against canvas counted the seconds that passed. Ted began to squirm, twisting in his chair, his face growing flush. His eyes darted furtively again, but not at the defendant as one might expect, but back in the gallery to the face of Neville Bonner.

"Your Honour, please instruct the witness to answer the question," McTavish had grown impatient. The judge said nothing and stared at McTavish, who forwent the judge's instructions he'd requested, and bellowed the question again.

"How did you get your brother home, across miles of wild country, Ted? It's thirty miles to Bailey's Pass Ted. Thirty miles of thick forest and hills and valleys. Answer the question!"

He moved closer to the stand and stared hard into Ted's blinking, moistening eyes. Leaning in, McTavish shouted, "How did you get him home Ted!"

The rustle of canvas and utter silence.

Suddenly Ted's dam broke. "All right!" he blurted, a defeated whimper softly signalled his surrender. "I didn't get him home…"

His eyes looked up at McTavish, glistening with shame. Ted sniffled and wiped his sleeve across his nose, lowered his eyes once again and continued.

"Pitt built the sling to drag behind the horse and Pitt applied the turny-cat for his wounded knee. I don't know how to do any of that stuff." His hands flew to his face and tears streamed down between his fingers.

"He didn't just flat out attack us." Ted continued, shaking his head, eyes squeezed shut. "It was Trevor's idea to rob him. He pointed one of his pistols at Pitt's back…" his voice dropped to almost a whisper, "That's why Pitt shot him.

"Ma was…she was grateful to Pitt for gettin her boy home. We asked him to stay if he needed. Ma even fed him breakfast."

McTavish turned to look at Rosco and smile. Though I could only see the back of his head I knew that Rosco smiled back. Percy, the dreaded Percy Rawlins, dropped his hands to his head and buried his face. Judge Francis Henry slumped back in his chair. The gallery remained quiet, letting Ted's words sink in.

"Right then." McTavish wasn't finished yet. "Back to your

Uncle Casper. Mr. Pitt didn't back shoot him, like you testified, did he Ted?"

He shook his head vigorously, his words were sobs with recognizable sounds.

"No sir. It was a duel fair-and-square. That man is fast. Pitt dropped him before my uncle could finish twitching a finger... I'm sorry... I'm sorry Mr. Pitt." For the first time Ted raised his eyes to look at Rosco and the tears flowed freely.

"It's all right Ted," some said they heard Rosco reply. "I understand, Teddy," was plainly heard by all.

McTavish walked to stand beside Ted, and placed an empathetic hand on his quivering shoulder. He stared out at the gallery and declared, "Ted, I only have one more question for you, and I want you to look at your mother when I ask it. Do you understand me Ted?"

"Yes... I do... I understand."

Ted raised his eyes to look back in the gallery at the hooded, bowed head of his mother. Again, as she'd done the day before, she had seated herself between Neville, who scowled and looked down-right droop-faced, and Millie, who, as always, shimmered like a frosty morning on a sun-filled day. Marjorie did not raise her eyes to meet her son's gaze, but all other eyes darted wildly from mother to son and back again.

"Did Rosco Pitt kidnap and rape your mother, Ted?"

This time Ted did not hesitate. He choked back his tears and as McTavish had requested, looked straight at his mother.

"No."

The gallery erupted. The gavel pounded. The court became chaos.

"No!" Teddy shouted, but the crowd grew louder and drowned out the words that followed, but from this reporters vantage point, his lips seemed to say, "It was Neville!" and the finger he pointed seemed to confirm that theory.

"I have no further questions. Your Honour!" McTavish shouted.

The court recessed for an additional fifteen minutes.

✽ ✽ ✽

Again the mob. Again fifteen minutes became thirty. Again I move away from the chorus of the crowd who gather. I move into a world where steam rises from the slush and the sky hangs low and glides overhead, dull, grey and damp.

I look across the street and see God's high tower is masked in mist, engulfed in the clouds that have rolled down from the mountains. I glance down the rutted road of Randy River proper but no figure moves from behind the mercantile. The movement appears beside the jailhouse where Reggie Burell is back to his task, preparing to erect the large centre-beam to span the top of the gallows. The wood glistens white and wet.

I approach Reggie. He sees me coming and passes a brush to another, who continues to wipe wet snow off of the squared length of oak. Other men make busy threading rope through a system of pullies, a simple but effective rigging to hoist the beam high to the appropriate height.

"Hello there Mr. Burrel," I greet him. He walks towards me, or sludges his way through the slush, and shakes my hand. His shake is firm and natural, but his eyes go slitted, whispering suspicion.

"Mr. John Maximillian," he said. "Your reputation proceeds you. Please, call me Reggie."

We exchanged small words about the weather. Reggie was thankful the wind had died and though heavy with moisture, the air was still, motioning to the cross-beam around which the men now fastened the ropes.

"Well," I said, turning slightly to watch the men do their work, "I hope the task goes as planned, now that the wind has settled. That cross-beam has a key role to play in this days events."

Reggie observed me for a moment, tilting his head, his eyes finding mine. "Between you, me, and that crazy Appaloosa running circles over yonder, this beam was born to hold in and of itself and will have no say in any case, as to the completion 'as planned,' as you say Mr. Maximillian. No sir, the accountability of any construction, if and when I am involved, directly and solely rests on my shoulders and I can assure you sir, the gallows will stand as planned, and the hanging will go, 'as planned.'"

I tapped my finger on my chin. Reggie did the same to the brim of his hat. We parted ways and I start back to the courthouse tent, where the flaps have been pulled and the mob files in. The Marshal watches me enter. We tap our fingers.

* * *

The gallery rises, the judge hurries in, the jury fills the box and the trial resumes.

"May we approach the bench, your Honour." McTavish stands to make his request. Rosco remains seated. Judge Henry nods and Percy joins the two men in a whispered gathering at the bench, but McTavish's whispers are frantic, and find the ears of many.

"But your Honour, based on the perjured testimony alone, you must find solid groons for dismissal!"

And...the gavel came down.

"The jury will strike that comment from your memories." Judge Henry turned to Percy. "You may call your next witness."

What followed was a parade of witnesses of various ages and statures, but what they were a witness to was a bit muddled in this writer's mind: a peach pie stolen from a window sill; a mysterious man eyeing some chickens; a fast-moving horse racing through the trees, too fast to see the rider, but a Union hat, at least, to be certain.

Then came Marcel LaFontaine, he rendered fat, sold the soap, and lived just outside of Randy River proper in a "box of sticks" of his own. His eyes were a permanent pink, reddened by the continuous exposure to the lye required for his craft. He claimed, the man, none other than Rosco Pitt, barely avoided "an ass full of buckshot," when Marcel had spied him "defecating in my garden!" He was "pawzo-tivly, abso-lutely certain the man I shot at was that man right there." Marcel pointed at Rosco, just to be clear.

"When was this, Mr. LaFontaine?" McTavish asked.

"It was the day before poor Trevor got shot. I remembers it clearly," Marcel declared.

"Well now Mr. LaFontaine, do you think, perhaps, your testimony might get a wee bit cloudy if it is known, for a fact, that on that day in question, Mr. Pitt was no where near Randy River. On that day, Mr. Pitt wawsny even in the Valley of Many Rivers. What if I was to tell you, Mr. LaFontaine, that a witness places Mr. Pitt still on the hem of MissT's skirt – um, excuse me – I mean still in the high country. What would you say to that, Mr. LaFontaine?"

"I'd say that witness is a liar," Marcel replied, unperturbed by McTavish's assertion.

McTavish tensed. His back stiffened and his shoulders rose. He turned and faced the gallery, his anger surging, reddening his already ruddy complexion.

"Your Honour, let the record show that this witness, like the witness previous, has perjured himself. I, Laughlin McTavish was the man who was with the accused on the day before the shooting of Trevor Trowley, and I can attest to the fact that the accused was in no proximity to Mr. LaFontaine's garden."

He spun quickly and moved toward Marcel. "I am that witness," he uttered a low growl, "and I am no liar. I have no further questions for this man, your Honour." He spat the last with venom.

"Your Honour. I object." Percy rose slowly. "The attorney for the defence is testifying now… really your Honour?"

"Objection sustained," Judge Henry nodded, adding, "And the record will reflect no such thing, Mr. McTavish. Sit down.

"You may call your next witness, Mr. Rawlins."

"Thank you, your Honour. The prosecution calls Mr. Neville Bonner to the stand."

Silence fell and eyes turned to watch the man rise, smiling and nodding to all. Bonner made his way to the witness stand casually strolling up the middle aisle of the courtroom. As he smiled and nodded and met the eyes of the many, some nodded signs of support while other people visibly lowered their heads and would not hold his gaze for long.

He posed a formidable figure with his long grey cloak and crisp, black suit of clothes. His hair was slicked back and fell to a row of bending curls across the collar of his shimmering, white shirt.

"Thank you, Mr. Bonner, for taking the time today to lend your testimony to this court as we pursue justice in this tragic case of savagery and murder. My questions sir will be brief. And," Percy shot a glance at the defence table, "hopefully the counsel for the defence will grant you the same respect, given your important stature in this, our cherished community."

"Well thank you Mr. Rawlins. It is my only hope that my testimony will prove forthright and imperative to our pursuit of justice." Neville's southern drawl had suddenly become thicker. His eyes narrowed as he spoke, staring hard at the accused.

"Mr. Bonner, please tell the court how you came to encounter the defendant, and, if you could good sir, details surrounding the events that preceded the terrible assault on Randy River."

"Yes. Well, of course, on the day of, word of the shooting of both Trevor and Casper Trowley travelled fast, and fell to my ears at the breakfast table. I was aghast, to say the least. I immediately sent a wire to the U.S. Marshal's office and arranged to have watches set in and around Randy River and dispatched men to set pickets in the trails and forests to the north, south and the east.

"The day had passed without incident, though I know both Millie and I were both distraught and greatly concerned for the welfare of our friend the Widow Marjorie Trowley, what with being in the hands of a scoundrel and a murderer. Despite the burden of worried minds, that next evening came the Harvest dance. Millie and I had planned to attend and, as is the way here in Randy River, keep on carrying on despite the previous day's tragic events. I had returned home to fetch Millie for the dance, and that's when I discovered this man sitting in my parlour, smoking my cigars and drinking my brandy. Snug as a bug in a rug, he was." Neville graced Rosco with a look of disdain.

"So, you arrived home to find the defendant in your parlour?" Percy turned wide-eyed to the jury. "Whatever did you do, Mr. Bonner?"

"The ladies, neither Millie nor Marjorie would speak. I could see the fear on their faces and their cries for help in their moistened, doe-like eyes. It was apparent to me that Marjorie had suffered greatly. I clearly saw the bruising and I knew the woman had been beaten badly. But I remained calm, concluding that would be the best course given the danger of the situation. I welcomed the man into my house. I feigned empathy for the man's plight and when I saw he had calmed himself and appeared at ease, giving him a sense of control, as I did, I conspired with Millie to get poor Marjorie away from him. It was my hope, in her absence and with both Marjorie and my sister out of danger, that I would then be able to subdue this man."

"Brave, Mr. Bonner, very brave indeed!" Percy fawned over Neville's self-proclaimed heroics, inserting a dramatic pause and a wide-eyed expression for the gallery, before continuing on with his questioning. "But it didn't quite work out that way. Did it Mr. Bonner?"

"No. No it did not." Neville continued his testimony. "We talked long into the night, as I recall. I probed for a path to end it all peacefully. I offered the man money. I offered him safe passage out of the county. As we continued our discussion the man partook of my brandy in excess. Suddenly he began to rage, realizing much time had passed since Marjorie and Millie had left the parlour. He demanded the woman be returned to his side. I tried to stall the man's anger, soothing him with calming words but he would have none of it. It was then the man assaulted me. He took me by complete surprise and I greatly regret my naivety, letting down my guard as I did." Neville looked down, he sobbed slightly, his hands going to his face as he cried softly, though no tears pooled in his eyes. The man's sorrow was as dry as a drought.

"The next thing I knew I came-to on the floor of the parlour. The sun was up and from upstairs I heard the floor settle as heavy steps crossed in my room. The man, I knew, had found my Gatling gun.

"I was groggy. The world was spinning and I could feel blood dried and cracking that had flowed from my broken nose. I hurried out into the street, desperately seeking assistance."

Neville paused again, hands going to his face and soft sobbing interrupting his words. Percy glanced at the jury, then softly consoled Neville, who finally raised his dry eyes.

"I heard the sound of breaking glass. I knew… I knew what this scoundrel was going to do next and I saw the church letting out and the men approaching me on the street and I tried to warn them off but I was too late. The bastard opened up on them. He raked the street with that gun and I made a dash behind the mercantile but the men on the street were caught unawares and I watched him – that man right there – Rosco Pitt – cut them down to pieces with that devastating weapon."

Percy let the silence linger. He moved to the jury and standing directly before them he repeated Neville's final words: "cut them down to pieces… I have no further questions, your Honour."

"Thank you Mr. Rawlins," Judge Henry said, turning to Neville. "If you could continue to make yourself available Mr. Bonner, the court will call a brief recess prior to the start of the cross examination." He pulled out a pocket watch from beneath his black robe. "We will break for lunch. A 30-minute recess – court will reconvene at 1 p.m." The gavel came down.

"All rise."

※ ※ ※

The day was growing long. Outside the court the crowd

lingered, their conversations melding into each other creating an apprehensive hum in the air. I moved away once again from the mob, my feet sucked deep by the mud that had emerged from beneath the melted snow.

Across the way the circus appeared to be packing up. Figures could be seen hitching horses to wagons and collecting their camp in preparation of departure. I saw no more a lonely clown standing forlorn by the fire.

A sudden ruckus across the street drew attention. Millie Bonner appeared in hot pursuit of the Widow Trowley, who plowed the mud as she made her way down the street to slip inside the livery. Mille remained on the street, appearing stunned and dumbfounded.

"Excuse me Miss Millie," she turned to my approach. "Is everything all right? Is the Widow okay?" I nodded toward the stable.

"She... she said she was leaving. She just got up and said she was leaving! Mr. Maximillian, please," she continued, eyes wide and pleading, "please speak to her. She needs to testify. This whole affair has been very trying for her, I know, but Neville will be furious if she doesn't testify, Mr. Maximillian."

I calmed her. I told her not to fret, as women sometimes do, and I would see to the Widow Trowley.

"Rest your mind, ma'am. I will go and speak with her. Calm yourself pretty lady. Get yourself out of this mud and leave the widow to me." I placed a gentle hand on her shoulder and offered an assuring glance.

"Thank you Mr. Maximillian," Millie said, sparing one last look at the livery stable. "Your are a gentleman in a place where such chivalry is dead. Thank you kind sir." She turned and trudged through the mud as she made her way back to the court.

At first the stable was dark, but I heard her right away. As my eyes adjusted to the dim light of the livery, I saw her emerge, leading Jax to the back double-doors of the stable. She saw me, my silhouette I imagine, standing still in the dull light streaming in from the street. I saw her hand move to the brim of her hat, and touched my finger to my chin in return.

Marjorie opened wide the doors of the stable. She'd ripped off her court-day attire and beneath was dressed ready to ride, a heavied holster hanging ominous from her side.

She moved with grace as she mounted the magnificent Jax, brewed black and rumbling, the beast scuffed the threshold, eager for the charge. In a "click" the stallion bolted, across the muddied corral and over the back fence. A whistle pierced the air and I watched, an easy grin creasing my face, as Mr. Andrews appeared and fell in at a gallop beside them. Due west they raced, to the tree line.

Back out front the mob had thinned, spreading out and moving up and down the muddied road. Some admired the gallows, commenting on the whiteness of the oak and the loft of the centre-beam. While others, taking full advantage of the 30-minute lunch break, had found their wagons around the church a suitable place to eat their sandwiches, drink their coffees, and make their predictions. Small fires hosted circles of small groups, and the chatter was a mix of prophecy and conjecture, at best.

I moved down the street, towards the wagon with the gun, its canvas cover damp and lifeless. As I approach I hear the snicker and then the fart. Inside there sits a man, his name is William.

"But if your gonna include my likeness in one of them thar chronicles, Mr. Max," he said with a grin, "I'd be appreciative if you would call me Wildman Willy Barber, son of a preacher and a Memphis whore." He barked a quick, short laugh. "Imagine that!"

The man stretched his full frame from one side of the wagon to the other, bringing into question the loft of his height had he been standing. His boots were crossed, toes stretching the canvas, and his hands were folded behind his head, stretching the canvas on the other side. Behind and beyond Wildman Willy, stood the ominous golden gleam of the Gatling gun, its lethal end fixed on the jailhouse door. Willy noticed my admiring of the gun.

"She's a beaut aint she?" he said, leaning slightly to his left and farting yet again.

He laughed. "There's more than that gun in here that's lethal at the moment. Apologies Mr. Maximillian. Had me some of Millie's chili last night and, well, didn't quite sit right with the boys, my selves included." He smiled, sitting up and straightening his back. "What's can I do you for today's, Mr. Maximillian?"

"Well," I said, scratching my head. "I lost my hat this morning and thought I'd take this break in the trial to see if I could retrieve it, Willy. You didn't happen to see a dark, grey Derby with a black band go flying by earlier, did you?"

I reached into my coat as I spoke and pulled out a pouch of pre-rolled tobacco, courtesy of Freddy, and offered one to Willy, who smiled, nodded, and proceeded to climb out of the wagon. It was then that Freddy himself stepped out from the side of the wagon and promptly, quietly and discreetly dispatched of Wildman Willy.

Though I did not witness the method of Freddy's assault, the blood-dipped blade he dropped from his hand told enough of the tale.

Freddy exchanged his garments for Willy's, and surprisingly, they were a rather good fit. Together we tossed Willy's limp body into the wagon and Freddy climbed in behind him. He spared me a glance, touched the brim of his hat, then settled in at the grips of the golden gun. My finger went to my chin.

I checked my watch as I moved across the street. The 30-minute recess was nearing its end but such time restraints were inconsequential at this juncture. "Once set in motion, what will be will be..." Rosco had said.

At the jailhouse door I pause. People are beginning to move back towards the court. Across the street Willy's hat sits on Freddy's head behind the six barrels of the gun, a shadow.

No one pays attention as I open the door and enter the jailhouse. Inside I move quickly. My mind doesn't race. It doesn't hurry ahead in panic, but quietly goes about the task at hand.

I see Rosco's Sharps, leaning and gleaming inside the glass gun case, boxes of shells stacked neatly beside the stock. Once retrieved, I move back outside, head down, trudging through the mud, I enter the chapel.

'This is the house of God.'

The thought looms large in my mind in capital letters. I move to a door, barely visible in the dark shadows of the pulpit. It opens with a whisper and I slip inside to climb the spiral stairs.

'This is God's high tower.'

The thought whispers in my mind as I clamber up into the steeple, lean the gun, and stack the ammunition on the floor beside it. I peek out from the window in God's high tower. Below the crowd has gathered, awaiting for court to reconvene. The gallows gleam white and beyond is the expanse east: an open field; a tree line; and beyond winds the Randy River. Mist rises where the river runs hidden by the trees. I look back at the rifle and shudder.

I get back to the tent just in time. The last one to enter, I touch my chin for the Marshal, who proceeds to touch the brim of his hat. I take my seat.

Murmurs. Gavel. Silence.

"Court is now in session," the Marshal announced.

"Um… Mr. Pitt, where is your counsel?"

Judge Henry had noticed but no one else had, until now. The gallery took to gossip and the murmurs rose again. McTavish was not seated at the defence table. Eyes darted around the courtroom. McTavish was no where to be found. Rosco stood up slowly and cleared his throat.

"Your Honour, may I approach the bench?"

"Your Honour, I object!" Percy raised his grievance. "This is highly unusual."

"Unusual. Yes, but over-ruled," Judge Henry nodded at Rosco. "Mr. Pitt, you may approach."

The murmurs drowned out the whispers so what was said is not known. They conferenced for several minutes, the gallery growing restless. Finally the gathering dispersed and all parties assumed their previous positions.

The gavel came down. "It would appear the attorney for the defence has taken ill," Judge Henry announced.

"On account of Millie's chili." Rosco made that fact apparent, turning to face the gallery as he said it with the most genuine look of concern that one could imagine. Laugher erupted and again the judge brought the gavel down.

"Yes." The judge begrudgingly acknowledged, "Millie's chili."

Millie appeared beaming with pride, as her part was now entered into record.

"Mr. Pitt, in his own defence I might add," the judge made it clear, "you may proceed."

"Thank you, your Honour." Rosco bowed deeply to the judge, then turned and did the same to the gallery. Chuckles threatened and the judge sounded the gavel. Only once was sufficient.

Rosco glared at Neville, who had been sitting on the witness stand fully entertained by the events unfolding before him. Finally, after a long staring match that saw the witness blink first, "The defence has no questions for this witness," Rosco spat with disdain.

At that moment, if I'd had a pin I would have dropped it, for the conditions were perfect to test that adage.

Neville's eyes became slitted. His mouth formed a grim line across his pointed face. Percy side-eyed Rosco, a cautious, wavering smile quivering on his lips.

"Mr. Pitt. Though I'm hesitant to do so, I would advise you to allow me to call a recess until such a time as your counsel can be located." Judge Henry offered his advice but Rosco merely shook his head.

"No questions your Honour. No recess your Honour. May we please proceed?"

"Very well," Judge Henry paused for another second, studying the defendant. "Mr. Bonner, you may step down. Mr. Rawlins, you may call your next witness."

"Thank you, your Honour. The State calls the Widow Marjorie Trowley."

Gradually, as it became apparent to all that the Widow Trowley was also not answering the call, that the Widow Trowley was no longer in court, not even the wrath of Judge Henry could quell the eruption.

Eyes went to Millie. She fluttered and flailed, oh goodness oh my, then bathed in the attention.

Marjorie was quite distraught at the testimony of her brother, she declared, shimmering her eyes and tilting her head. "My poor, dear Marjorie. She fled from me. I tried to stop her, but she was inconsolable," she proclaimed loudly, adding, much to my dismay, "Mr. Maximillian was there. Tell them good sir, how you aided my plight."

She pouted at me, flashing those emerald eyes. I must admit I was taken, but the questioning mob shook me from my trance.

"Yes," I told them, but my pursuit of the widow into the livery proved futile. "I did not see her inside, and hurried back to court," I explained.

Judge Henry bellowed, tossing his gavel aside. "Order in the court! Order! Order! God damn it shut your cake-holes! All of you! Order in the court!"

Finally, with an exasperated nod from the Judge, Marshal Morrison pulled his pistol and fired one report through the canvas ceiling above. He stood there, still holding his gun in the air, smoke drifting from the barrel, and when he was certain he had everyone's full attention, he holstered his weapon, quietly smiled at all the faces and said, "Please folks, order in the court." The gallery complied.

"Thank you, Marshal Morrison." Judge Henry's face wrinkled with questions as he turned to address Percy.

"It appears your witness is not present in court Mr. Rawlins. What do you propose?" He turned and glanced at Rosco, sitting back calmly in his chair, boots crossed beneath the table, hands twiddling thumbs looking patiently at the judge.

"I have no objections, your Honour," Rosco said, as if anticipating an unspoken question.

Percy requested to approach the bench. The judge allowed

it, and Rosco shuffled to join them, shackled and cuffed. After a few moments of straining ears and unheard whispers, Percy announced the State would forgo the witness, "for the sake of expediency, and as we are quite certain we have proven our case."

"Your Honour, I object!" Rosco stood up quickly, tilting dangerously in his shackles but finding finger-tip purchase on the desk.

Judge Henry looked down his nose, his eyes piercing and cold. "Mr. Pitt," exasperation hung on his words. "We just conferred on the matter. What... no wait, strike that." Judge Henry sat taller and straighter in his chair. "Objection over-ruled. Sit down now Mr. Pitt.

"Very well then Mr. Rawlins. Closing arguments?"

Percy turned and looked long and hard at the jury. Again, he side-eyed Rosco and grinned. "As I said, your Honour, we feel the State has proven its case. The State rests."

Gasps from the gallery rose and fell. Then stood Rosco.

"The defence rests, your Honour." Rosco bowed again to the judge; bowed again to the jury, then added, "Although, your Honour, there is something I would like to say, on a personal note, if I may, your worship?"

"You may not," the Judge denied Rosco's request. "Ladies and gentlemen of the jury." He spun on the bench to look at the twelve, "Do you require an allotment of time to reach a verdict?"

The foreman rose. He was a slight man of an average sight, just one of many who reside in the realm that is Randy River, a jury of his peers, they said.

"We do not, your honour. We are prepared to render our verdict immediately."

Despite himself, for though the foreman of the jury was fair in his tone, the glancing smile that played on his lips told a tale and yet gave nothing as to how the tale ends.

The walls of the tent billowed by the massive gasp that ascended from the gallery. The scene became a tableau of justice, delivered as such in the wilds of the West, a courthouse scene with chaos erupting, finger pointing and mouths wide shouting, all frozen in frame.

"What do you say?" the judge asks, so slowly it seems to be not real.

"The jury finds the defendant guilty on all counts but one, your Honour. On the charge of rape and battery, we find the defendant not guilty, your Honour."

The chaos ensued. I looked to one face, and he looked back. Rosco smiled. Even as the judge pounded the gavel, he smiled. When some in the gallery began to throw refuse, he smiled. Though he heard the scorn and the hiss of the community at large, he smiled. There were those voices who blessed the now convicted man. Their were words clearly heard:

"God bless you, Rosco Pitt," and "God speed, Rosco Pitt."

Even when the ruckus died down and the gavel ceased to pound and the people found their chairs, Rosco remained standing, facing them, still smiling.

It was Millie who stood back up, despite Neville's failed and concealed attempt to silence her. It was Millie who stood up when all else were quiet. She did not look at the convicted man, though she spared him a glance as she departed, but she looked to the gallery at large, tilted her head in the way that she does, and said, "God forgive us for what we do today." She turned quietly, and with her head held high, she disappeared through the flap in the tent.

"Mr. Pitt, please face the bench."

Rosco tipped his finger where his hat would be. I touched my finger to my chin. Marshal Morrison quietly moved closer to stand behind the defence's table. Rosco nodded to him then turned slowly to face Judge Henry.

"Having been found guilty by a jury of your peers, in the County of Randy River, this court here by sentences you to hang from the neck until dead. The sentence to be carried out immediately."

Again, chaos erupted. Again, opinions varied, but the most loudest consensus seemed to express a preference for stretching the neck. The Marshal moved quickly and took a firm grip of the condemned man.

"The jury is dismissed! This court is adjourned!" Judge Henry shouted over the deluge of sound. The murder of crows fled the scene.

CHAPTER 18

A view from God's high tower

From above I watched the gathering of people swell around the canvas, a human pond rippling with motion, undulating with sound. Two figures emerged from the far end of the tent. They are immediately joined by six others, appearing armed and cautious. One of the two figures crouches to the ground and makes busy at the feet of the other. The Marshal has removed the shackles from around Rosco's ankles.

The crowd can be seen to part, as the group of eight figures begin to move down the street. Ahead of them a path opens, then closes quickly behind them as they seem to glide threw the sea of humanity. Beyond this scene departs a trail of wagons, rolling slowly to the trees to the south. The circus left town opting not to compete with the spectacle of the hanging to come.

The once vocal crowd watches in silence. No proclamations of eternal damnation rise in the air from the street below. Down the street of Randy River proper, away from the throbbing din of the spectacle, the road is empty with all heads now crowding the space before the gallows. Hushing whispers fill the still air as a silence descends and all eyes watch the procession move through the people towards the gleaming white oak of the gallows, a length of rope dangling pencil-thin from the centre-beam.

High in the lofty perch of God's high tower, across from me, not bothering to peer over the edge of the sill, McTavish lies stoic, rifle at the ready, grasped in his hands, mouth open slightly. He sees with is ears for now, counting on my whispered narrative to keep him apprised.

Suddenly, a figure emerges on the stage of the gallows. The cloak and the thinness of the man tells me immediately the name Neville Bonner. Another figure joins him, a hooded figure, face shrouded by a cloth, just the eyes and mouth exposed – the hangman. I tell McTavish and his expression remains unchanged.

The procession reaches its destination at the foot of the stairs of the gallows. The crowd pushed in tighter as the six armed figures turned to face the mob, while Marshal Morrison guided Rosco slowly up the stairs. When they reached the threshold, even my distant eyes could see the sudden hesitation of Rosco – could see the man visibly shift back in his stance and turn his gaze to the length of rope, that now appeared to be drawn on the sky like a thin line of lead.

Movement from down the street, which just moments ago was empty, drew my attention away from the execution to see a small group of people emerge from The Bonner House. Millie and the house staff had started making their way up the street, reluctantly it seemed, to join the spectators. I pulled my watch from my waste coat – 'about five more minutes.'

Back on the gallows, Bonner approached the handcuffed figure of the accused, Rosco Pitt. Though I couldn't see his expression, I was sure Neville was grinning as I watched him wave an arm and introduce the condemned man to his executioner, the hangman.

Neville moved close to Rosco, he leaned in to whisper when suddenly Rosco's head pivoted backwards then jerked suddenly forward, smashing into Neville's face and knocking him down on the platform. The hangman rushed forward and pummelled Rosco with heavy fists then kicked his unshackled legs out from underneath him. The crowd gasped, laughed and cheered then broke into applause as the Marshal launched forward whipping the barrel of his gun up and under the chin of the hangman, who immediately could be seen raising his hands and stepping back.

After a few moments both men got up. Rosco seemed no worse for wear while Neville grasped a bloodied white rag held firmly to his face. It appeared, from this writer's vantage point, that Neville's nose was broken again.

Again I pull out my watch. 'Three minutes.'

The hangman moves forward and with the Marshal's hand, they guide Rosco to the working end of the hangman's noose. For a moment I see his face clearly, framed by a loop against a gun-metal sky. Rosco smiled, then spit a spatter of blood onto the gleaming white oak. Neville, bloodied and gasping from his mouth, approached holding a hood. Rosco glared at him from behind the noose and Bonner stopped dead in his tracks, instead passing the hood to the hangman who received a similar glare. Rosco would have no hood.

The noose was placed around his neck and the hangman stepped back to place his hand upon the lever. The Marshal shifted Rosco's position, making sure his friend was standing dead-centre of that trap door. He placed his hands on Pitt's shoulders and gave him a shake. The two men stood facing each other. The crowd remained silent, honouring the kinship to which they now played witness. It was like the whole world stopped to watch.

"Shame!" One voice, an unknown voice, rose from the crowd – the voice of a child.

"Lets get on with it!" Neville bellowed.

The Marshal glared at Bonner for just a second then turned to the condemned man. "Do you have any last words, Mr. Pitt?" He stepped back and to the side.

Rosco stood looking out at the crowd, the noose now a collar, yet he did not waver. "Just one Quentin," he replied, loud and clear for all to hear, "Just one wor…"

KAAABOOOM! Kaboom kaboom kaboom!

The world shuddered. The wave of the blasts shattered windows up the street and shook the very ground beneath the feet of those gathered before the gallows. The series of explosions sounded the beginning of the end. All heads spun to look down the street and see the four explosions ripple through the plaster of The Bonner House, one after the other in rapid succession. The concussion sucked the air and the house for tired eyes and weary souls came crashing down on itself. Thick dust and smoke plumed out from beneath the rubble and began a slow rolling crawl up the street, while flames began to lick the air from beneath the crumbled structure.

"Pull the lever!" Neville raged, even from the height of God's high tower, one could clearly see the bulging whites of his eyes. The hangman did as was asked. Suddenly Rosco disappeared through the trap door.

A solid crack split the air as the centre-beam snapped and collapsed upon the gallows, bringing down the entire structure beneath its weight, and all those who once stood upon it.

Dust and debris, as it had done at the Bonner House, plumed out from the collapsed timber, blanketing the crowd and causing them to disperse. The crowd flinched then scattered feebly, slipping and trudging through the mud, trying to move quickly off the street, seeking their wagons or finding safe cover. But the Sons and the cattle company boys did not give ground. Numbering about twenty, weapons now drawn, all crouched and guarded, spinning this way and that, they sought out the unseen threat.

As the dust slowly settled, my eyes became glued to movement beneath the gallows' ruin. The Marshal and Neville both climbed out of the rubble. Morrison appeared injured, his leg trailed limp behind him. Bonner stood tall and drew his pistol. By the time the Marshal realized his peril it was too late.

The shot rang out, cracking in my ears and ringing my bells. Down on the dusty street Neville fell where he stood. Marshal Morrison turned his head to God's high tower and touched a finger to the brim of his hat. Beside me, McTavish shifted and reloaded the Sharps. His grin split wide and his eyes sparkled as he nodded at my gaze.

The death of Neville Bonner could not be celebrated. The Sons of the Confederacy and the Cahill Cattle Company boys had regrouped and began opening fire. Some eyes had spied McTavish take the shot and all guns responded upon God's high tower.

The Marshal ducked for cover back beneath the rubble of the gallows as our position was pummelled with bullets, causing both McTavish and I to cling to the floor and cover our heads. Seconds seemed minutes as the onslaught continued; then came music to our ears. The Gatling gun sounded.

Freddy raked the road and men fell, some dead, some pretending, but they fell just the same. Others made a struggled dash, some towards the church. They were quickly dispatched by McTavish and his Winchester. Some sought refuge in the jailhouse, but Freddy proceeded to mow them down without prejudice.

Once the dust had settled again and a few of the stragglers were permitted to scurry out of town, as did most of the looksie-loos, Freddy finally relented and silenced the gun. McTavish took a few more long-range shots with the Sharps, picking off two more men fleeing east, while the Marshal moved through the street and the debris of the gallows seeking out the dead and the living.

"The fight's not up here no more," McTavish stood to survey the street. "We best get back down."

※ ※ ※

There is much to be said in the aftermath. Slowly stragglers emerged, looksie-loos looking then leaving the scene fast. The dead littered the mud, cow-poke dusters and grey coats predominate the unmoving. From some the moans rise periodically – the wounded wail. Some crawl pathetically through the mud on their bellies, but for the most part only stillness assaults the eyes of the living.

As McTavish and I exit the church and move towards the jailhouse, Millie's tear-stained countenance catches my eye, as she and two of her girls move among the bodies, trying their best to aid the wounded, and avoid the eyes of the dead. Millie seems to take special care in the avoidance of her now-dead brother.

Maddie walks apart from them, and delivers aid of her own. She brings peace to the wounded with the blade of her knife, which finds the throats of many and silences their cries.

The Marshal rises once again from the ashes. He drags his leg behind him as he limps through the mud and makes his way to the wooden porch at the jailhouse. Freddy clambers out from the covered wagon, still wearing Willy's hat and duster. He starts to make his way across the street, surveying the carnage he'd wrought with Neville's gun. Slowly we all work our way to the jailhouse and move behind the building where we gather in silence to the rear of rubble that had once been the gallows: the Marshal, Freddy, McTavish, Maddie, and me, John Maximillian.

Only one body had been found in the debris of the gallows, and a consensus was reached to leave him where he lay, and let him rot. The mask was never pulled. We did not care to know. The hangman would be left to those, if any, he'd left behind in this world.

Behind the rubble, the Marshal eyes the ground. McTavish joins him. Maddie crouches and points towards the east, to the distant tree line. The tracks, she said, "head off towards those trees, yeah," to which McTavish agreed.

"Aye. Two horses, moving fast and straight across the open land towards the river beyond them trees."

"I recon they'd turn south at the river," the Marshal said. Freddy, McTavish, Maddie and I looked at the Marshal and saw the resolution in his eyes. "Thinking I'm gonna have to follow."

McTavish eyes Morrison, a mix of suspicion and consideration painting a pondering across his face. "Maybe leave them be,

Quentin. What are you going to do if you find him?"

There was a long pause then. From the street the sounds of wagons and the mingling of men drifted to our ears.

"That's a good question, Lachey," Morrison removed his hat and looked again to the trees. "I'm not sure."

"Aye. Well, some questions are best left not answered, Marshal. Me, I'm goin' hame. MissT is calling me and," he paused to look at Maddie and me, "we've got some journals to find. Isn't that right, Mr. Maximillian?"

"Aye... I mean yes," I tried to smile. "I'm eager to get started on that Mr. McTavish." I nodded at Maddie, who, having no longer any reason to remain, what with the end of The Bonner House, decided to return to the high country from which she'd came.

"We are one with the mountain yeah." Maddie's eyes fell fondly on Freddy. "What are you doing, Peckerwood?"

Freddy kicked the dust for a moment, finding fascination in his tattered, old boots. Then his eyes rose to meet ours and with a new-found confidence he told us of his plan.

The Marshal could use a deputy, he proclaimed. "Imagine that! Me, a U.S. Marshal." Proudful, and deservedly so, Freddy's eyes took a moment to meet the eyes of each of us. With out words he thanked us.

"Y'all changed my life," he said, as the tears welled up in all of our eyes.

With that we moved back to the street, retrieved our respective mounts from the livery, and mounted up. From high in our saddles we bid our adieus, each of them touching a finger to the brims of their hats, and me tapping a finger to my chin. Our mouths said our goodbyes but our eyes all agreed, we would meet again.

EPILOGUE

TORTURE CHAMBER: Ghastly skeletal remains found beneath The Bonner House

By
John Maximilian

A gruesome discovery found beneath the crumbled remains of the well-known Bonner House – For Tired Eyes 'N Weary Souls, has been uncovered during a recent investigation by the U.S. Marshal's office, Northwest Region.

"We found the bones in a secondary chamber that tunnelled off the foundation and basement of the structure," said U.S. Marshal Reuben Calhoun.

The Bonner House, which was blown up during the attempt to hang a condemned murderer, was well known in the valley as an excellent dining and accommodation experience for many a tired eye and weary soul.

"This came on the heels of an official report of sedition in the area of The Valley of Many Rivers, connected to a group of militants called the Sons of the Confederacy," the Marshal added.

In the days leading to this investigation, the community of Randy River, a small, outpost community founded by one-time and recently deceased Southern sympathizer Neville Bonner, was the scene of a violent spree perpetrated by a mysterious mountain man named Rosco Pitt.

Pitt, who stood trial and was condemned to hang by the neck until dead for a series of gruesome murders, escaped his captors and fled the hangman's noose. Today, the man is a fugitive and at large, where-a-bouts presently unknown.

It is not known at this time the identities or causes of death of any of the human remains found, but Marshal Calhoun said the bones, upon examination by Federal physicians, showed signs of scratches and breakage that "was most likely the result of deliberate torture.

"The investigation will continue," the Marshal concluded.

❋ ❋ ❋

Notes from J. Maximillian
It has been said that Rosco Pitt was the death of Randy River. In less than a year following the days of violence and the trial of the man from the mountain, the last of the settlers of Randy River packed up their belongings in a bullet-riddled wagon that once housed a golden Gatling gun, and made slow progress south, away from The Valley of Many Rivers.

Despite an investigation by the U.S. Marshals' Office, there were no further developments in the case of the human remains found beneath the rubble that had once been The Bonner House – For Tired Eyes N' Weary Souls.

There was, however, a small skirmish resulting in the death and capture of several, heavily armed militants operating under the banner of the Sons of the Confederacy. In addition to charges of sedition being laid against the group, the U.S. army also seized a large cache of weapons and ammunition, including, says the report, "a gold-plated Gatling gun."

At the time of this writing I have received no word from Marshal Quentin James Morrison, who, accompanied by Deputy

Marshal Fredrick Simmons, had set out to find the man once known as the murderous villain Rosco Pitt.

At the time of this writing, "I am one with the mountain," as a wise man once said, and have found comfort in the high country in the company of an ornery Scotsman and a woman named Maddie, the princess of the mountain, I have come to call her affectionately.

Time moves slow on the folds of MissT's skirt. We are yet to find the lost journal of Rosco Pitt, but there is plenty of time, here on the mountain.

"Tomorrow," McTavish has promised. "Tomorrow."

John Maximillian, a writer of chronicles.

The End

BOOKS BY THIS AUTHOR

Tusk: A Beringia Story

The story starts now, in eastern Siberia. Archeologists find a tusk buried in sediment in a cave known to have been the home to humans at the dawn of our modern times. On this tusk there are etchings, scribed by hands unknown, its purpose mysterious, but as shown by the pictures on the walls of the cave in which it was found, for some, the meaning is clear.

The tusk tells a story, told by a gifted storyteller, and shared around the fires of a clan. It tells the tale of the seer Hooyip and the never-ending struggle he and his clan must face with the dawn of every day, just to survive. It's an epic tale of ancient love, struggle, and the strength of humanity, set against the brutal world of the Mammoth Steppe.

Set at the dawn of modern humans, near the end of the ice age, the story begins in a system of caves in northeastern Siberia. Hooyip dreams of the mammoths and the herds moving across the land of Beringia, and at the evening fires begins to urge the clan to follow the herd; follow Hooyip's mammoth.

The telling of the tale unveils the brutal society, ancient mysticism, and our earliest, primal emotions, that formed the building blocks of our societies today. But most of all it is simply a story – and as the Russian said, "I'll bet it's a good one."